"ELEANOR THE PRIVATE EYE IS UTTERLY ENDEARING"
The New York Times Book Review

"Engrossing . . . Entertaining . . . Mrs. Roosevelt is once more her bright, cheerful self, committed to justice and as tactfully strong as ever."

Baltimore Sun

"A fine White House whodunit . . . First rate . . . Roosevelt doesn't hesitate to tell all."

Grand Rapids Press

"Elliott Roosevelt has really hit his stride . . . He makes a reader believe, even while knowing better, that his mother actually did all the things in *Murder in the Rose Garden*."

Sacramento Union

"Most enjoyable . . . Roosevelt has fun as he strolls evocatively and with aplomb through the corridors of power and murder."

Detroit News

ELLIOTT ROOSEVELT

MURDER IN THE ROSE GARDEN

AVON BOOKS ◆ NEW YORK

AVON BOOKS
A division of
The Hearst Corporation
105 Madison Avenue
New York, New York 10016

First Avon Books Printing: June 1991

Printed in the U.S.A.

RA 10 9 8 7 6 5 4 3 2 1

To my loving wife, Patty

1

"It is a marvelous thing, and a compliment to our country, that the next Queen of England is going to be an American," said Senator Everett E. Cranshaw. "And so American an American—so typical an American woman."

"I am not altogether sure," said Mrs. Roosevelt with a warm smile, "that Mrs. Simpson represents quite the typical American woman."

The senator chuckled. "Bessie Wallis Warfield Simpson. Her Majesty the Queen! May God bless her!"

The President grinned. "Scrawny woman, I've always thought. To be perfectly honest, I have never been quite able to understand what the Prince—excuse me, His Majesty Edward the Eighth—finds so fascinating in her."

Now Senator Cranshaw laughed aloud. "I am afraid," he said, "I can lay no claim to any special ability to judge the qualities peculiar to the fair sex. The King is smitten with her, though. No question about that. And, in spite of the objections of a few small-minded English politicians, the next Queen will be Queen Bessie. Or Queen Wallis. Or maybe they'll give her a new name, as they often have their monarchs. Queen Victoria the Second . . . ?''

"No," said Mrs. Roosevelt. "Queen Victoria was a queen regnant. If—Oh, never mind. She will not be Victoria the Second, though. Count on it."

The President was shaking his evening martinis and was not subtle in his anxiety to change the subject. "Queen of Hearts," he said. "The queen of one heart, anyway."

"I trust you gentlemen will excuse me," said Mrs. Roosevelt. "I have an engagement."

Senator Everett Cranshaw rose and bowed as Mrs. Roosevelt rose from her chair. She nodded and smiled at him, then at the President, and then hurried away along the second-floor hall of the White House, toward the elevator—a quick, decisive figure in blue-and-white silk crepe, white shoes, clutching in her left hand the white gloves she had worn outside this afternoon and had never quite found time to be rid of.

"Well, Everett . . ." said the President as he watched the First Lady turn the corner into the elevator vestibule. "You will partake, I assume?"

The senator glanced at the silver cocktail shaker, at the drops of condensation now forming on it, and nodded happily. "I will, indeed, Mr. President. I will indeed, and will regard it as a great honor."

President Roosevelt sat in his wooden wheelchair. His valet, Arthur Prettyman, had put the gin, vermouth, ice, and olives on a table where they were handy for the President to mix his evening martinis. The senator from Maine, a Republican, felt honored to be invited to this private, one-on-one meeting with the President—even though he knew he was there to be persuaded to vote for the tax changes the President was asking from the pre-election session of the Congress. He and Franklin Roosevelt had been schoolboys together, at Harvard; and though they had not often seen each other since had kept track of each other's careers and were pleased they knew each other.

"My son Elliott," said the President, "is thinking of taking a trans-Atlantic flight on this new German airship. The Hindenburg. Always had an interest in aviation, you know."

"Politically—" the senator began.

"Yes, I know," the President interrupted. "Politically, it wouldn't be a very good idea. Herr Hitler is not very popular in this country. For good reason. But I would like to know what role Zeppelins will play in the future of air transportation."

"Mr. President—"

Senator Cranshaw stopped. He stood. The President's private secretary, Marguerite LeHand, had come down from her quarters on the third floor of the White House. The rather tight skirt of her summery white cotton dress showed the shape of her legs as she walked briskly toward them.

"You know Missy," said the President.

He did. He took the tall, attractive woman's hand and squeezed it, and she sat down and reached for a glass and the ice tongs. She would not take a martini but would pour herself some whiskey over ice, with a little water. She was casual about it, he noticed. She did not ask the President's by-your-leave before she poured herself a drink.

There was gossip about the President and Missy LeHand. The senator did not take it seriously—though some of his Republican friends did. The most conspicuous and cogent argument against idle talk was the simple fact that Mrs. Roosevelt accepted a close personal relationship between her husband and his thirty-eight-year-old secretary and seemed to have no objection to any element of the alliance, whatever it was. Miss LeHand—beyond any question and whatever else might be true—was an exceptionally attractive woman. What was more, she was obviously devoted to the President.

"You are leaving town shortly, I understand, Mr. President," said Senator Cranshaw as he accepted his first martini from the President.

"Yes, a little cruise," said the President. "New England waters."

"Maine waters, I hope," said Cranshaw.

"Indeed," said the President. "Start in Maine, return to Maine. Sailing from Pulpit Harbor, out to Nova Scotia, back to Eastport. Not a bad itinerary for some sea air and fishing, don't you think?"

"Is Mrs. Roosevelt—?"

"No. She'll stay home and mind the store. She's much more the politician than I am, you know. And incidentally, Everett, would you like an endorsement when I stop in Maine?"

Cranshaw laughed. "Really, Mr. President. The kiss of death. Maine Republicans would nail me to a cross."

"To a *wall*, Senator," said Missy. "Not to a cross."

The senator laughed again. "I stand corrected."

"You Republicans *bear* a cross, Everett," said the President. "Your candidate this year—Governor Landon."

"No heavier a burden than Cactus Jack Garner," said Cranshaw. He referred to the Democratic candidate for re-election to the vice presidency. "That old man can't even mumble intelligently."

The President had poured his own martini and now raised his stem glass and saluted Senator Cranshaw. "To 1936," he said. "To the election of 1936. May the best man win."

"Amen," said the senator, sipping from his glass.

Missy sipped whiskey, then asked—"Would you like to put a little money down on the election, Senator?"

"Off the record, Miss LeHand," the senator said. "Off the record, strictly. The President will be re-elected. It will be close, I think; but the President will be re-elected."

She laughed. "Then we can't bet," she said. "Because

I don't just *think* the Boss is going to be re-elected. I *know* it."

While the President was relaxing upstairs and entertaining an old friend from his school days, Mrs. Roosevelt was presiding over a small dinner in the private dining room on the first floor. Harry Hopkins sat at the table, eating oysters even though they were out of season, washing them down as was his habit, with swallows of bourbon. Her other guest was Mary McLeod Bethune, the eminent Negro leader, president of Bethune-Cookman College which she herself had founded.

Mary Bethune was, as a Negro policeman once described her, "black as a black shoe." Tonight she wore, as she often did when she came to the White House, a large orchid at her shoulder, on her yellow silk dress. She was a regal figure, a formidable and eloquent advocate of social and economic justice for her people.

She was the fifteenth in a family of seventeen children, and some of her older brothers and sisters had been sold in slavery. Mrs. Roosevelt relied on her for the most intimate glimpses she could get of a tragedy she herself could begin to understand only through friendships with people like this. Mrs. Roosevelt and Mary McLeod Bethune had become close personal friends as well as coworkers for change, and they enjoyed each other's company and the small, private luncheons and dinners they occasionally shared.

Both of them understood that this dinner was for the purpose of discussing what Negro leaders could do to support the President in his campaign for re-election. Mary Bethune, as always, had a few things to point out to the First Lady.

"The problem, you see," she told Mrs. Roosevelt, "is that there are white WPA projects and Negro WPA projects, housing projects for whites in white neighborhoods and for

Negroes in Negro neighborhoods . . . Do you see? Even in these federal programs, we are segregated.''

"Harry . . ." said Mrs. Roosevelt.

"The problem is," said Hopkins, his mouth full of oyster, "that if we'd asked the Congress to fund programs with whites and Negroes living and working side by side, we'd never have gotten the funds at all, would never have gotten the programs off the ground."

"Some kinds of change come slowly," said Mrs. Roosevelt, shaking her head.

"Our first job was to get things started," said Hopkins. "Now we can begin to think of greater justice in the administration of these programs."

"If we are re-elected," said Mrs. Roosevelt.

"You will have the support of my people," said Mary Bethune. "If you haven't done all we could hope for, you have done more than anyone since—"

"Abraham Lincoln," Hopkins interrupted, his mouth again filled with oyster.

"I was thinking of Theodore Roosevelt," said Mary Bethune with dignity.

Mrs. Roosevelt laughed. "Harry," she said. "Don't—"

"Don't count your colored votes before they are cast," said Mary McLeod Bethune.

"Don't take them for granted," said Hopkins. "That's what the Republicans have done for seventy years—assumed Negroes would vote for Republican candidates because Lincoln signed the Emancipation Proclamation. Well, we are working on a new Emancipation Proclamation."

"I shall believe it, Mr. Hopkins, when I see it," said Mary Bethune. "In the meantime, I know the vast majority of my people will vote for President Roosevelt and not Governor Landon. If more of us could vote . . ." She paused and smiled sadly.

"Voting rights," said Mrs. Roosevelt. "Make a note, please, Harry."

"It's a note that's been in my mind for a long time,"

said Hopkins. "Someday our party will have to take a stand for colored people's voting rights. If we did it this year, the party would split wide open, and the Republicans would elect Alf Landon. I'm sorry," he said, nodding toward Mary Bethune. "If we announced our support for a voting-rights act this year, the southern states would bolt the party."

"Put it on the agenda," said Mary McLeod Bethune. "A day will come."

Mrs. Roosevelt did not linger long over a meal when she could avoid it. Her schedule was too full for her to give an hour to coffee and brandy, unless perhaps the conversation were constructive. Her talk with Mary McLeod Bethune and Harry Hopkins *was* interesting and useful, but they did not prolong it after dinner, and Mrs. Roosevelt bade good night to her guests a little after nine. She escorted Mary Bethune to the South Portico and, with a fond kiss on the cheek, handed her over to the White House driver who would take her to her hotel.

By then the President was in bed. His dinner tray had been put aside. He had been helped into his pajamas by his valet, who had also put aside his braces. He sat propped against three fat pillows, enjoying his last cigarette of the day.

Missy was with him. They were listening to a movement from a Beethoven symphony played on a remarkable new phonograph that had been sent to the White House by RCA. The device was capable of playing records in succession, dropping them from a stack, one by one onto the turntable. One could listen to twenty minutes or half an hour of music before it was necessary to touch the phonograph. RCA had also sent a score of albums. The President was fascinated with the machine and appreciative of the music, and lately he had been enjoying music with his dinner almost every evening.

Missy had been to her suite on the third floor and had

changed into a light-blue nightgown, covered by a matching cotton robe. She was as comfortable as the President and enjoying the music just as much.

Shortly, when the stack of records was played, she would help him to lie back. She would make sure he was comfortable and that all he needed was at hand before she left him for the night. She was glad that he was about to take a sailing vacation. She had seen him fall just before he took the podium to make his acceptance speech at the Democratic Convention in Philadelphia, and she had seen him shaken as she had never seen him shaken before. She was concerned about him and thought he needed rest.

He particularly favored the music he had selected—the choral movement of Beethoven's Ninth Symphony—and was following the rhythm with small movements of his hands and mouthing the words being sung by the chorus— "Freude schöner Götterfunken . . ."

When the telephone rang, he ignored it, and she picked it up.

"Miss LeHand?"

"Yes."

"Stan Szczygiel."

He was a veteran agent of the Secret Service who, thank God, pronounced his name "Siegel." She glanced at the President, who was listening to the music and as yet paying no attention to the telephone call. "What can I do for you, Stan?" she asked.

"Can I speak to The Boss?"

"Not unless it's urgent."

"Okay. You judge. The night police have found a body in the Rose Garden. Whatta you think? Important enough to tell him?"

Missy glanced at the President. He was absorbed in the music, all but unaware of the telephone call. "I doubt it. Unless—Well . . . Who is it?"

"A woman," said Szczygiel. "Nobody that anybody knows, I guess. Not anybody on the staff. Nobody prominent. The whole question is, what's she doing lying dead in the White House Rose Garden?''

''Not important enough to spoil his sleep,'' said Missy. ''If anything develops that really needs his personal attention, call me. I'll be back in my rooms in half an hour or less.''

''Okay, Miss LeHand. And we keep it quiet, right?''

''Until we can talk about it, Stan.''

''I understand. We'll take care of it discreetly. So . . . Good night.''

Mrs. Roosevelt, while bidding her guests farewell at the South Portico, had noticed flashlights and a flurry of activity in the Rose Garden between the main house and the Executive Wing. As soon as she was back inside the house she hurried through the ground-floor hall and into the colonnade. By now, electric lights on tripods had been set up, and she could see the whole scene:

In the Rose Garden, just under one of the windows of the Cabinet Room, a woman dressed in black lay sprawled face down in a rose bed—quite obviously dead. Secret Service agents and uniformed White House policemen scurried about, one of them taking photographs with a big camera that seemed to explode with light when one of its flashbulbs went off.

Stanlislaw Szczygiel rushed toward Mrs. Roosevelt. ''Oh, Ma'am,'' he said. ''You don't want to see this.'' He tried to place himself between her and the sight of the body.

Sczcygiel was sixty-two years old, and had begun his White House career under President Theodore Roosevelt—as he had once told Mrs. Roosevelt. He was a squat, square man, both of face and physique; and perhaps his most memorable feature was his oversized gin-reddened nose.

''Mr. Szczygiel,'' she said firmly. ''I have seen dead bodies before.''

Szczygiel frowned, but he gave up his attempt to prevent the First Lady from seeing. "I'm afraid she's been murdered, Ma'am," he said. "Strangled."

"She looks murdered," said Mrs. Roosevelt. "I mean, the bodies of people who die of natural causes don't look . . . broken. Who is she?"

Szczygiel reached into his jacket pocket and pulled out a slip of paper. It was a driver's license. "Her name is, uh—" He squinted over the typed name. "It's Tally-a-fero."

Mrs. Roosevelt snatched the license from his hand. "Vivian . . . The name is pronounced 'Tolliver,' Mr. Szczygiel. 'Tolliver,' not 'Tally-a-fero.' "

"Do you know her, Ma'am?"

"Not exactly," said Mrs. Roosevelt. "I've met her several times. She is—was—the daughter of the late Senator Jefferson Taliafero, of Mississippi. She was a maiden lady and came to Washington with her father. When he died, she stayed on. She is—was—something of a Washington hostess. Her home in Georgetown has been a sort of salon where prominent people have gathered. And—*Murdered!* Who could possibly have had a motive for murdering Vivian Taliafero?"

"We have a suspect in mind," said Szczygiel.

"Who?"

"Well . . ."

"You can tell me, Mr. Szczygiel. I have a bit of experience in these matters, and since murder has been committed in the precincts of the White House, almost outside the President's office window you might say, I intend to take an interest in the investigation—if for no other reason than concern for the President's safety. If, after all, murder can be committed— Well. You understand my concern."

"I do indeed, Ma'am," Szczygiel conceded. "Well, Miss . . . uh, you say it's pronounced 'Tolliver.' Miss Taliafero has been dead less than an hour, we would judge. The autopsy may make it possible to be more certain about that. The policemen who make rounds about the building are certain she was not lying there when the sun set or during the twilight hour. It's been dark for about an hour.''

"And you suspect whom, Mr. Szczygiel?''

Stanlislaw Szczygiel glanced around as if he were about to disclose a confidence he did not want anyone but the First Lady to hear, though almost every man taking part in the investigation knew who was suspected. "It's Mr. Hausser, Ma'am,'' he said. "Mr. Frederick Hausser. He is under arrest. He'll be taken to the District jail shortly.''

"Fritz *Hausser* . . . ? Oh, Mr. Szczygiel, I hope you are certain of the facts behind your suspicion. Mr. Hausser is—''

"A fine young man,'' Szczygiel interrupted. "Even so.''

"Where is he now?'' asked Mrs. Roosevelt. "You say he hasn't been taken to jail?''

"As a matter of fact, he's in the Cabinet Room,'' said Szczygiel. "Being interrogated.''

"I want to see him,'' said Mrs. Roosevelt decisively, and she turned on her heel and walked on through the colonnade and into the West Wing.

Frederick Hausser was a forty-year-old lawyer, a graduate of Yale. He was tall, thin, pallid, with a prominent, bobbing Adam's apple. He wore round, gold-rimmed spectacles. His fellow workers in the West Wing considered him something of a joke, because he was a constantly worried hypochondriac who carried in his briefcase a small leather case crammed with a dozen or so bottles of pills. Fritz frequently felt a symptom that required a pill, and he would take out his case, select the right pill, and nervously swallow something—a pill to stop the cold he felt coming on, a pill to combat the headache he was sure was about to rage, a pill to calm his nerves, a liver pill, a diuretic, a laxative. . . . He was, on the other hand, respected as a thoughtful young lawyer. The final element of his reputation rested on the fact that he had inherited a small fortune and could have afforded to be—though he wasn't—one of the dollar-a-year men who served this President.

Tonight he sat at the big conference table in the Cabinet Room, handcuffed, nervous, miserable, suffering close interrogation by two uniformed policemen.

The policemen jumped to their feet when they saw the First Lady, and Szczygiel nodded his head toward the door. They left, and Mrs. Roosevelt and Szczygiel sat down.

"Mr. Hausser . . ." she said softly, shaking her head.

"I didn't kill her," said Hausser.

"You could go a long way toward making us believe that if you would just answer one simple question," said Szczygiel.

"But I can't," murmured Hausser.

Stanlislaw Szczygiel began to pick under the fingernails of his right hand, resting each right-hand finger on his left thumb and pressing the nail of his right index finger under the nail he wanted to dig. He tipped his head to one side and regarded Hausser with professional skepticism. It was a practiced attitude, almost an inherited one. He was a Secret Service agent. His father had been a Philadelphia policeman. His great-great-grandfather had come to America with Pulaski, to fight for General Washington; and after the war he had returned, bringing his family. He had intended to move west, where he would acquire a vast tract of land and become a gentleman farmer. In fact, neither he nor any of his descendants had ever made a home more than fifty miles west of the Atlantic Ocean, and none had ever lived anywhere but in a major city. Szczygiel was as tough a cop as any in New York City.

"Well . . . If you can't answer, you can't, I guess," he said to Hausser. "We'll send you along to the District of Columbia jail, then."

Hausser shook his head and blinked. Mrs. Roosevelt thought he was about to break down and cry.

"What is the question Mr. Hausser feels he cannot answer?" she asked Szczygiel.

"When we searched through the pocketbook of the victim out there," said Szczygiel, "we found one of Mr. Hausser's personal checks. It was made out to cash, in the amount of one hundred dollars. The question is, why did he give Miss Taliafero a check for one hundred dollars made out to cash?"

Mrs. Roosevelt looked at Hausser. "You can understand why they would want to know," she said.

"And you can't understand why I can't answer," said Hausser dismally.

"I have another question," said Mrs. Roosevelt. "Did you give Miss Taliafero the check here, in the Executive Wing, tonight?"

Hausser nodded.

"One of the secretaries saw a dark-haired woman dressed in black, matching Miss Taliafero's description, in the west hall," said Szczygiel. "Unfortunately, she isn't clear about what time that was. Anyway—"

"It doesn't make any difference," said Hausser. "I admit she came to my office. I told you she was there. We were together about ten minutes. Maybe less. Maybe only five. She arrived a little after eight o'clock. Maybe a quarter after. She left before eight-thirty."

"With your check," said Mrs. Roosevelt.

"With my check," he agreed.

"Well, Mr. Hausser, you do make it difficult for yourself by refusing to say why you gave her a check."

"I'm sorry," he said to Mrs. Roosevelt. "If I told you, you wouldn't believe it."

"In the circumstances, you might elect to risk that," she said.

Hausser blinked and shook his head.

Mrs. Roosevelt frowned. "I find it most difficult—almost impossible, in fact—to believe you are guilty of murder, Mr. Hausser. If, on the other hand, you can't offer an explanation for that check, I am afraid I can't do much for you."

"You'll be charged with murder," said Szczygiel.

"You can't prove I killed her," said Hausser bitterly. "If for no other reason—" He swallowed noisily. "If for no other reason, because I *didn't*."

2

Jimmy, Franklin, Jr., and Johnny were to accompany the President on his sailing vacation. Mrs. Roosevelt would go up to meet their chartered schooner on its return. He would be gone a long time for a newly renominated President at the outset of a tough campaign. It was his judgment that the American people would rather not hear his voice on the radio every day from July to November, not see him everywhere during a long campaign. However much professional politicians might disagree—and most of them did—that was his judgment and his decision.

On the morning after the body of Vivian Taliafero was found in the Rose Garden and Frederick Hausser was taken to jail as the prime suspect, Mrs. Roosevelt sat in her office looking at the editorials and polls. There was a consensus in them that Governor Alfred Landon would be elected President of the United States in November and that Franklin D. Roosevelt could go home to Hyde Park on January 20, 1937. She did not agree with her husband that this was the time to take a vacation. She did not share his ebullient confidence. She did not understand why he thought the middle of August would be plenty soon enough to launch his campaign for re-election—and that the campaign itself need not consist of much more than a few speeches.

"This country, after all," one of the editorials said, "is normally Republican. Since Abraham Lincoln was elected President in 1860, only three Democrats—Cleveland, Wilson, and Roosevelt—have occupied the White House. Out of nineteen presidential elections, the Democrats have won only five. Mr. Roosevelt's pretended confidence is that— pretended. In 1936 this nation will return to a sound, careful style of government. The wild experiments called the 'New Deal' will be over."

Mrs. Roosevelt turned to the newspaper accounts of the death of Vivian Taliafero. The Washington *Post* reported—

Miss Vivian Taliafero (pronounced "Tolliver"), daughter of the late Senator Jefferson Taliafero (D. Miss.), and a prominent Washington hostess for many years, was found dead on the grounds of the White House last night. Murder is suspected.

According to White House sources, Miss Taliafero died of strangulation.

Vivian Taliafero, 34, had lived in this city for the past sixteen years, having come to Washington to be her late father's hostess, her mother having died some years before the election of Senator Taliafero. Regarded always as an exceptional beauty, Miss Taliafero turned her handsome Georgetown home into a literary and political salon, after the fashion of the great French salons of the Revolutionary period. She was hostess to many of the most eminent and interesting men and women to have graced our city in the past two decades.

Among the prominent men who were often seen in

her parlor, sipping tea and discussing the great issues of the day, were the late Justice Oliver Wendell Holmes, Baltimore sage H. L. Mencken, former Massachusetts Senator Henry Cabot Lodge, and former Secretary of the Treasury Andrew Mellon. Presidents Harding and Hoover were her guests, as were dozens of members of Congress, Cabinet officers, and judges. The Taliafero home in Georgetown was also a favorite rendezvous for powerful lobbyists, who met Senators and Congressmen there.

"I learned with sadness this morning of the untimely death of a charming lady," said Chief Justice Charles Evans Hughes. "She was an ornament to our city."

Former President Herbert Hoover, contacted in New York, expressed himself as "shocked" to hear of the murder of Miss Taliafero. The news was so appalling, he said, that he did not have a formal statement to make at this time but said he would issue a statement later.

Police have a suspect in custody, but they declined to name him or suggest any motive for the murder. There has been no official comment from the White House.

Accompanying the news story was a two-column photograph of Vivian Taliafero. She was a short, slightly plump young woman whose best feature had been her striking brown eyes. Mrs. Roosevelt remembered noticing her eyes—vivacious, ardently expressive of a range of re-actions and emotions, yet soft and alluring. She had worn her dark-brown hair cut short, just under her ears, and in bangs over her forehead. She'd had a ready smile, yet there had always been something reserved about that smile. With her round, open face, she had never looked the part of a femme fatale. Still, something about her defied defini-tion—something hidden, even mysterious.

Mrs. Roosevelt was pleased that the name of Frederick Hausser had not been released to the newspapers. She found it difficult to believe that that slight, timid, hypo-chondriac young man was capable of murder. She disliked the thought that he was this morning locked in a cell in the D.C. jail. She had meetings this morning, but she resolved to take a little further look into the Taliafero murder case when she could find a few minutes later in the day.

"I have encouraged her to take a vacation while I'm taking mine," said the President. "But—"

"I think Missy's judgment is good," said Mrs. Roosevelt. "We all have much work to do this summer. Organizing . . ."

The President grinned mischievously. "You mean you've decided you like Washington?" he asked. "Not ready to move back to New York?"

Missy LeHand was laughing. Mrs. Roosevelt could not help but laugh, too. The President and Missy were in the swimming pool, which was located in the colonnade between the Executive Wing and the White House proper. The President and Missy wore almost-identical bathing suits—blue knit-wool trunks and white vests. Mrs. Roosevelt sat in a chair beside the pool, wearing a loose white dress that was comfortable in the summer's heat. She was sipping from a glass of lemonade. The dripping pitcher and extra glasses waited on a tray.

"If no one takes an interest in the campaign," she said, "we shall certainly be moving back to New York."

"There's an old adage in politics," said Missy. " 'You can't beat somebody with nobody.' "

"You are wrong if you suppose Governor Landon is nobody," said Mrs. Roosevelt. "And there's another saying, which is that this country is normally Republican."

"I read that editorial this morning, too," said the President. "But 'normally' means other times. These are not normal times."

"Maybe that's what you've achieved, Boss," said Missy. "You've brought it back to normal times, almost."

"Tell that to Gerald L. K. Smith," said the President. "Or Father Coughlin. Or Francis Townsend."

"Or William Randolph Hearst," suggested Mrs. Roosevelt with mock innocence.

The President laughed again.

A man in a tan suit came out of the Executive Wing and walked toward them. It was Stanislaw Szczygiel.

"Mr. Szczygiel!" Mrs. Roosevelt called to him. "Come join us for a glass of lemonade. I've been meaning to call you."

Szczygiel happily accepted. He sat down, and Mrs. Roosevelt poured lemonade for him. "Hot, isn't it?" he said.

"Come in swimming, Szczygiel," said the President. "We've got extra bathing suits in the office."

"Well, thank you, Mr. President," said Szczygiel, "but I'm afraid I—"

"Afraid's the word," the President laughed. "You Secret Service agents are always afraid to get wet."

"What news of the investigation into the death of Vivian Taliafero?" asked Mrs. Roosevelt.

"You know," said Szczygiel, "it's not exactly a Secret Service responsibility. It didn't involve a threat to the President, and the D.C. police and F.B.I.—"

"*Make* it a Secret Service responsibility," said the President. "If you need an executive order, I'll give you one in writing before I leave for my vacation. I don't want John Edgar Hoover snooping around the White House. In fact—Missy, type something up for me, will you? I want responsibility assigned to—Well, you understand."

"I do," said Missy a little grimly.

"Anyway," said Mrs. Roosevelt. "What's new?"

"Well, something that pretty well puts a cap on it, actually," said Szczygiel. "At least the D.C. detective in charge thinks it does."

"And who is that?" asked Mrs. Roosevelt.

"A Lieutenant Kennelly, Ma'am," said Szczygiel.

"Lieutenant Edward Kennelly?" she asked. "I have worked with him before. He's a fine man, though I think a little precipitate in making judgments."

"Ed Kennelly," said Szczygiel.

"And what is the new evidence he has found?"

"He went through Hausser's rented rooms. Found his checkbook. He has been writing a lot of checks to cash, for the past two years. If he thought he was being anonymous by writing them to cash, he was wrong. To be cashed, they had to be endorsed. We found two of them among his canceled checks—endorsed by Vivian Taliafero. It seems he's been paying her fifty dollars a month. When we asked him why, he refused to say."

Mrs. Roosevelt frowned. "That *is* curious," she said. "But it doesn't prove much, does it? I mean, really, it doesn't prove he killed her."

"It would prove much less if he would just tell us why he wrote those checks. We know the two were written to her. We can assume the rest were. The total of his checks to cash in the past two years is a little over a thousand dollars. Why?"

"You have a suspicion about that, I imagine," said Mrs. Roosevelt.

"I do."

"Blackmail," said the President from the pool. "On the other hand, old fellow, he may have bought something valuable from her two years ago and has been paying her off at fifty dollars a month. Say an automobile."

"Then why won't he tell us so?" asked Szczygiel.

The President nodded. "Blackmail . . ."

"Let us not jump to that conclusion," said Mrs. Roosevelt. "I've been thinking about the case, Mr. Szczygiel, and I have some questions. In the first place, has the autopsy been completed?"

Szczygiel nodded.

"The cause of death was—"

"Strangulation," said Szczygiel.

"Had she been struck or beaten in any way?" asked the First Lady.

The President began to laugh. "Come Watson, the plot's afoot! Sherlock Roosevelt is at it again."

"Well," said Mrs. Roosevelt, a bit ruffled, "I did manage to make some little contribution toward proving that poor Amelia Colmer didn't kill her husband, and that Alfred Hannah did not commit suicide. Didn't I?"

"Oh, you most assuredly did," said the President. He was bobbing up and down in the water of the pool. He spoke to Szczygiel. "She likes to stick her nib into police investigations. Thinks of them as little intellectual challenges."

"I like to prevent injustices," said Mrs. Roosevelt.

"That, too," said the President, and he swam away toward the far end of the pool, showing a strong, confident stroke.

Missy swam after him, and Mrs. Roosevelt and Szczygiel were left alone.

"My question," said Mrs. Roosevelt, "is whether Miss Taliafero was stunned or injured in any way before her killer began to strangle her."

"No, Ma'am," said Szczygiel. "She was not struck or beaten. She was simply strangled."

"Was she drunk?"

"No, Ma'am. She'd had a drink or two, according to the chemical analysis of her blood, but she was not drunk."

"Then, Mr. Szczygiel, is it not true that at the time of her death she was a relatively young, reasonably strong woman, capable of struggling?"

"Yes, Ma'am."

"Strangulation . . . Wouldn't she have kicked and struck out with her fists and . . . and struggled?"

"One would expect so."

"And scratched maybe. Maybe even have bitten?"

Szczygiel nodded thoughtfully. "I see your point."

"Has Mr. Hausser any scratches, bites, or bruises on him?"

Szczygiel shook his head. "I took him to jail myself. They stripped him, of course. I didn't see any marks on him."

"Ah . . . And what would you estimate as Mr. Hausser's weight?"

"Oh—Not more than a hundred thirty, I'd guess. Maybe less."

"A slight man. Probably not terribly strong," she said.

"I'd judge not," said Szczygiel.

"And Miss Taliafero weighed . . . ?"

"A hundred twenty, I think the autopsy report says."

"So a hundred-thirty-pound man strangled a hundred-twenty-pound woman to death, without having first stunned her by a blow to the face or head; and he did so without suffering the least bruise or mark to himself. Indeed, he did so with such force that she did not even recover breath for an instant so she could scream."

"I take your point," said Szczygiel.

"What is more, being employed in the Executive Wing, he murders her on the grounds of the White House—and that after she was seen in the Executive Wing by at least one witness."

"Well, he may not have known she was seen."

"But it was likely she would be. The Executive Wing is not a very private place."

"True."

Mrs. Roosevelt shook her head firmly. "What is more, having just given her a check, he kills her and leaves the check in her purse to be found by the police." She shook her head more firmly. "That doesn't make much sense, Mr. Szczygiel."

· "You've thought the matter through rather carefully," said Szczygiel.

"Well, it's a good thing someone has," she said.

"I take your point," said Szczygiel, and he began to pick at his fingernails.

"Let us get Lieutenant Kennelly on the phone," she said. "I think I'd like to go over to the jail and see if *I* can persuade Mr. Hausser to be more forthcoming about why he wrote that check."

"Mrs. Roosevelt," said Szczygiel to Lieutenant Kennelly, "has made a strong point about Miss Taliafero's having suffered no injury except those to the throat."

"May I see the autopsy report?" she asked.

"Of course," said Kennelly. "Uh . . . maybe I should take out the photographs. Pretty ugly, you know."

Mrs. Roosevelt's chin rose. "I have seen dead people before, Lieutenant Kennelly," she said.

Kennelly handed her the file. She stared at the photographs more than at the typed pages. There were four eight-by-ten glossy black-and-white prints—one of the naked body lying on its back, one of it lying face down, one close-up of the injuries to the right side of the throat, another of the injuries on the left.

"A tragedy," Mrs. Roosevelt whispered. "So young. And beautiful."

"Yes," said Kennelly. "She was. I never saw her alive, but even from those pictures I can see she was a beauty."

"Are we absolutely certain," asked Mrs. Roosevelt, "that she suffered no injury but the strangulation?"

Kennelly nodded. "Since your call, and while you were on your way over here, I telephoned the coroner and asked him how carefully he'd checked for other injuries, like to the head. Nothing else."

Mrs. Roosevelt was reading the autopsy report. "Unless I misunderstand these terms," she said, "I am reading that great force was applied to the throat. Cartilage of the larynx and trachea ruptured. Collapse of those organs. Ruptured veins and arteries." She shook her head. "Do you really believe Mr. Hausser had the strength to do this?''

"It's possible," said Kennelly. "People's adrenaline flows when they are involved in this kind of thing.''

"Is that a scientific fact, Lieutenant, or—''

"No, Ma'am.''

She flipped the pages. "Does anything in here suggest how tall the murderer had to be?''

"No, Ma'am," said Kennelly. "But in a strangling the victim is usually wrenched to the floor or ground. It would be unusual for the two people to remain erect.''

"Then the killer's clothes would have been stained by the grass or the soil of the rose bed," said Mrs. Roosevelt. "And I didn't notice any dirt or stains on Mr. Hausser's clothes last night.''

Kennelly grinned. "I hope his lawyer is as persuasive as you are,'' he said.

"Does he have a lawyer?''

"Not yet. We can hold him three days without letting him make a phone call, and that's what we plan to do. Maybe he'll get enough worried to break down and tell us something.''

"Well, let's see if my powers of persuasion are sufficiently strong to encourage him to tell us why he wrote checks to Miss Taliafero," said Mrs. Roosevelt. "I should like to see him alone if that's possible.''

Frederick Hausser was brought into Lieutenant Kennelly's small, spartan office; and Mrs. Roosevelt was left alone with him. Hausser was dressed in a pair of worn gray coveralls and was barefoot. He sat down facing Mrs. Roosevelt across the detective's desk, and before he spoke he exhaled a melancholy sigh.

"The evidence against you, Mr. Hausser, is not very strong," she said. "I believe they would release you if you would give them a reasonable explanation for the check. Of the several checks, actually, since they know you wrote at least two others to Miss Taliafero.''

"They've taken away my medication," said Hausser. "I'm feeling asthmatic and need my Asthmador powder."

"You wrote the checks to cash," said Mrs. Roosevelt.

"Besides I—It's embarrassing to have to say this, but I haven't had a bowel movement since I've been here."

"I shall ask them to have a doctor examine you. Why were you giving Miss Taliafero fifty dollars a month?"

"I am most reluctant to say."

Mrs. Roosevelt smiled. At last he had shifted his attention to the subject. "Everyone understands you are reluctant. But sooner or later you are going to have to answer the question."

"I suppose I could tell *you*," he said. "Maybe you won't draw the conclusions the police would draw."

"I shall try," she said, "not to draw *any* conclusions."

Hausser sighed again. "The matter was really . . . rather innocent," he said. "The police and the public will think otherwise. They'll leer. They'll assume the worst."

"Mr. Hausser, *I* shall assume nothing. Now, please—"

He nodded. His Adam's apple bobbed. "I . . . That is, Vivian and I . . . We became involved in a wicked relationship. I imagine you know what I mean. I said it was innocent. Actually, of course, it wasn't. We committed adultery, Mrs. Roosevelt." He closed his eyes for a moment. "I am ashamed. And she was. I was of course entirely willing to marry her, but she insisted she could not marry—though she never said precisely why. After a month we broke off the relationship, by mutual agreement. We were never intimate again."

Mrs. Roosevelt frowned and waited for him to continue. He didn't. She had to prompt him:

"The checks, Mr. Hausser?"

"Oh. Well, this was most embarrassing to her. You see . . . Vivian was short of funds. What her father left her had proved insufficient. Unfortunately, she had developed some expensive habits—entertaining constantly, betting on horses, and so on. Of course, she liked expensive clothes.

She—Well, she suggested that, in view of the fact that I *had* after all compromised her honor, I might like to help her out a little. And . . . we set an amount. I gave her fifty dollars a month.''

"Why were her checks made payable to cash?"

"To avoid embarrassment to her, she said. She was ashamed to be taking money from me."

"You gave her this money voluntarily, of course."

"Oh, yes! Entirely voluntarily. Certainly you are not suggesting Vivian was . . . was *blackmailing* me?"

"Others have suggested it," said Mrs. Roosevelt dryly.

"Of course. You see. That is just what I fear—assumptions like that. An assumption of blackmail destroys Vivian's reputation. Besides . . . Besides, it establishes a supposed motive for me to want to do her harm."

"You have a reputation in the Executive Wing for being a man of independent means," said the First Lady. "Is it not true that you have a personal fortune?"

A pink blush came across his pallid face. "I, uh, do have resources. But what difference does that make?"

"I suppose fifty dollars a month is not a great deal of money for a man of independent means," said Mrs. Roosevelt. "Not enough to move a man to kill."

He nodded nervously. "That is true," he agreed.

"One further question, then. Why did Miss Taliafero come to your office last night?"

"To receive a check," he said. "I must confess I had let the date slip by and had not sent her a check when I should have—when I meant to. She came to the office and asked for it. To make it up to her for the inconvenience, I gave her this month's money and next month's in advance.''

"And she left your office alone?"

"I accompanied her to the door to the colonnade. I . . . must confess, Mrs. Roosevelt, that I wanted to kiss her." He closed his eyes again. "I wanted to touch her once more. But I didn't. She walked out of the Executive Wing, and I went back to my office. And within minutes—Within minutes she was attacked and murdered.''

Frederick Hausser did not open his eyes. Tears appeared and ran down his cheeks. He sobbed quietly.

"I should appreciate your looking at something, Lieutenant Kennelly,'' she said when Hausser had been taken back to his cell and Kennelly and Szczygiel had returned to the office. "Let's look at Mr. Hausser's checkbook.''

"Of course,'' said Kennelly. He pulled the checkbook from a drawer of his desk.

"Now,'' said Mrs. Roosevelt. "He wrote a check to Miss Taliafero in June, did he not?''

Kennelly nodded. "Second of June.''

"And May?''

"Third of May.''

"So. Going back through them, the checks were always written during the first few days of the month, were they not?''

Kennelly nodded as he flipped through the pages. "Yes. Very faithful guy, Hausser. Methodical.''

"July then?'' asked Mrs. Roosevelt.

"Oh . . . No. No, not until . . . *yesterday*. No fifty-dollar check the first week of the month. Then this one for a hundred dollars written yesterday.''

"It confirms his story,'' said Mrs. Roosevelt. "I'm going to explain what I mean by that, then suggest you release him, Lieutenant. I don't think we've got the right man.''

3

The next morning the President boarded his special car, which was then attached to a train bound for Boston, where the special car would be detached and put at the rear of another train. Each of these trains acquired the special designation POTUS—meaning President of the United States—and acquired special clearances through switching and railroad-traffic systems, to expedite the President's travel.

Mrs. Roosevelt accompanied the President to the Bureau of Printing and Engraving, where the presidential car was drawn up to a loading ramp by a siding. There it was possible for the President's wheelchair to be pushed aboard the car without lifting. He used it often.

The President and Mrs. Roosevelt shared a warm kiss aboard the car just before she returned to the presidential limousine for the return drive to the White House. "Wish me good sailing, Babs," he said. "And good fishing. And, as for you—Well, take better care of yourself than you usually do. Take some rest from time to time. And, Babs— Let the detectives do the detective work."

"Is that advice given for my benefit, or the detectives'?" she asked with a cheery smile. "God bless you, Franklin. Don't run your ship on the rocks."

Back at the White House, Missy LeHand intercepted Mrs. Roosevelt almost at the door. "J. Edgar Hoover is here," she said. "He's with Szczygiel and Baines. I need hardly tell you why."

Mrs. Roosevelt drew a deep breath. "Ask Mrs. Nesbitt to put out some coffee and juice, and some rolls or toast, in the private dining room. Then tell Mr. Hoover to meet me there."

"Uh . . . the Boss signed the order," said Missy. "Baines has it. He's probably shown it to Hoover by now."

Having taken only the two minutes required to deposit her hat and gloves in her sitting room, Mrs. Roosevelt returned to the first floor and went to the private dining room—the room where two evenings ago she had dined with Mary McLeod Bethune and Harry Hopkins.

Hoover was waiting, pacing the floor with his hands clasped behind his back. Nattily dressed as always, he wore a cream-colored double-breasted suit with a blue shirt and necktie, and two-tone shoes of tan and white.

"Mr. Hoover," she said. "What a pleasure."

"It's a pleasure to see you, Mrs. Roosevelt," he said. "As always."

"Coffee?"

"Actually—Well, yes, thank you."

She poured two cups of coffee. Mrs. Nesbitt had sent up some slices of melon, too, and she put slices on two plates and put them at two places on the table. "I've just seen the President aboard his train," she said.

Hoover sat down. "I, uh, came to offer the services of the Bureau in the Taliafero murder case," he said. "But it seems the President has signed an order conferring rather unusual jurisdiction on the Secret Service. Do you happen to know why?''

"I know very well why, Mr. Hoover," she said. "The President expressed himself quite firmly. He doesn't want any of your resources diverted from your war on the gangsters. Also, he wants you to focus your attention on subversives—Communists, Nazis, all such kind of people."

"Well, I—"

"The Taliafero case is a little sideshow, Mr. Hoover," she said. "It may generate an unfortunate amount of publicity, too. The President wants to spare you all that."

"I could spare one or two agents."

Mrs. Roosevelt smiled and shook her head. "The President was most firm about it, Mr. Hoover. You have achieved such marvelous success dealing with larger matters—"

"Well, thank you," said Hoover with a flustered grin.

She took a bite of melon. "Tell me about the arrest of Mr. Karpis," she said. "Public Enemy Number One, and you arrested him personally!"

"Yes. Yes," said Hoover.

"Then found you had no handcuffs," she said with an innocent smile.

It was an embarrassing little mistake he and his agents had made. They had captured the armed and dangerous criminal, then discovered that not one agent had thought to carry handcuffs. Hoover liked to present a public image of total efficiency, and he had been abashed to have to let reporters see his men leading Karpis away with his hands bound behind him with a necktie.

"We had the guns," said Hoover weakly.

"And the shrewd intelligence and the courage to find the man and arrest him," she said. "So let our Secret Service agents worry about the murder of Miss Taliafero. If your help is truly needed, I shall wire the President and secure his consent to amend the executive order."

* * *

"Because of the executive order, the D.C. police have asked Szczygiel or Baines to go with them when they enter Vivian Taliafero's house," said Missy.

"Surely they have done that already," said Mrs. Roosevelt.

"Apparently not," said Missy.

"Well, I should like to go with them myself," said the First Lady. "Unhappily, I am meeting Jim Farley for lunch."

"Suppose *I* go," said Missy.

"Oh, I couldn't ask—"

"The President is out of town," said Missy. "I can go, and I can give you a personal report of what I see. Besides, a woman might observe something a man would overlook. *You* might. And I might. It's a woman's home that's going to be searched, and a woman—"

"I am convinced," said Mrs. Roosevelt. "If you want to, Missy. I should consider it a favor if you went."

Agent Stanlislaw Szczygiel and Detective Lieutenant Edward Kennelly were not sure Missy LeHand's presence was any great favor to them, as they entered the house in Georgetown. But they were subtle about it, and if she guessed how they felt it was a guess, nothing she could read on their faces or in their voices.

The house was on a tree-lined brick street. The house itself was brick: old, soft, eroded, pastel-colored brick. It was small, but it was not modest. It had stood there for at least a hundred years. Like many of the houses along the street, it had a cast-iron hitching post at the curb. A low brick wall separated a narrow front garden from the street; and to the sides and behind that wall rose to eight feet in height, affording the house total privacy.

Kennelly opened the front door with a small tool, to which the lock readily yielded. The door opened on an entrance hall, from which a graceful set of stairs rose in a gentle curve to the second floor. To the right of the hall, through double doors, was a formal living room, furnished in a Federal style. To the left was a formal dining room. The hall led to a kitchen and pantry on the rear of the house, and a small, intimate study furnished with sedate leather-covered armchairs.

"So this is the famous Taliafero salon," said Missy, looking around. "She entertained the best and the worst this town has to offer."

It was true. Szczygiel knew it. He had spent hours poring over old newspaper accounts of the Taliafero salon. By that small fireplace in which coal, not wood, had been burned, Douglas MacArthur had stood chatting with Henry Stimson about the state of the nation's army and navy. On that sofa, perhaps—or if not there, then in one of those wing chairs by the fireplace—J. P. Morgan had sat and sipped whiskey and talked money with Richard Whitney, president of the New York Stock Exchange. Senator Huey P. Long had been here often—until he was assassinated in his own state capitol ten months ago. Louis Brandeis and Benjamin Cardozo, justices of the Supreme Court, had continued to come here after Justice Holmes was no longer able. It was in this parlor, the newspapers said, that Al Smith had met the panjandrums of the Liberty League and accepted from them the text of the speech that would ruin, finally and forever, whatever shreds were left of his sagging reputation for intelligence and integrity.

"All very respectable," said Szczygiel. "What moved somebody to kill her?"

Missy led the way upstairs. Her instinct suggested that anything irregular in a woman's life would be found in her bedroom.

It was a rather ordinary bedroom—except in one respect. The centerpiece was a magnificent four-poster bed with a fringed canopy above. Vivian Taliafero's dressing table was crowded with a not unusual collection of cosmetics, combs, brushes, and perfumes. Her closet was packed with expensive clothes. The candles on her night tables would fill the air with scent when lit.

What was unusual was that the wall to the left of her bed, as you faced it, was one huge mirror, floor to ceiling.

"Vanity, hmm?" said Kennelly. "She must have enjoyed the sight of herself."

Missy stood before the mirror, looking at her own image and at the image of the bed behind her, and frowned curiously. She had heard of mirrors on ceilings, but . . . Abruptly an idea came. She rushed out of the room, turned, and entered what was apparently a closet to the side of the bedroom.

It was not a closet. It was what her sudden idea had suggested. Inside the hall door was a second door. Beyond that was a narrow chamber that faced—It faced the back side of that huge mirror: a two-way mirror. Anyone entering that chamber and closing that second door would be in the dark and would be invisible from the bedroom while enjoying an unhindered view of bed and occupants. Anyone who wanted a show—whatever show Vivian Taliafero presented on that bed—had a perfect view of her stage.

The chamber was furnished with just three items—two tall tripods extended to their fullest length, and a short stepladder.

"My God," muttered Kennelly when he entered the chamber and saw what Missy had found. "A salon my achin' backside. The place was a bordello!"

"Hmm-umm," said Missy. "A blackmail factory. Whoever did whatever they did on that bed, was witnessed from here—and, what do you want to bet, *photographed.*"

"Uh . . . no, I think you're ahead of things on that score," said Szczygiel. "There wouldn't be enough light. And a time exposure . . ." He grinned. "It wouldn't get what you wanted."

"Better look into the science of photography, Szczygiel," said Missy. "It's very different from what it was even two years ago. Faster films . . . Even film that will react to infrared light—invisible light, to the subject being photographed. Anyway, maybe some of the subjects lay on the bed in the sunlight from those windows.''

"Maybe it was just shows," Szczygiel suggested. "Some people were allowed to come in and watch—"

"We shouldn't guess," said Missy. "But a lot of possibilities are here, in this mirror wall and this observation room. I would guess our innocent salon hostess was running something much more profitable than a salon.''

"I want fingerprints off every bottle on that dressing table," said Szczygiel to Kennelly. "And off those bed posts, too.''

"Both sides of the mirror," Missy suggested.

"Both sides of the mirror. Not downstairs. God knows whose prints are in that parlor. But this bedroom . . .''

They searched the bedroom thoroughly, being careful not to introduce their own fingerprints into the collection they expected they might find. Then they went through other rooms.

The bathroom was unexceptional. It might well have been the bathroom of a maiden lady who never received gentlemen callers on her second floor. A guest bedroom seemed to have been only the place where Vivian Taliafero stored clothes. The air of the room was heavy with the odor of mothballs, and the closet was filled with winter clothes. The bed was stacked with them. Still more clothes hung in paperboard wardrobes that stood around the bed.

"I notice something odd," said Missy.

"As do I," said Kennelly.

"No jewelry," said Missy. "Expensive clothes in quantity, but no jewels. Odd.''

"Unless there's a safe somewhere on the premises," said Szczygiel. "I think we have to look for a safe.''

"Or maybe she had a safe-deposit box in some bank," said Kennelly.

"We keep looking," said Missy grimly.

There was no attic. A dusty crawl space above the ceiling could be entered by means of a pull-down stairway, but a glimpse up there showed that no one had disturbed the dust for years.

There was a cellar. They entered it from a door in the kitchen and went down, expecting to find a supply of wines. Instead, they found a brick-paved and -walled laboratory. A photographic laboratory. Bottles stood in ranks on rough wooden shelves: the chemicals with which negatives were developed and prints made. There were trays and tanks, an enlarger, safelights, light-tight boxes of film and photographic paper, plus of course the cameras, four of them—all the stuff for making pictures. It confirmed what they had suspected upstairs, that cameras had been set up behind that see-through mirror and compromising pictures had been taken.

But there were no pictures. No negatives. No prints. A safe cabinet, which might have contained them, was empty. If this photographic laboratory had made the most scandalous pictures of the century, none remained to be seen.

"Obviously," said Szczygiel, "she had a confederate. Had to have, to take the pictures—that is, assuming she was the costar on the bed. And her confederate heard of her death and rushed here to clear out every last picture, before *we* arrived."

"Conjecture," said Missy. "But a very likely conjecture. Very likely."

Missy, who knew something about photography, was examining the cameras—two Leicas equipped with f:1.5 lenses, a Rolleiflex with an f:2, and a Graflex with an f:3.5. The Leicas shot 35mm film, the Rolleiflex produced 2¼ × 2¼ roll-film negatives, and the Graflex used 4 × 5 sheet film. The Rolleiflex was equipped with a synchronized flashgun capable of firing infrared flashbulbs. These expensive cameras could hardly have been better chosen for making pictures of bedroom activity in low light.

"And while the confederate was at it, he or she cleared out any other valuables Vivian Taliafero had—jewels or whatever," said Kennelly.

Missy glanced around the laboratory. "Whether that is speculation or not, obviously someone has been here before us."

"I want fingerprints from everywhere," said Szczygiel.

Kennelly allowed himself a little smile. "Apt to get some interesting ones," he said.

Szczygiel shrugged. "I could kick myself for not hurrying out here night before last. We might have found a ton of evidence. We might have caught the confederate in the act of stealing it."

"I bet he's destroyed every item of it by now," said Kennelly.

"I doubt that," said Missy. "If he took photographs from this house, and if they were what we think they were, they are extremely valuable. If Vivian Taliafero was a blackmailer, and if someone killed her to stop the blackmail, that someone has a surprise coming."

"It is difficult to believe," said Mrs. Roosevelt when Missy reported to her the evidence that Vivian Taliafero had been running a blackmail factory in her Georgetown home.

Agent Szczygiel came to the First Lady's office just as Missy finished her report. He had more facts to tell:

"We've just finished an examination of Vivian Taliafero's bank records," he said. "Hausser's checks were the only checks made out to cash that she ever deposited."

"Then maybe your surmise is wrong, Missy," said Mrs. Roosevelt.

Missy shrugged.

"Probably not," said Szczygiel. "Each month Miss Taliafero deposited the same three checks—the one from Hausser, one from the federal treasury, representing payment of her survivor's rights to her father's senatorial pension, and one from a Biloxi bank, representing the monthly income from a trust fund her father had established for her before his death. The total was a little more than two hundred dollars a month. Not enough—not nearly enough—to support the lady in her Georgetown home in the style to which she was accustomed.''

"I'm not certain exactly what that proves, Mr. Szczygiel," said Mrs. Roosevelt.

"Lieutenant Kennelly," Szczygiel went on, "sent men to make some inquiries. From the labels in some of her expensive clothes, they could tell where she bought those clothes. She drove a Ford she bought from a Georgetown automobile dealer. Labels on champagne bottles told where she had bought her wines and liquors. The D.C. detectives checked out two couturiers and the automobile and liquor dealers. Miss Taliafero was a very good customer of each. She paid all her bills with cash.''

"Still—"

"She spent sixty-five dollars last month on wines and liquors," said Szczygiel. "At just the two couturiers that were visited, she spent one hundred eighty-five dollars. She bought her Ford in November—and paid six hundred and fifty dollars in cash. Besides, in her closet there were two or three furs, a score of pairs of shoes, a—"

"Well over a thousand dollars' worth of cameras and camera equipment, I should guess," said Missy.

Szczygiel shook his head emphatically. "People who live on $200 a month don't have things like that.''

"She owned her home," said Mrs. Roosevelt.

"She didn't inherit it from her father," said Szczygiel. "She was paying off a mortgage at eight-five dollars a month. She wrote checks for that. She paid for her insurance with checks. She was a member of the Pavilion Club and paid her dues and monthly luncheon bills with checks. She employed a housemaid, who was paid by check. You see—"

"A housemaid?"

"Yes. Unemployed now and very tearful about it."

"That maid must have known something about what went on in the house," Missy suggested.

"Swears she didn't," said Szczygiel. "She says her duties, chiefly, were to prepare food and serve guests. The cellar door was kept locked, she says, and she insists she didn't know what was down there. Also, she says the door into the room behind the see-through mirror was always locked, so she never guessed what that was. When Kennelly's men asked her about the big mirror, she said it wasn't a see-through. In fact, she said she'd never heard of such a thing as a see-through mirror."

"This maid is available for further questioning, I suppose," said Mrs. Roosevelt.

"Yes. Her name is Amy Curtis. A Negro girl."

Mrs. Roosevelt shook her head sadly. "It is difficult to imagine a woman like Miss Vivian Taliafero involved in such nefarious activities as the evidence seems to suggest. I hope some other explanation of the facts will turn up."

"You have always tried to think the best of people," said Missy.

"Well, I *do* try to," said Mrs. Roosevelt. "Sometimes people disappoint us. More often, they don't. I retain my optimism about the human race."

"Fingerprints," said Stanlislaw Szczygiel. "Kennelly has made a card file of them."

He handed a stack of cards to Mrs. Roosevelt, who read them over with growing dismay. "Oh, Mr. Szczygiel, this is *dreadful!*" she whispered hoarsely.

"Well, please do notice that most of the prints were taken in the kitchen and in the living and dining rooms," said Szczygiel. "Only the cards with the red checkmarks represent prints taken in the bedroom or the upstairs bathroom."

"But these men—" She scowled over the names on the red-checked cards. The fingerprints of Secretary of Trade Herschel Rinehart, a member of the Cabinet, had been taken from a water glass in the bathroom. Those of a judge of the United States Circuit Court had been found on the tiles just above the bathtub. Those of an assistant attorney

39

general had been taken from one of the posts of Vivian Taliafero's four-poster bed.

"Their careers could be ruined if their names got out."

"Their names aren't going to get out, Ma'am. Unless . . ."

"Unless what?"

"Well, they are all suspects in the death of Miss Taliafero. There's no avoiding that. They're all suspects."

Mrs. Roosevelt tossed one card to Szczygiel—the card bearing the name of the member of the President's Cabinet. "He's not," she said. "He left Washington for Boston the day before Miss Taliafero was killed. He made a speech there that evening and one at noon the day of the murder. He could not possibly have returned in time to have been in the Rose Garden and strangled the poor woman."

"All right," said Szczygiel. "That leaves the other two. I'll have to interrogate them. I have no choice but to do that."

The First Lady glanced over the rest of the cards once more. "These men are all innocent, I should think," she said. "After all, Miss Taliafero *did* conduct a salon in her parlor and dining room. By no means all the men who went to her house were there for improper purposes."

"I tend to agree," said Szczygiel. "Of course, none of them are absolved from suspicion by—"

"Surely you don't mean to question all these gentlemen?"

"No. Still . . . our murderer could be among them."

She handed him the cards. "Fingerprints . . ." she mused. "What prints were found on the photographic equipment in the cellar?"

"Ah, that's an interesting point," said Szczygiel. Having returned the index cards to his jacket pocket, he began to pick his fingernails. "Someone made an effort to wipe off all the fingerprints on the cameras and other equipment. He was pretty thorough, too; but you'd have to guess he was in a hurry, and he didn't get them all. He left his prints inside one of the cameras, also on a part of the enlarger. And—'' He smiled. "Also on the back side of the see-through mirror."

"Excellent," said Mrs. Roosevelt.

"No. I'm afraid not," said Szczygiel. "Whoever our subject is, he has never been fingerprinted. There is no record of his prints in the files of the D.C. police or in the F.B.I. central files. He's never been arrested apparently, never worked for the government, never served in the armed forces."

"Oh, dear," sighed Mrs. Roosevelt.

"We can match these prints against the prints of any suspect, and of course if they match we have a case. But—" He shrugged. "Until we have prints to match them against, I'm afraid it's not much help to have them."

"Were there other unidentifiable prints in the house?" she asked.

"Yes. One set on the clock by her bed. The rest downstairs."

"It is simply not true that *everyone* has been fingerprinted," she said. "I've observed that fingerprint identification is not universally useful, as many people assume."

"No," said Szczygiel. "It isn't. And now, I suppose, I have no choice but to confront Judge Kincaid and Assistant Attorney General Wolfe."

"And perhaps I shall ask a few more questions of Mr. Hausser."

Frederick Hausser had returned to work in his office within hours after he was released from jail. He went home, bathed, dressed in fresh clothes, and was back behind his desk a little later, as if nothing had happened. He had never been a gregarious man—didn't think his job required it—and he felt no pressure to explain to anyone in the office why he had been arrested and held overnight in the District jail. Two days later he still had not discussed it with anyone.

Mrs. Roosevelt knocked gently on his open door, then walked in. Hausser literally sprang from his chair.

"Sit down, Mr. Hausser," she said cheerfully. "You are no longer the prime suspect. May I sit down and chat with you for a moment?"

"Of course," he said, sinking back into his chair.

She glanced around his office. The offices in the Executive Wing were anything but luxurious. Indeed, the whole wing was in a state of seedy disrepair, owing to long-time reluctance on the part of Congress to appropriate money to remodel it. Hausser's scarred old wood desk sat on a carpet so worn that patches of coarse-woven yellowish backing showed through the threadbare maroon pile. His bare-wood swivel chair shrieked when he leaned back in it. An oscillating fan rattled on a window sill. A strip of flypaper hung from the ceiling—with a score or more of dead flies stuck to it—but a fly swatter lay at hand on the desk, and half a dozen more dead flies lay on the floor and even on top of a stack of papers.

"Washington is an uncomfortable place in the summer," she said conversationally.

"It's very bad for me, really," said Hausser. "I may move to Maine. Besides . . . Perhaps I shouldn't mention it, but I'm sure I picked up a rash in the jail. Bedbugs maybe."

"Frankly, Mr. Hausser, if you had been more forthcoming Tuesday night, you would not have gone to jail."

"I felt I had to keep Miss Taliafero's reputation clean."

Mrs. Roosevelt sighed. "I cannot be certain, Mr. Hausser, if you are the most naive man I've ever met or a very shrewd man with a clever way of telling lies."

"Please, Ma'am!"

"Mr. Hausser, you are not entirely out of trouble. I am going to ask you a few more questions, and if you do not give honest and complete answers you may find yourself in jail again."

He flushed, and the muscles along his jawline began to twitch. "I . . . I have told you the truth," he protested.

"I must have more of the truth," she said. "You said you had a—I believe you called it a 'wicked relationship' with Miss Taliafero."

"I am ashamed to say that I did."

"Where, Mr. Hausser? Where did you do it?"

Hausser's lip trembled. "Why, in her home," he said.

"In her bedroom?"

"Yes . . ."

"When you were in that bedroom, did you notice that one wall of the room was an exceptionally large mirror?"

He nodded feebly. "Vivian had a joke about that—that she was so vain she needed an outsized mirror to admire herself adequately."

"Do you know what was behind that mirror? What *is* behind it?"

His mouth hung open as he shook his head.

"Not a wall," she said. "A room. A dark room. From behind that mirror you could be watched, doing whatever it was you did with Miss Taliafero. Not only that. You could be photographed—and almost certainly were."

He could not have been more stunned if she had slapped him. For a moment his mouth moved, forming words for which he had no voice; then he gurgled in his throat and stuttered—"If anyone but you said that to me, I'd call it a lie."

"I can arrange for you to go to the house and see for yourself," she said. "Behind the mirror is a room where cameras were set up to photograph whatever happened in the bedroom. In the cellar is a complete photographic laboratory, with cameras and other equipment particularly suited for such photography. The police have found everything but the negatives and photographs themselves. They seem to have been hastily removed from the house after Miss Taliafero's death."

"But, Mrs. Roosevelt, for what purpose?" he cried.

Then he closed his eyes and removed his eyeglasses. "Never mind, I'm afraid I know for what purpose."

"Do you?"

"Well, I can guess," he said, rubbing his eyes with both fists.

"Mr. Hausser, I want a straightforward answer. Did Miss Taliafero ever show you photographs she had of you? Or did she tell you she had such pictures? Is that why you paid her fifty dollars a month—to prevent her embarrassing you with photographs showing you engaging in illicit intimate activity?"

He shook his head. "I swear to you, Mrs. Roosevelt," he muttered, "that I had no idea until now that she made any such photographs. She never mentioned any such thing to me. I gave her money because I cared for her and because I believed I had done her a grievous wrong."

"It appears, Mr. Hausser—though it is not yet proved—that she received money from several other gentlemen."

"Because she had pictures of them," he whispered.

"Yes. So it would appear."

Hausser sat shaking his head. His little spectacles lay on his desk before him, and he planted his elbows to either side of them and dropped his head into his hands.

"Do you wish to amend your statement in any way?" she asked gently.

"Not really," he mumbled. "Maybe . . . Maybe, thinking back, I should acknowledge that it was really *her* idea that I give her money. I guess I really didn't play the gallant gentleman and offer it. She said I had compromised her reputation and honor, that in Mississippi men were *shot* for doing a thing like that, and that—But, Mrs. Roosevelt, I swear to you she never mentioned any photographs. I swear it!"

"You also continue to swear that you didn't kill her."

"No, I didn't! I didn't. God, no!"

"Well, somebody did," said Mrs. Roosevelt. "Tell me all you can. I mean, the details of your relationship with

Miss Taliafero. Obviously I don't mean the details of your intimacy. I mean the details of how you met her and so on.''

Hausser picked up his glasses and re-seated them on his nose. Facing the task of recounting facts seemed to invigorate him a little, and he reached for a thermos carafe and poured two glasses of ice water. He pushed one glass across the desk toward the First Lady.

"Well . . ." he began. "I met . . . Vivian. I came to call her by her first name. I met Vivian at the Pavilion Club, actually. At the buffet, on a Saturday noon. Someone introduced us. Senator Cranshaw, now that I think of it. She and I talked, and before the lunch was over she invited me to her salon. Oh, that was an honor! I felt I had really *arrived* in Washington. So I went to Georgetown on the following Wednesday evening—not wanting, you know, to appear the first evening when I might have. She received me as if I were an important person. She actually inquired as to why I hadn't come Monday or Tuesday. I drank champagne in her parlor, and ate hors d'oeuvres. And she introduced me to General Hugh Johnson and to Congressman Martin Dies.

"That evening. Another evening I met Senator Huey Long. Also Vice President Garner. I—"

"How did the relationship between you and Miss Taliafero develop into an intimate one?" asked Mrs. Roosevelt.

"I suppose it was the third time I went to her house. I didn't dare go more than once every two weeks or so, you understand, so I suppose I'd known her a month or six weeks, and—Well . . . She asked me to stay after the other guests left. She said we hadn't had an opportunity to become better acquainted. I'd had a good deal of champagne, I suppose. We sat down on her couch together, and she asked me about my work, about my family, about my education. And—Well, it was quite sudden. She kissed me! She said I was the kind of man it was difficult to meet in Washington, and she said she wanted to know me better.

"I . . . We didn't go to her bedroom that night. But the next time, just a couple of days later, we did. We didn't even wait until the other guests had left. She slipped up beside me and said she couldn't wait any longer. She took my arm and led me to the stairs. I was quite embarrassed. I suspected others knew where we were going, and why. But we went upstairs."

He stopped. He closed his eyes again, and squeezed out tears.

"You needn't tell me about what happened upstairs," said Mrs. Roosevelt.

He swallowed. "I guess I am a fool," he whispered. "I was in *heaven!* I didn't care what might follow from the adventure. Whatever it was, it was worth it! She was an angel . . ."

"And later you went back downstairs."

"Yes, Congressman Dies was standing by the fireplace with a drink in his hand. Bourbon, not champagne. He sort of leered at me and said, 'Welcome to the club, young man.' I was so naive I supposed he meant welcome to Vivian's salon. Now I suspect—"

"Yes," said Mrs. Roosevelt. "It would be the best thing he's done in Washington."

"Another man said something of the sort. Senator Valentine. He greeted me with the same kind of leer and laughed and said something to the effect—My Lord! He said something about—His words were, 'They take pictures at the Olympics, son. Hope you performed in gold-medal style.' "

"Senator Steven A. Valentine . . ." she mused.

"Senator from the U.A.W., as they say," Hausser suggested.

"Worse things are represented in the Senate," said Mrs. Roosevelt.

"I was insufficiently intelligent to understand what he was telling me."

"By then it was too late," she said.

"Either Senator Valentine was also being blackmailed, or he was an accomplice," said Hausser darkly. "How else could he have known she took pictures?"

"That thought has already occurred to me, too, Mr. Hausser. How indeed did the senator know?"

Judge Beresford Kincaid turned impatiently on his heels, causing his voluminous black robe to swirl around him. "I suppose so, Mr. Szczygiel. In my chambers. And very briefly."

Stanlislaw Szczygiel had approached the judge as he came off the bench and walked into the narrow corridor between the courtroom and the clerk's office. The Circuit Court was in recess for the summer, which did not mean the judges had a long summer vacation. Judge Kincaid had spent the week hearing motions. Now it was Friday afternoon, and he made no secret of his impatience to be out of Washington as quickly as he could. He was taking a long weekend at an estate in Virginia, where he expected to cool himself in the pool, drink long, cold drinks, and be spared the endless convoluted arguments of litigants. He was annoyed to be approached by an agent of the Secret Service.

He knew why he was being approached.

In his office—grandly called "chambers" but only a dusty little room filled with hot air stirred by a fan—Judge Kincaid pulled off his robe and sat down in his sweat-drenched shirt. The judge was sixty-eight years old, a once-powerful man with broad shoulders and hard muscles, now softened and a little rounded by the years. His face was red. His thick hair was white. His eyebrows were like big white brushes, dramatic in contrast with his ruddy skin. He lit a cigarette and glowered at Stanlislaw Szczygiel.

"I'll be as brief as I can, Your Honor," said Szczygiel. He was nervously picking at his fingernails. "Under an Executive Order signed by the President, the Secret Service bears principal responsibility for investigating the murder of Miss Vivian Taliafero."

"An order of questionable legality," the judge rumbled.

Szczygiel turned up his palms. "As that may be," he said. "Nevertheless, we are investigating the case, with the cooperation of the District of Columbia police. An element of that investigation has been a fingerprint examination of Miss Taliafero's home in Georgetown."

"I should imagine you've found a 'Who's Who in Washington,' " said Judge Kincaid.

"Yes. We are most interested, though, in the fingerprints we found upstairs, in Miss Taliafero's bedroom and her adjacent private bathroom."

The judge drew deeply on his cigarette, then put it aside in his desk ashtray. "Go on."

"We found *yours*, sir."

The judge smiled sarcastically. "She asked me for a private conference in her bedroom, so I could advise her on a problem she felt she had with the way the Biloxi bank was administering her trust." Then his smile disappeared. "Just where were my fingerprints found?"

"On the tiles above the bathtub," said Szczygiel soberly.

"The woman was a poor housekeeper. Or that colored girl of hers was. It's been months since I was in that tub."

"Did she show you the pictures?" Szczygiel asked.

Judge Kincaid's chin rose slowly, and the skin of his face flushed a darker red. He scowled. "I was a district attorney for thirty years before I was appointed to the bench," he said. "I know all the interrogator's tricks there are. So don't ask me if I saw some pictures. Tell me what pictures you mean."

"Pictures of you, sir—taken from behind the big mirror in the bedroom."

"Have you seen any such pictures, Szczygiel?" the judge demanded.

"No. Only the means for taking them."

"Then maybe there are no pictures of me."

"Maybe. That's what I was asking you."

The judge inhaled cigarette smoke and pondered visibly for a moment. "I think I'll take that question under advisement," he said. "That's one of the privileges of judgeship—I don't have to rule on anything immediately."

"Are you prepared to admit you had an intimate relationship with Miss Taliafero?"

The judge leaned back in his chair and contemplated Szczygiel with skepticism and a measure of contempt. "I am prepared," he said, "to admit that I took a bath in her tub. Let me know when you can prove anything else."

An hour later he confronted Assistant Attorney General William Wolfe. Wolfe, too, was anxious to be away from his office, to begin his weekend; and he was curt and hostile.

"I hardly knew the woman, Szczygiel. Are you harassing every man whose fingerprints you found in her house?"

Stan Szczygiel was less impressed with an assistant attorney general than he was with a judge of the Circuit Court. "Only ones whose fingerprints were found on her bed," he answered.

Wolfe was a slick man—slick black hair held in place with a scented dressing, pencil mustache, high-styled double-breasted suit that seemed to keep its crisp shape in spite of the damp heat of the July day. He smoked his cigarettes in a holder, perhaps in imitation of the President, but unlike the President he kept the holder in his mouth while he talked, and the cigarette wobbled around melodramatically.

"Is the Secret Service investigating adultery?" he asked. "Your fingerprint evidence will hardly make *that* case, much less anything else."

"One straightforward question, one straightforward answer, okay?" said Szczygiel. "Was Vivian Taliafero blackmailing you?"

Wolfe first grinned, then laughed. "How could she have blackmailed me, Szczygiel? I'm an unmarried man! If she had incontrovertible evidence that I was in her bed, she couldn't blackmail me."

"She *had* incontrovertible evidence," said Szczygiel blandly.

"Really? And you have seen this evidence, I suppose."

"No, but I know it exists."

"Do you, now? Okay. Anything else, Mr. Szczygiel? I am bored with this conversation, really, and am of course under no obligation to continue it."

Szczygiel turned down the corners of his mouth and shrugged. "No obligation," he agreed. "But—Well . . . You're a smart-aleck, Wolfe, and you're not as big a cheese as you think you are. You've just claimed the number-one position on the list of suspects."

"Who the hell do you think you are, Szczygiel?" Wolfe barked, rising from his chair. "Let me show you what you are. I'm going to throw your ass out of here, and let's see how much stink you can raise about it."

Wolfe stalked around his desk, grabbed Szczygiel by his lapels, and jerked him out of his chair. Abruptly then he loosed his grip and sat down awkwardly on the floor, clutching his belly—into which Szczygiel had just driven a hard fist.

Stan Szczygiel smiled contemptuously. "Tough man are you, Mister Assistant Attorney General? I'm investigating the murder of Vivian Taliafero by authority of a direct Executive Order signed by the President. I make reports. I'll be writing one about you tonight. Let's see . . . How will I describe you? 'Arrogant, not too bright, probably not the murderer of Vivian Taliafero because he's all bluster and wouldn't have the guts to strangle a woman.' And . . . Oh, yes. 'A sucker for a short left.' "

5

The President wired:

ADVISE MRS. NESBITT TO MAKE ALL 1936 TUNA
SALADS DURING NEXT TWO WEEKS STOP AF-
TER THIS FISHING EXPEDITION THERE WILL BE
NO MORE TUNA STOP FOR WHICH I SHALL BE
DULY GRATEFUL STOP CHICKS MAKE FINE
SAILORS STOP SUN COOPERATING STOP ALTO-
GETHER A MARVELOUS HOLIDAY SO FAR STOP
MOUNT SIEGE GUNS AND HOLD FORT STOP
LOVE STOP

Mrs. Roosevelt showed the wire to Missy as they sat
down together for a simple Friday-evening dinner, which
consisted, ironically, of tuna salad and corn on the cob. It
had been served on a card table in the sitting hall in the
private suite.

"Except for a bit of time given to the problem of the murder of Miss Taliafero, I've spent my day working on some of the problems of the campaign," said Mrs. Roosevelt. "I have to say that, so far as I can determine, the only group that is really well advanced in its planning is the women's committee."

"What troubles me," said Missy, "is that eighty-five percent of the newspapers in this country are owned by Republican families or Republican-controlled corporations. I know the Boss is worried about that, too."

"I am troubled," said Mrs. Roosevelt, "about his somewhat blasé attitude toward the campaign. As you know."

"He's been giving some orders," said Missy. "Did he tell you that he ordered Henry Wallace to see that the price of cotton does not drop below twelve cents between now and November?"

"I know he did," said Mrs. Roosevelt. "I'm not sure how he thinks the Secretary of Agriculture can achieve that."

"He said that's Henry's problem. He told him he doesn't care how he does it, so long as he does it."

"The Republicans are going to make a major campaign issue of Social Security," said Mrs. Roosevelt. "They say we are taking money from the working man and putting it in a government fund which may never repay him."

"Social Security may be the best thing this administration has done," said Missy, lifting her glass and taking a sip of iced tea. "I can't believe the Republicans really want to repeal it."

"Well, that's how they're talking. They say the Act should be repealed before the first withholdings are taken in 1937."

"They'll have to elect a Republican Congress as well as a Republican President," said Missy.

"Speaking of electing a Republican Congress," said

Mrs. Roosevelt, "what do you know of Senator Valentine?"

Missy was eating an ear of corn, and she paused to chew and to use a napkin to wipe a bit of butter from her mouth before she answered. "Steve Valentine? They won't beat him. I'd say that's as safe a Senate seat as we have."

"But his character . . . What do you know about that? Anything? I mean, have you heard anything?"

"Well . . ." said Missy. "Family man. Father of three. Devout Presbyterian." She paused and smiled wickedly. "There are a few rumors around that not all is as it seems."

"Mr. Hausser says Senator Valentine was at Miss Taliafero's house one evening when he, Mr. Hausser, went upstairs with Miss Taliafero; and when they came down the senator made a remark suggesting he knew about the hidden cameras and all that. I am a bit concerned about the newspaper coverage. One paper has already editorialized that we should have allowed the F.B.I. to investigate the case."

"I would be more interested in that if I knew the origin of the suggestion."

"Let's keep our suspicions to ourselves. The question is, will Mr. Szczygiel and his associates be able to solve the case, or will it drag on indefinitely."

"The longer it drags on, the worse," said Missy. "I mean, the more chance some reporter will discover the dreadful scandal in the background."

"It already involves a federal judge," said Mrs. Roosevelt. "Plus an assistant attorney general and two members of Congress."

"Two?"

"Well . . . Besides Senator Valentine, Representative Dies also made a strange comment to Mr. Hausser."

Missy put aside her corn cob. "I have a thought," she said. "Unless you think it's entirely inappropriate, I'll make a quiet inquiry."

"Your thought is—?"

For a brief moment Missy drummed her fingers on the table, as though pondering whether to continue with her idea, to express it, or just to drop it. Finally she said—"The Alex Bushnell suicide."

Mrs. Roosevelt grimaced. "What a distressing business!"

"You know I was a friend of Betsy's."

"I . . . I do recall, yes."

"I say, *was* a friend. I should say, *am* a friend—though I rarely see her anymore. Betsy was extremely bitter about what happened. She became reclusive at first and didn't want to see her friends. I understand now she is anxious to re-establish old friendships. I think I should pay her a call."

"What has this to do with the death of Miss Taliafero?"

"Betsy told me at the time of Alex's death, that he killed himself because some horrible scandal was about to erupt, that would have ruined his career. Well, it never did. Now I wonder what the scandal was."

"You don't think—?"

"I don't know," said Missy. "But I think it's possible. I think I should find out. Have you any objection?"

"No," said Mrs. Roosevelt. "I know you will handle it tactfully."

Mrs. Roosevelt remembered Alexander Bushnell very well. He had been one of the young men who had volunteered his services to the Democratic campaign in 1932, in spite of the fact that his family had been Republicans for three or four generations. He had come to Washington in 1933, one of the young attorneys who took prominent positions in the New Deal—he, eventually, at the new Securities and Exchange Commission.

He had been born in 1897 and so was just thirteen years younger than she was, and he had been born and reared in a milieu much like her own—Manhattan, a prosperous though not immensely wealthy family. He had been educated like the President, at Groton and Harvard. In 1917, the twenty-year-old Alex had enlisted in the army, trained at Camp Yaphank, and had been commissioned a second lieutenant just before his regiment was shipped to France. He was wounded slightly at St. Mihiel and came home a hero. He finished his education, was admitted to the New York bar, and joined Elihu Root's law firm.

All very respectable. Then he married badly. Unsuitably. Or so his family believed. He married Betsy Sullivan, the daughter of a Connecticut state senator reputed to be a bootlegger. What was worse in the eyes of the Bushnells, the Sullivans were Catholics.

Betsy Sullivan Bushnell was of the new generation of women, who seemed almost effortlessly to have claimed and established an independence Mrs. Roosevelt herself had been compelled to struggle to attain. The young woman had enjoyed her freedom as nothing more than her due and apparently had cared not a fig about the hostility of the Bushnells. She was chic, she smoked cigarettes and drank in public, she salted her conversation with au courant slang, and she had opinions of her own, which she expressed a bit shrilly in Mrs. Roosevelt's judgment.

Alex had been a slim, almost ascetic young man who probably had found it difficult to cope with his wife's flippant derision of the austere Bushnells. *He* had been the family friend. Although Mrs. Roosevelt had sometimes envied Betsy's easy, self-assured poise, she had found it difficult to become close to her. She had sent her a note of condolence when Alex shot himself, and two months later had invited her to a small dinner at the White House. Betsy Bushnell had not acknowledged the invitation.

"Fancy seein' you," said Betsy to Missy. "Just happened to be in the neighborhood, I bet. Is the visit official or unofficial?"

Missy had arrived at Betsy's small white frame house

on N Street about seven-thirty. Betsy came to the door in a white sateen slip, which she wore with a pair of white satin high-heeled slippers. She had a cigarette in her hand.

"Haven't seen you for a long time," said Missy. "Something came up that made me think of you. And no, I didn't just happen to be in the neighborhood. I came."

"Well, come in. Like a drink?"

"I wouldn't mind," said Missy. "The President is on vacation, and I just had dinner with Mrs. R. Iced tea."

Betsy led her into the small living room, where she switched off the radio. "Having a bourbon and water myself," she said. "What can I do for you? I've got gin. Maybe a bit of Scotch. Besides bourbon."

"Bourbon and water will be perfect," said Missy.

While Betsy was in the kitchen, Missy glanced around the living room. Betsy lived modestly. Her furniture was drab and some of it well worn, as though it had been bought secondhand. She'd heard the Bushnells had refused to supplement the little that Alex had left.

Betsy returned with Missy's drink, a generous slug of bourbon with a little water. Her hair was blonde, as always—a little more blonde than always, in fact, showing evidence of the application of peroxide. She had gained a little weight; her jawline was indistinct now, and she showed a diminutive second chin.

"Yer health," she said, lifting her own half-empty glass. Missy nodded and sipped.

"So," said Betsy. "Still workin' for the Roosevelts, I understand. You must love 'em."

"They've been more than kind to me," said Missy.

"Yeah. Well, I work myself, y' know. Nothin' glamorous like at the White House, but . . . What the hell?"

"What do you do, Betsy?"

"Sell this stuff," she said, nodding toward her glass of bourbon. "Workin' in a liquor store. Not nearly as much fun now that it's legal. My old man sold it when it wasn't, y' know. That's when there was money in it."

"You've decided to stay in Washington, I guess."

"You better believe it. You wanta know why? Because one of these days this city is gonna be the most important in the world, most important and most exciting in every way. You watch. It's gonna happen."

"Why, do you think?"

Betsy tipped her glass, finished her drink, and stared into it as though it had betrayed her by being consumed so quickly. "Because there's gonna be another war," she said. "Another world war. You watch and see. And when that happens, this is gonna be the roaringest boom town this country's ever seen."

Missy laughed. "The Boss ought to hear this."

"Don't kid yourself that he doesn't know it. And you know it, too, even if you don't wanta admit it."

"What makes you think that, Betsy?"

"Look at the map of Europe," said Betsy. "What a screwed-up mess they made of it after the last war. Sooner or later the Russians are going to come after what was stolen from them in 1919. So are the Germans. So are the Hungarians. And when a war gets started over there, it'll spread like it did last time." She shook her head. "It's gonna be a *big* war. And Washington's gonna be the center of the world . . . Anyway, why did you come to see me?"

"I need to ask you something about Alex," said Missy simply.

Betsy shrugged. "Ask anything you want. I've got no emotions left about him. Wait till I get me another drink."

Betsy went to the kitchen again, and Missy had a moment to review her thoughts about how to ask what she wanted to ask.

"Okay, kiddo," said Betsy when she dropped once again into her lopsided armchair beside the radio. "Shoot."

"I need to ask you something about how he died," said Missy. "About *why* he died. It's because there's a chance something similar is happening to somebody else."

Betsy lit a cigarette. The clumsiness of her hands as she struck a match and held the flame to the cigarette suggested to Missy that the emotional content had not entirely gone out of her memories of Alex's sudden suicide.

"I'm sorry to have to bring this up," said Missy gently. "I wouldn't do it except that it may be important."

Betsy inhaled smoke, then reached for her drink. "Ask anything you want," she said curtly.

"What made him do it, Betsy? Specifically . . . was he being blackmailed?"

"Somebody was trying," said Betsy. She smiled bitterly. "They didn't understand that Alex was a man you *couldn't* blackmail. It wouldn't have made any difference what anybody'd had on him, he wouldn't have paid blackmail. That was the Bushnell in him. It was just . . . unthinkable to him."

"Can you tell me the details?"

"Why not? It couldn't make much difference now."

"It might, to somebody else," said Missy.

"Okay. I got an envelope in the mail one day. In it were two pictures—I mean, two photographs, big shiny prints. They showed Alex on a bed with a woman. Neither of them had any clothes on. More than that. They, uh . . . Well, you can imagine what they were doing."

"Who was the woman?"

"I don't know. Anyway, when he came home I showed these pictures to him. I was mad as hell. You can understand that, can't you? I was mad as hell." She sighed. "Well, he begged my forgiveness. But I was pretty tough. I said I'd think about it. He went to work the next day and the day after that. Then one evening he got a phone call. It was a reporter from the *Times*. He had the same kind of pictures of Alex and wanted to know what was going on. Alex told me that was who had called. He asked me again if I forgave him. I said I did. He said he had to go out. And out he went, and I never saw him alive again."

"Did he explain to you how he happened to be photographed with this woman?" asked Missy.

"Oh, yeah. He said she was a respectable woman and he'd let himself develop an infatuation for her. He said he'd only been to bed with her one time. He said he'd been just shattered when she demanded money. And of course he refused to pay her anything. So she—She started circulating the pictures. Sooner or later it would have blown up into a scandal, he'd have lost his job, and he'd have been unwelcome back at his law firm. The Bushnells would have been all over us, cluckin' 'We told you so,' and all that. His solution was to kill himself."

"And you never found out who the woman was?"

Betsy shook her head emphatically.

"What became of the photographs?"

"I tore my set up shortly after I confronted Alex with them. The reporter called me two days after the funeral and told me he'd done the same with his and would never mention the matter again."

"There were rumors," said Missy.

"I wish the story'd gotten out, to tell you the truth," said Betsy. "The high and mighty Bushnells think Alex shot himself because he at last realized what a bad woman he'd married."

"Can you describe the woman in the pictures?"

"Not really. Her back was to the camera."

"If you saw the room where it happened, would you be able to recognize it from the pictures? I mean, the wallpaper, the windows, and so on?"

Betsy shook her head. "The pictures were taken sort of from above, so you couldn't see anything but the bed. Just the two of them, was all you could see. All in good, clear focus, with good light. It was no casual job of picture-taking."

"I want to show you a picture of a woman," said Missy. She took from her purse a small picture of Vivian Taliafero, supplied her by Szczygiel. "Could that have been the woman with Alex?"

Betsy frowned at the picture for a long moment, then said—"It could have been. But who could tell? Dark hair . . . That's really all I could see that I see here. Who is this?"

"Vivian Taliafero."

"Murdered."

Missy nodded. "I'd appreciate your keeping quiet about what I've told you."

"I see what you think. If there's any truth in it, she deserved it, the bitch."

Missy drew a deep breath. "I'm afraid I have to agree with Mrs. Roosevelt, who says nobody deserves to be strangled, no matter what they may have done."

"Mrs. Roosevelt is a lady," said Betsy.

"That's true," said Missy. "That's very true."

"Stan . . ."

Missy had decided to stop by the Secret Service office on her return to the White House, to return the picture of Vivian Taliafero she had taken to show to Betsy Bushnell; and entering the office she found Stanlislaw Szczygiel asleep, with his head on his desk.

"Oh! Oh, I'm not asleep, Miss LeHand. Just resting my eyes."

"Sure. Why are you on duty so late, anyway?"

Szczygiel looked up at the clock. "I'm not," he said disgustedly. "Somebody thought it would be funny to let me sit there and sleep all night. There are two kinds in the Service these days—smart-aleck kids like Deconcini who think a thing like that is funny, and sobersides like Jerry Baines who'd take it as evidence I ought to retire. Speaking of on duty, are *you* still?"

"Strictly speaking," said Missy. "I'm on duty twenty-four hours a day, seven days a week. But the Boss is off sailing this week and next, so I should be able to manage a sixty-hour week."

"I'd like to know where some people find those 'bureaucrats' who are supposed to work only half time," said Szczygiel. "Not in the White House, I can tell you. Not in this presidency, anyway. There are people working in the West Wing right now—and the Boss is away."

"I don't know about you, Stan, but I could use a drink," said Missy. "I've had two bourbons and water today, and those were mixed with cheap bourbon. Care to join me in a little nip?"

"Where, Miss LeHand?"

Missy puffed out her cheeks as she blew an impatient sigh. "Stan . . . I'm Missy. Or Marguerite at least. If we're going to have a drink together—Or am I preventing you from getting home? Is Mrs. Szczygiel—"

"Rosie died eight years ago," said Stan.

"I'm sorry. Do you want to have a drink?"

"Or six," said Stanlislaw Szczygiel. "But where?"

"Out of the White House stock, where else," said Missy. "And I have a sitting room in my squalid suite on the third floor."

"I have a bit of news," he said as they walked through the hall toward the pantry. "William Wolfe has cleared out. I suggested to Kennelly that they keep an eye on him, and they went to the boarding house where he lives to see if he was there. The landlady said he'd packed his bags and left about two hours before. I guess I made him nervous by calling him chief suspect."

"Well, if he wasn't, he is now," she said.

"Right."

They went to the White House pantry on the ground floor, the domain of the formidable Mrs. Nesbitt. An old Negro butler still dozed at the center table in the pantry, but he was up in an instant at the sight of Missy and went scurrying around looking for the wherewithal to make up a snack tray.

"A privilege that goes with the job is a key to the White House liquor cabinet," said Missy to Stan. She opened the locked cabinet, revealing a modest supply of champagnes, brandies, and other spirits. "Your choice, sir. Napoleon brandy?"

"Brandy I can live with or without," said Stan. "But I do covet that bottle of Beefeater gin."

"Gin it is," she said. "And what has George found for us?"

"You wouldn't want none of that tuna salad, would you, Miss Missy?" George asked.

"I had it for dinner, George," she said. "It's one of Mrs. Roosevelt's favorites. You wouldn't be trying to get rid of it, would you—so it's not left for your lunch tomorrow?"

"Ohh, Miss . . ."

"I'm going to do us all a favor, George," said Missy.

She took the big bowl of tuna salad from the table, kicked the lid off a garbage can, and dumped it in.

"Ohh, Miss . . ."

"Admit it, George. You didn't want to have to eat Mrs. Nesbitt's tuna salad."

The big black man grinned happily. "I have to say, in eighteen years workin' in the White House, I have nevah *seed* such rotten awful meals as what is served to the President of the United States. Uh . . . You won't repeat that, Miss?"

"I will," said Missy. "But I'll say *I* said it. Tell me, George, which President got the best meals?"

"Well, that would have to be Mistah Hoover, Miss. Missus, she knew what was good and what wasn't. Now, Missus Roosevelt, she's a fine woman, but—"

"But what she doesn't know, or care, about food and drink would constitute the encyclopedia on the subject," said Missy. "I once heard her say she could not understand how, in this day and age, anyone could spend *twenty minutes* deciding what to serve at a banquet."

George laughed. "President'll eat anythin', she say. Don' care what he eat."

"He *cares*, George, I promise you," said Missy.

"Po' man," said George mournfully.

She and Stan would not let George carry their bottle and small tray all the way to the third floor. They took it up themselves. Missy's suite there was small. Her sitting room was comfortable but tiny. Mrs. Roosevelt had offered to arrange more spacious quarters for her, but Missy had pronounced herself satisfied with what she had. She had a degree of privacy she would not have had if she had been accommodated on the second floor. Yet, she was available twenty-four hours a day should the President need her.

She had no kitchen. They had brought ice on their tray. She did have a small green bottle of vermouth. Stan drank his gin straight. Missy made martinis that would have amazed the President—simply by pouring a splash of vermouth into a glass of ice cubes and filling the glass with gin.

"Your conversation with Betsy Bushnell proves something worth proving," said Stan.

"Which is?"

"If Alexander Bushnell was in fact being blackmailed by Vivian Taliafero—and I have no doubt the woman in the Bushnell photos was none other—then it proves she and her confederate were ruthless enough to publicize the sexual peccadilloes of prominent men. In fact, Bushnell may have been the test case. 'See, fellows, I *am* capable of making good on my threats, and look what happened to the man who tried to hold back on me.' Once Bushnell shot himself, the others paid more quickly."

They were eating some smoked salmon. It was something the President had asked for a few days ago, and there had been some left over—possibly because Mrs. Nesbitt did not know what to do with it.

"Speculation," said Missy. "The woman in the pictures sent to Betsy Bushnell may not have been Vivian Taliafero.''

''No,'' said Stan. ''No, there may have been two women in Washington having themselves photographed in those particular circumstances—and from a high angle, so as not to show too much of the background. Remembering the step-ladder in the chamber behind the mirror? It could be a coincidence.''

''I am afraid to guess,'' said Missy, ''who else may appear in photographs from the Taliafero blackmail factory. In this election year—''

''I am supposed,'' said Stan Szczygiel, ''to be a nonpolitical officer. But—''

Missy grinned and dug her elbow into his arm. ''We'll burn those pictures if we get our hands on them, won't we, Stan?''

''Democrats and Republicans alike,'' said Stan.

''Of *course*,'' laughed Missy. ''Why, of course.''

6

It was an old joke—but one based on fact—that the British Foreign Office for a long time paid its diplomats assigned to Washington the special hardship supplement that was paid to personnel sent out to serve in a tropic clime. This July Saturday showed why. By the time Mrs. Roosevelt woke, a little after eight, the temperature was eighty degrees. The dehumidifier that was supposed at least to keep her bedroom reasonably dry was overtaxed. Its drip pan had overflowed during the night, wetting the floor and rug, and still the air in her room was sticky and oppressive.

Franklin suffered more from the heat than she did. That was one reason why he was now at sea in the cool dry air down east. He had not urged her to come with him. He and the boys would have more fun sailing and fishing—and eating, drinking, and laughing at their own special rough humor—if she were not along. And she, for her part, would enjoy what she meant to do these two weeks, even if temperatures did reach the nineties each day and the humidity did stick at one hundred percent.

On that July Saturday, she had a full schedule—

Dictating at least one "My Day" column, and probably two or three.

Answering a stack of letters that had accumulated the past two days.

A speech to a conference of the National Farm Wives Union at noon at the Mayflower Hotel.

She had a memo that morning, reporting a comment by Harold Ickes—"The President smiles and sails and fishes and the rest of us worry and fume." She sent him a note—"Worry, please, Harold, but don't fume. Worry is often productive of good results. Fuming never produces anything but jangling nerves and ulcers."

The heat bore down on her as it did on everyone else. She drank lemonade, fluttered a woven-straw fan, and worked on.

She was often interrupted, of course. The telephone rang. Unscheduled visitors asked for a moment of her time—which invariably turned out to be much more than a moment. As the morning went on she accomplished less of her scheduled work than she had hoped, and the time for leaving for the Farm Wives luncheon meeting crept up on her.

She was about to close up her desk and send Tommy Thompson home for the day when Stanlislaw Szczygiel knocked on the door and asked if he could speak to her for a moment.

"Of course, Mr. Szczygiel," she said. "And can I offer you a glass of lemonade?"

"Thank you, Ma'am."

He sat down. He looked weary, she noticed. In fact, he looked a little sick. He accepted a glass of cold lemonade and drank it down as if he were burning with thirst.

"Well, Mr. Szczygiel. What news?"

"Has Miss LeHand reported what she learned from Mrs. Bushnell?" he asked.

"No. I haven't seen her since early last evening. I know what she thought she might find out."

"Well, she did," said Szczygiel. "It's very likely, if not certain, that the late Mr. Bushnell was being blackmailed by Vivian Taliafero and killed himself in consequence."

Mrs. Roosevelt shook her head sadly. "Alex Bushnell was a fine young man," she said. "One mistake . . . I'm afraid my sympathy for Miss Taliafero is diminishing."

"No one has claimed her body," said Szczygiel. "Lieutenant Kennelly asks if there is any reason why it should not be buried."

"I see no reason. Do you? Surely there will be a funeral. She had a host of friends."

"Who had no idea about the dark side of her life," said Szczygiel.

"Who had no idea," Mrs. Roosevelt agreed. "So they will want to honor her memory. The White House must not seem to be standing in the way. Tell Lieutenant Kennelly to release the body to a funeral director."

"Yes, Ma'am. Other than that, I have nothing much to report. You will probably hear bad talk about me. I had to punch an assistant attorney general in the belly Friday afternoon."

"Oh, Mr. Szczygiel!"

"Well . . . He grabbed me by the lapels and was going to throw me out of his office."

"Mr. Wolfe? Indeed. Well, I am sure you exercised good judgment. Do you regard him as a suspect?"

"Yes. He's aggressive. Hot-tempered. I told him he wouldn't have the courage to strangle a woman, but that was to goad him. He's definitely a suspect. Especially since he's skipped."

"Skipped?"

"Within an hour or so after my confrontation with him, he packed his bags and left his boarding house."

"Not a vacation? Not a coincidence?"

"No. I asked the D.C. police to put out a wanted bulletin on him."

"And what of Judge Kincaid? How did he react to being questioned?"

Szczygiel grinned. "He's a tough, shrewd old boy. He told me I didn't have any evidence that could link him with the crime. Which is true. But we have to think of him as a suspect."

"My suggestion to you and Lieutenant Kennelly, Mr. Szczygiel, is that you concentrate a bit on the confederate we believe Miss Taliafero must have had. Surely we can find out who was behind that mirror."

"I'm meeting Kennelly at noon. We're going to interrogate the housemaid."

"That will prove productive, I should think. I wish I could accompany you. I am making a speech at noon, however."

"When will you be finished? We can wait for you."

"I'm not certain when I shall be finished. Say two or two-thirty. I don't want to put you to any great inconvenience, Mr. Szczygiel."

"It will be none, Ma'am. Kennelly and I will be pleased to wait until two-thirty."

When Mrs. Roosevelt left the Mayflower at 2:20 she sent the White House car back without her and left with Stan Szczygiel in a Secret Service car. He telephoned Lieutenant Kennelly just before they left the hotel and picked up the D.C. detective on the street in front of headquarters at 2:35.

"The hotel," said Mrs. Roosevelt, "is air-conditioned, which is very pleasant. I shouldn't be surprised if every major public building in Washington is air-conditioned in a few years."

"We can begin with the White House," said Szczygiel.

"I rather imagine it will begin with congressional offices," she said.

They had decided to interview Amy Curtis at home, rather than to require her to come to police headquarters. She was waiting for them. Her family—parents, two brothers, two sisters—made their home in the first floor of a small frame house, and another family lived upstairs. Her mother and one sister were at home. The others were at their jobs.

"Miz *Roosevelt!* My *Lawd!*" the girl's mother shrieked. "Oh, my *Lawd!*"

The mother was a plump black woman, wearing a voluminous cotton dress in a flowered pattern. The girl was lighter, taller, and slender, with a lofty dignity that contrasted with her mother's gawky amazement at seeing the First Lady. To Amy Curtis, a visit by Mrs. Roosevelt was pretty much the same as a visit by anyone else, and she would try to make her comfortable but would not lose her composure.

"I . . . Oh, let me make some *tea,*" said Mrs. Curtis.

"That would be very nice," said Mrs. Roosevelt. "If it isn't too much trouble."

"I'll make a pot of tea. Or . . . We got gin, if you'd rather."

"I'd rather," said Szczygiel.

"Uh . . . Well—Yes, gin," said Kennelly.

They sat down in the small living room—Mrs. Roosevelt in a wooden rocker, Szczygiel and Kennelly on the couch, and Amy facing them from a straight-back chair with a cane seat. Her dress was like her mother's—shapeless, flowered, modest.

"We've come to ask a few questions about Miss Taliafero," said Mrs. Roosevelt.

Amy Curtis nodded. She regarded them with a skeptical, not-altogether-friendly face.

"It appears," said Mrs. Roosevelt, "that Miss Taliafero

was involved in criminal activity. We've no reason to suppose you knew that or had anything to do with it. We are, though, trying to find out just what went on in Miss Taliafero's house. What we learn may help us to find out who killed her, and why.''

Amy Curtis raised her chin, and her face was rigid. ''I does my job and minds my own business,'' she said.

''You—'' Kennelly began, but he was interrupted.

''Yes, of course,'' said Mrs. Roosevelt. ''We understand that. But you may have observed something that can help us find out who killed Miss Taliafero.''

The young Negro woman glanced around the living room of the house where she lived with her family, as if to suggest to these her inquisitors that she had her own problems and was not interested in buying anyone else's.

''We know you don't know who killed her,'' said Mrs. Roosevelt. ''We are looking for what detectives call clues.''

''I *knows* what clues are,'' said Amy.

''Let's be specific, then,'' said Mrs. Roosevelt. ''Miss Taliafero took men to her bedroom. The mirror by the bed was transparent from behind, and a man—we suppose it was a man—behind that mirror took pictures of what happened on the bed. Those pictures were later used to extort large amounts of money from the men who had been photographed. What we want to know is—''

''What you want to know,'' the young woman interrupted, ''is who is behind that glass and takes those pictures.''

''Exactly.''

Amy Curtis sighed. ''Miz Taliafero pays me a good wage,'' she said. ''Part of my duties is to keep my eyes on my work and see nothin' but. That's what she tells me the day I come to work. I figure that's because lots of famous men come, and some of them get drunk in her parlor. She tells me never to open that door—the one you now say goes into the room behind the mirror. I try to open it. Curious, you know—who wouldn't be? It's locked. She say, never go down in the cellar. I find that door is locked, too. So, I do my job, collect my money, and mind my own business.''

"Fine," said Mrs. Roosevelt. "But let's talk about who was in the house. Miss Taliafero had to have a confederate. We're looking for the name of a man, or a woman, who—"

"Takes the pictures," said Amy Curtis.

"Took the pictures," said Kennelly gruffly.

"Lots of men comes to visit Miz Taliafero," said Amy. "Lots of 'em. Some comes two, three times. Some comes *all* the time. Some is famous men, I see. Some . . ." She shrugged. "Who they? I don't know. I'm powerful ignorant."

"Like a fox," said Kennelly.

"Maybe I do be a fox," said Amy Curtis resentfully. "I not work in . . . I not work in no cathouse and not *know* it's a cathouse."

"What were your hours, Miss Curtis?" asked Mrs. Roosevelt.

"I come to work at four in the afternoon, work till midnight."

"What were your duties?"

"Chief cook and bottle washer," said Amy. "First thing I clean up, if I didn't have time to do it night before. Then I make some sandwiches and cut up some cheese and stuff, to make a tray for the gentlemen that come. When the gentlemen start coming, I'm the serving maid, fetch drinks and all. Sometimes Miss Taliafero go out to dinner, and that gives me time to do some more cleaning. Keep making sandwiches. Keep pouring drinks. Eight hours. Six days a week."

"Surely you were aware that Miss Taliafero was . . . How shall we say? Was *entertaining* gentlemen in her bedroom."

"Believe it or not, I work there a long time before I

figure that out. Miz Taliafero, she pretty artful. She slip away, not gone a long time. Gentlemen she not invite upstairs, I don't think they ever know.''

"It *would* be hard to believe,'' said Mrs. Roosevelt, "that men like Justices Holmes and Brandeis would have continued to visit Miss Taliafero's home if they had even suspected she was involved in dissolute conduct in the house.''

Szczygiel and Kennelly exchanged glances, unsure if Mrs. Roosevelt was serious and naive or astute and jocular.

Mrs. Curtis returned, carrying a cup of tea for Mrs. Roosevelt. "You care for cream or sugar?'' she asked.

"No. This is lovely. Thank you.''

"An' you gentlemen want your gin on ice, or what?''

"Over ice,'' said Stan Szczygiel. "That'll be great.''

Kennelly nodded. "Wonderful,'' he said.

"Let me ask you this question, Miss Curtis,'' said Mrs. Roosevelt. "What if a visitor arrived while Miss Taliafero was out to dinner?''

"That happen sometime,'' said Amy Curtis. "You know, it generally understood that guests welcome like from six to ten, any day but Sunday. But sometime she go out, not there at six.''

"Could *you* let her guests in, then?''

Amy nodded. "Sometime did,'' she said. She grinned. "One time let a gentleman in that didn't know Miz Taliafero, isn't supposed to be there. He know about Miz Taliafero, figure he can get a free sandwich and a drink.'' She chuckled. "He get 'em, all right. Miz Taliafero come home, he go out the back door, quick.''

"All right. Then could anyone else let guests in?''

"Well . . . Sometime Mister Skaggs, he let 'em in.''

"Who is Mr. Skaggs?''

"Joe Bob Skaggs. He a particular friend of Miz Taliafero. Come the house a lot of times.''

"All the time?'' asked Szczygiel. "Every day?''

"Oh, no. Just a lot of times. More than other gentlemen, I suppose."

"Who was he?"

"Southern gentleman. From Biloxi, Mississippi, I believe. Talks southern. Calls me nigger."

"What else can you tell us about him?" asked Mrs. Roosevelt.

Amy shrugged. "Cripple. Uses two canes. Kinda hunched over all the time."

"Could he have been the photographer?"

"Well . . . Could be, I suppose. Could be maybe."

"Did you ever see him go upstairs?" asked Kennelly.

She shook her head. "Don't recall. Suppose he might. Don't recall."

Mrs. Curtis returned once more, carrying three glasses of gin on ice. She handed one to Szczygiel, then one to Kennelly, then raised the third glass in toast, smiled, and said—"Pray for cooler weather."

The two men drank appreciatively from the heavy slugs of gin she had poured over chunks of ice chipped from a block with an ice pick.

"Amy he'pful?" she asked.

"Most helpful," said Mrs. Roosevelt.

"Be nice if somebody could he'p Amy," she said. "She lose a good job when Miz Taliafero gits killed."

"Well, I wish I could offer a place at the White House," said Mrs. Roosevelt, "but I'm afraid all our staff positions are filled."

"We too plain folks for White House," said Mrs. Curtis. "Jus' a simple job for some nice lady."

"I'll inquire around," said Mrs. Roosevelt.

"It could be an ugly confrontation," said Stan Szczygiel.

They had placed telephone calls to D.C. police headquarters and to the F.B.I. and had learned that Joe Bob Skaggs lived in Alexandria, Virginia, just across the Potomac. Mrs. Roosevelt had just suggested she would go with the two officers and sit in on their interrogation of Skaggs.

"Well, unless you are afraid he'll pull a gun," she said, "I should like to come with you."

"I'm not afraid of that," said Szczygiel. "I am only thinking of the *appropriateness* of the First Lady's being involved—"

"Balderdash, Mr. Szczygiel. This First Lady is no shrinking violet—as indeed many others have not been. Besides," she added with an ingenuous smile, "I shall be accompanied, not only by an agent of the Secret Service but also by a detective of the District police."

"I understand from Jerry Baines that when you are determined to take part in an investigation, you take part in an investigation. So—"

"That's been my observation as well," said Kennelly.

"Aren't we wasting time, gentlemen?" asked Mrs. Roosevelt sweetly.

Szczygiel drove a Secret Service car, a black Ford, across the bridge and into Alexandria. None of them knew the streets, and Szczygiel stopped beside a parked Alexandria police car and obtained directions. The officers recognized Mrs. Roosevelt peering from the back seat and offered to lead them to the address.

Joe Bob Skaggs's house was on a tree-shaded residential street. The sidewalks were paved with brick, and the house itself, in Georgian style, was of soft old brick, orangish in color. Although the houses in the neighborhood looked comfortable, all of them were in need of repair, some more, some less. Skaggs's house was marked by chipped and peeling white paint on all its woodwork, also by a broken window patched with wood.

"Y'all like us to come in with you?" asked one of the Alexandria policemen.

Szczygiel shook his head. "You might hang around, though, until we see if he's here and how he reacts."

"We'll be in the car," said the Alexandria man.

Mrs. Roosevelt accompanied Szczygiel and Kennelly to the door. She stood on the stoop while Szczygiel knocked. No response. The house was quiet.

"Not home, I guess," said Szczygiel.

He knocked again, rapping hard with the brass knocker; and they could hear the sound echoing through the house; but that was all they heard.

Mrs. Roosevelt noticed a woman leaning against the Alexandria police car, talking earnestly with the two officers inside. Immediately one of the officers came out of the car and hurried to the door stoop.

"That's a neighbor," he said, nodding back toward the woman who still talked to the man left in the car. "She saw the police car and came out. She says Mr. Skaggs hasn't been seen for two days, says the house is dark at night, and says that's unusual for him. She says he's a crippled man and is always home nights—sometimes late but always home."

"It would be as well," said Szczygiel, "if she doesn't recognize Mrs. Roosevelt."

"She doesn't. She asked if that was a member of the Skaggs family."

"I have a suggestion," said Kennelly. He turned to the Alexandria man and said, "Kennelly, District police." He pulled his identification. "This fellow Skaggs is a suspect in a murder committed in the District. I think we better go in."

The officer looked at Szczygiel, as if to get some kind of confirmation from him. Szczygiel nodded.

"Okay," said the Alexandria officer. "The name is Miller, incidentally." He tipped his head to one side and looked at the door knob and lock. "We can break her. I'll get a bar from the car."

While Miller returned to the car for his crowbar, Kennelly bent over the lock and inserted a small steel tool. He pulled up a hinged handle and with it exerted pressure on the inside parts of the lock. Gradually he increased the pressure, until the lock broke with a snap. By the time Miller had returned, Kennelly had opened the door.

Miller stared wryly as Kennelly replaced the tool in his pocket. "Damn," he said. "How do the cops and burglars tell each other apart in Washington?"

The house inside proved surprisingly different from the house outside. It was furnished with conspicuously expensive antiques. The floors were covered with oriental rugs. It was evident that Joe Bob Skaggs was a man of taste, who lived well.

Or had lived well. His body lay face down on the floor of his living room.

"Bludgeoned," said Kennelly. "Beaten to death with the proverbial blunt object." He squatted beside the body, examining it without touching it. "Not recently, either. I'd guess two or three days ago."

The two canes Amy Curtis had said the man used were on the floor just beyond his outstretched hands. One of them was broken. One could guess he had raised it to defend himself, and his attacker had hit it with the death weapon. It was obvious that the attack had been brutal. Joe Bob Skaggs had been a slight man, aside from having only partial use of his legs. His head had been caved in by at least half a dozen vicious blows.

"We should leave," said Szczygiel to Mrs. Roosevelt. "You really don't want to be here when—"

"Officer Miller," she said to the Alexandria policeman. "You don't have to summon help for a few minutes, do you? After all, the man has been dead for some time, and a few more minutes before the official investigation begins—"

"I understand you, Ma'am," said Miller. "No, we can wait a few more minutes."

"And, uh, it would be better that your report not include the information that I was here."

"It will not contain any mention of you, Ma'am."

"Thank you." She spoke then to Szczygiel. "I really think we should look around here before we leave. We may find—"

"Pictures," Szczygiel muttered under his breath.

Miller retreated, aware that the Secret Service agent and the First Lady wanted to talk out of his hearing.

"Possibly," she said. "And—Do we dare remove them?"

"That," said Szczygiel, "depends on whether or not they can be carried in a small truck."

"If they could be carried in my handbag . . . ?"

"Then we had better take them with us," he said.

She nodded. "That's what I think."

Because she was wearing white gloves, it was Mrs. Roosevelt who opened closets and drawers in the house. When fingerprints were taken, it was just as well that those of an agent of the Secret Service not be found. Kennelly remained in the living room, talking with Miller, while she and Szczygiel made a quick examination of the premises.

They found photographs. They could in fact hardly have overlooked them; the pictures and negatives were spread over a bed and the bedroom floor.

"Shocking!" she gasped as she picked up the twenty or so prints and began shoving them into a manila file folder that also lay on the floor. Again, only she could pick them up without leaving new fingerprints on them. She averted her eyes. "Honestly, Mr. Szczygiel . . . Curious as I am to know who these men are, I cannot bring myself to look at such pictures."

"Careful not to wipe fingerprints off them, Mrs. Roosevelt," said Szczygiel. He was on his hands and knees on the floor, crawling from picture to picture, staring intently at every one for as long as he could before she grabbed it and pushed it into the folder.

"If you could get your hands into my gloves, I would

ask you to gather these up," said she. "They are . . . They are *sickening*."

"Here's Fritz Hausser," said Szczygiel.

She glanced at the picture. "Oh! How can I ever confront the man again?"

"There are some other gentlemen you are going to be embarrassed to confront," said Szczygiel.

In her office at the White House, Mrs. Roosevelt used scissors to cut a half-dollar-size round hole in a piece of heavy paper; and Szczygiel and Kennelly moved the paper around on the photographs so she could see the faces of the men in the pictures—without having to see anything more.

"There is a boring sameness about all of them," said Kennelly. "You could never identify Vivian Taliafero by these pictures. They—"

"I have no doubt," said Mrs. Roosevelt, "that Miss Taliafero and Mr. Skaggs destroyed any photographs in which she could be identified."

"And there are none here," said Szczygiel, "of Alexander Bushnell. If any of their pictures caused a suicide, they destroyed the evidence."

"Do you realize," she asked, "the impact it could have if these men were publicly identified? I wonder, frankly, if we would not do a better service to our country if we simply burned them all, now—even if that means the murderer goes free."

"We must not forget, Ma'am, that the murderer has now struck twice," said Szczygiel. "I'll accept your decision as to what we do with—"

"And so will I," said Kennelly.

"But I think," Szczygiel continued, "we must at least get the fingerprints off these photos before we destroy them."

"And write down the names," said Kennelly.

"Very well," said Mrs. Roosevelt. "Write down Frederick Hausser. Judge Beresford Kincaid. Senator Steven Valentine. Representative Gordon Pierce. Senator— This is most distressing. The President respects him so much. But . . . Senator Everett Cranshaw. And, of course— Even worse. Because his fingerprints were on the water glass . . . Secretary Rinehart. I don't think I shall even tell the President that a member of his Cabinet is involved in . . . But write it down. Herschel B. Rinehart, Secretary of Trade.''

"Ma'am," Szczygiel interrupted. "I just now remember this face." He pointed at a face he had centered in the hole in the paper. "Admiral Horan."

"Admiral Richard Horan," said Mrs. Roosevelt sadly. "I know his daughter."

"And this man here," said Szczygiel. "I've never seen him, to my knowledge."

"Nor have I," said Kennelly.

"Oh, I have," said Mrs. Roosevelt. "If I could possibly find any joy in seeing a man's face among these, I would find it now. That is Burton Oleander, president of the Association of Coal-Fired Utilities. He made a vast fortune through electric-utility holding companies, and now he's chief lobbyist for the holding companies. He has repeatedly called the President a Communist."

"And worse," said Kennelly. "I've heard his name often."

"Well, write it down," said Mrs. Roosevelt. "That makes eight names on our list."

"Eight suspects," said Szczygiel. "One of them, almost certainly, is the murderer."

Mrs. Roosevelt smiled at him. "Actually, Lieutenant," she said quietly, "I rather suspect the chief suspect is not on the list."

"Not . . . ? Why?"

Mrs. Roosevelt glanced at Szczygiel, then looked back at Kennelly. "Someone killed Miss Taliafero," she said. "We have assumed—I hope correctly—that the motive was her extensive blackmail enterprise. But killing her did not terminate the blackmail. She didn't have the photographs on her when she died. The killer hurried to her house in Georgetown and ransacked the cellar darkroom, looking for the prints and negatives of the incriminating pictures. He didn't find them. So then he went looking for Mr. Skaggs—having somehow learned that Mr. Skaggs was the confederate and likely to have the photographs. He went to Alexandria and killed Mr. Skaggs, maybe in an angry confrontation, demanding the photographs, or maybe just in cold blood. In the house he found the prints and negatives, and—'' She paused. ''And what would he then do, gentlemen?''

''For me,'' said Kennelly, ''I'm just listening. I got an idea what he did, but maybe you got a better idea.''

''He sorted through what he found and removed *his own* photographs,'' she said. ''Isn't that what he would do? He removed the evidence Miss Taliafero and Mr. Skaggs had used to blackmail him—the same evidence that established him as a suspect in her murder and all but *proved* he killed Mr. Skaggs—and left the rest of the evidence for the police to find. Isn't that what he would do? Otherwise, why would he have stayed in the house after he killed Mr. Skaggs and searched for the photographs?''

''Which leaves us with what suspects?'' asked Szczygiel.

''Three,'' she said. ''Mr. Wolfe's fingerprints were found on the bed, yet his pictures are not here. Secretary Rinehart's fingerprints were found in the bathroom, on the drinking glass, yet his pictures are not here. Congressman Martin Dies welcomed Mr. Hausser to 'the club' after Mr. Hausser had an intimate hour with Miss Taliafero, and his pictures are not here. Am I wrong in supposing those three men are more likely suspects than those whose pictures we have found?''

''A damned impressive analysis,'' said Kennelly to

Szczygiel. "I think she's got a point. I guess we ought to look hard at Wolfe and Rinehart and Dies."

"Not to the exclusion of the others, though," said Mrs. Roosevelt. "Theories must never be allowed to get in the way of facts."

7

Mrs. Roosevelt sat down to breakfast with Missy on Sunday morning. Postmaster General Jim Farley had been invited to join them, but the invitation had been casual, and Farley had sent word that he would be unable to come. He did not say why.

Breakfast was served beside the pool, where Mrs. Roosevelt and Missy sought refuge from the heat by swimming. Missy was a strong swimmer, as she had learned to be in past years when she had been required by the President to keep up with him as he swam from his little yacht *Larooco*, in Florida waters, and later in the pool at Warm Springs and in the pool here in the White House. Mrs. Roosevelt wished she had learned to swim as Missy did. In her young years, women were expected to enter the water only swathed in yards of heavy fabric, and with that impediment she had never learned to swim as well as her husband and children. Lately even the First Lady of the

Land could risk being seen in a loose, skirted swimsuit, with a white rubber cap to protect her hair, and she had begun to swim more freely.

This morning she wore a green and white cotton suit, and Missy wore something less modest, the two-piece suit—tight blue trunks, white vest above—that was almost a uniform for women on the nation's beaches and around swimming-club pools. Both of them wore rubber swim caps.

They had climbed out of the pool when breakfast was served, and they sat comfortably wet on wood-and-canvas chairs and ate fruit and cereal, nothing heavier, and drank iced tea.

Mrs. Roosevelt described to Missy what she had seen yesterday. They talked about the men displayed in the ugly, obscene photographs found in Joe Bob Skaggs's house.

"I agree with you," said Missy, "that the murderer is unlikely to be one of the men in the pictures you found. Whoever killed Skaggs would certainly have taken his own picture with him when he left."

"Even so," said Mrs. Roosevelt, "it is shocking to see who appeared in those pictures. Senator Cranshaw, for example. He and the President were at Harvard together. A married man . . . lovely children." She shook her head. "I—"

Missy interrupted. "Please forgive me," she said, "if I say you are a little naive. Vivian Taliafero was an attractive woman and obviously made it a point to be—Well . . . I was going to say attractive. The better word is seductive."

"Yes, I—Yes, I suppose so. I'm afraid I have little understanding of exactly how a woman achieves that. It is true that I am naive."

"Forgive me, Eleanor," said Missy. "In many ways you are the least naive person I know. Even the Boss is sometimes more naive than you. But it would be naive to wonder how Vivian Taliafero could seduce a man. She had what it takes.''

"Senator Valentine?"

Missy shrugged. "Easy enough, I'd think. His mousy little wife and his loud children might well lead him to look for occasional relaxation somewhere else."

"And Judge Beresford Kincaid?" asked Mrs. Roosevelt. "Surely he—"

"I don't know much about the judge," said Missy. "Nothing, in fact. And again, why not? Mata Hari had nothing on Vivian Taliafero, apparently. There is no discreet way to say it. The redoubtable Miss T offered a man everything he could want."

"I'm looking at the list for a man capable of murder," said Mrs. Roosevelt.

"Look at the list another way," said Missy. "Is there a man on it who is *not* capable of murder?"

"A cynic would say that any man or woman is capable of murder, I suppose," said Mrs. Roosevelt. "Still . . ."

"Admiral Horan," said Missy. "Why not? An athletic sort of man. Capable of violence, I'd think."

"I see no option," said Mrs. Roosevelt, "but to inquire into the whereabouts of each of these men at the times when the two murders were committed. We can eliminate those who—"

"Let's not assume," Missy interrupted, "that both murders were committed by the same man. We know of at least ten who had motive to kill her, but it wouldn't have done any of them much good to kill her when the photographs were in the possession of Skaggs."

"I do, though," said Mrs. Roosevelt, "assume they were committed by a *man*. A woman might have killed this pair, to protect her husband's reputation and career, but I cannot imagine a woman strangling Miss Taliafero and bludgeoning Mr. Skaggs. That takes a man's physical strength, does it not?"

Missy shrugged. "Knowing what I do about Vivian Taliafero, I think I would have been capable of strangling her. And so far as Skaggs is concerned, how much strength did it take to beat a small crippled man to death with a club? Not much, I'd think. That murder at least could have been committed by a woman.''

"It was brutal," said Mrs. Roosevelt. "Whatever may have motivated the man who killed Mr. Skaggs, he did it with vicious brutality."

"Capable of murder . . ." Missy mused. "And also capable of brutality. We must review our list with that in mind."

They continued to discuss the mystery while they ate their breakfast. When the heat oppressed them, they slipped into the pool and swam a lap or two, then returned to the table.

When Stanislaw Szczygiel appeared, both of them urged him to go into the Executive Wing and don one of the bathing suits the President kept in a closet there. He did. He reappeared somewhat embarrassed in blue trunks and white vest, showing a pale but solidly muscled body. He had a nose like W.C. Fields's, and an unruly shock of hair that fell over his forehead, but he carried almost no extra weight.

Mrs. Roosevelt ordered another breakfast, and Szczygiel swam half a dozen laps and came out wet and sat down with them.

"Working on Sunday morning, Mr. Szczygiel?" asked Mrs. Roosevelt.

"I am working? Swimming and enjoying breakfast with two such charming ladies? I hadn't thought of it as work."

"A gallant gentleman," Missy observed.

"One carrying a bit of information," said Szczygiel. "The fingerprints of the late unfortunate Joe Bob Skaggs match those on the cameras in the Taliafero house. We are surprised?"

"We are not surprised," said Mrs. Roosevelt. "To the contrary. If they had not matched, we should be obliged to start over with entirely new premises for the investigation, would we not?''

''Then what we surmised is what we know,'' said Szczygiel. ''Vivian Taliafero lured men to her bedroom, allowed them certain liberties; and Joe Bob Skaggs, behind the mirror, photographed the goings-on.''

''And created . . . How was it that Dorothy Sayers titled her charming mystery? *Clouds of Witness*. Well, we seem to have clouds of suspects.''

''Well said, Ma'am.''

''Could we . . . Should we create a chart? Would it not assist us in sorting out the various suspects?''

An hour later, in her office on the second floor of the White House, Mrs. Roosevelt led Missy and Stan Szczygiel through the creation of a chart:

Suspect	Where Tues. Night	Where at Death Skaggs
Cranshaw	White House	?
Kincaid	?	?
Valentine	?	?
Hausser	Executive Wing	?
Horan	?	?
Pierce	?	?
Oleander	?	?
Wolfe	?	?
Rinehart	?	?
Dies	?	?

''Dare I suggest,'' asked Mrs. Roosevelt, ''that our mystery will be solved when we eliminate the question marks from the chart?''

''Let's hope it's that simple,'' said Missy.

That Sunday Senator Everett Cranshaw attended church in his home town, then went to the shore, set up an easel, and spent the middle part of the day painting. He had returned to Maine on Friday, though he would have to catch a train back to Washington on Monday morning. As he painted, his wife sat wrapped in a cotton blanket against the chill breeze from the ocean, and his children scampered around the rocks and sand, keeping just back from the cold sea waves that broke on the shore. The senator was a miserable man. Usually, when he was miserable, he confided in his wife, or in someone; he was a naturally outgoing man and habitually trusted others to help him solve his problems. But he could confide in no one about the problem presented by the death of Vivian Taliafero. All he could do was wait for the inevitable catastrophe.

Judge Beresford Kincaid sat by a huge swimming pool just behind the house of his second cousin Adam Beresford. He felt a little immodest in his one-piece bathing suit—that is, trunks without vest—but he did what the other guests did; and he wondered if some of the women might even appear that Sunday afternoon in the new *two-piece* suits that had appeared lately—a sort of halter containing their breasts, with tight shorts around their hips. He hoped they would. He sipped from an odd drink his cousin insisted was appropriate for morning—tomato juice with a shot of vodka in it, which was called a Red River. His wife had not come with him this weekend. She was showing her sketches at a sidewalk show in Alexandria.

The judge, too, was distraught with worry. Damn the day he had been stupid enough to fall into the clutches of Vivian Taliafero!

Senator Steve Valentine wished he could have left Washington on this oppressive July weekend, but he was obligated to meet with representatives of United Auto Workers, who demanded his time both Saturday and Sunday. He sat in a crowded, ill-ventilated, smoke-choked conference room, keeping his patience only with difficulty as officers of the union squabbled angrily about nothing very important. Senator Valentine's mind was but little focused on the debate. He could not put aside the image of those ugly pictures that conniving woman had used to blackmail him. Who had them now?

Frederick Hausser had been invited to spend Sunday afternoon at Chevy Chase Country Club. He did not swim, or play golf or tennis, but he could sit under an umbrella, sip cold drinks, and chat; and he was constantly invited to country clubs to do just that—because families with marriageable daughters were anxious to have Becky or June or Patricia meet the young lawyer with the impeccable credentials and the interesting legacy. He would have liked to go to the country club, would in fact have liked to meet the daughter of the family who had invited him; but he felt a cold, or maybe even the flu, coming on and was staying home to fight it with a course of pills and a chest rub. He sat in bed, listening to the radio, sweating under the square of flannel he wore under his pajama coat. The flannel was saturated with Vicks salve. He could feel the aromatic salve penetrating his skin and gradually clearing his chest.

Hausser was not much worried about the Taliafero murder case. He had already been cleared, he supposed. He believed, though, that he had caught this cold or flu from being locked overnight in a grimy cell in a squalid jail.

Vice Admiral Richard Horan was attending a naval officers' conference at Annapolis—officially. In fact, he was in Silver Spring, spending the weekend with Betty Coughlin. He was fifty-five, she was thirty-four, and she was in love with him. She was not the first woman who had fallen in love with him, so he was not entirely surprised that she should; he had a reputation for being a handsome, athletic man, and he'd enjoyed affairs in succession. This might be something more nearly permanent. Betty was beautiful—chubby and loving and blonde and beautiful. For him, divorce was out of the question, so he spent as much time with Betty as he could and wished it could be more.

He had confided in Betty that he was being blackmailed

by Vivian Taliafero. When she read in the paper that the Taliafero woman had been murdered in the White House Rose Garden, Betty was pleased. When Dick—as of course she called him—arrived at her house on Saturday morning, she had told him she considered the murder great good news. They talked about it some more on Sunday afternoon.

"The problem is, who has the pictures?" he said. "If the police get their hands on them, God knows—"

"It would make you a suspect!" Betty gasped. She hadn't thought of that before—that Dick had a motive and might be a suspect in the killing of the Taliafero woman.

"Damn right," said the admiral.

"Are you worried?"

He nodded. "Damn right."

It was the weekend when Congressman Gordon Pierce, Pennsylvania Democrat, held his annual cronies party, a very private, even secret gathering of his closest political friends and campaign contributors. The party was held in a mountain cabin in the Poconos. The forty or so men who had come to the party had eaten four hams among other things, had quaffed two kegs of beer besides the liquor they had drunk, had played poker and shot dice, and had utterly exhausted the six girls he had hired to entertain. On Sunday afternoon, after the last guest was gone, he sat on the porch of the cabin with his brother and campaign chairman, George, and they talked about the disaster that was surely going to befall.

"What could she have thought would happen to her?" the congressman mused. "Sooner or later somebody is going to free himself from a blackmailer."

"But in the Rose Garden at the *White House!*" his brother protested.

"How much damage, George? We simply have to figure that the pictures are going to get loose."

"No, we don't have to figure that. We don't have to assume it. Even if the police get them, they don't have to make them public. The problem is, the pictures make you a suspect in the murder.''

"The problem is, I can't account for my time Tuesday night. I went to a picture. I sat in there in the dark and watched Wallace Beery and . . . And I haven't got any alibi.''

"Even so, they can't prove you killed the woman.''

"They don't have to. If it's announced I'm a suspect, then it has to be explained *why* I'm a suspect, and when that hits the papers I'm finished. I wonder if I shouldn't withdraw, let the party nominate somebody else.''

"No. We've got too much invested in your political career, big brother. We don't throw anything away until we have to.''

Burton Oleander played golf both Saturday and Sunday, carrying his considerable bulk around the course only by dint of considerable exertion and sweat. He had tried to interest one country club where he played in laying a little narrow-gauge railway parallel to the fairways, so a man could ride part of the distance from tee to hole.

On the course and at the bar after their rounds, he and his lawyer discussed their strategy in the event Oleander was charged with the murder of Vivian Taliafero. His lawyer was James Townley. They agreed that offense is the best defense.

"Just let somebody *dare* touch me,'' said Oleander.

Shortly after his confrontation with Stanislaw Szczygiel on Friday afternoon, Assistant Attorney General William Wolfe had driven out of Washington in his Chevrolet. He drove all night, then all day Saturday. Saturday night he stayed in a tourist cabin just outside Rome, Georgia, where he shaved off his mustache to alter his appearance.

But Szczygiel had learned he was gone and had asked the District police to issue a wanted bulletin on him. A description of Wolf and his car, including his license number, was telegraphed to state police departments and the principal municipal departments throughout the eastern half of the United States. Not many cars bearing District of Columbia license plates drove through northern Georgia and northern Alabama, and shortly after he crossed the Alabama line on Sunday morning Wolfe was stopped by an Alabama state trooper. By noon he was locked up in the county jail in Gadsden, Alabama.

Sheriff Buford Wallace put in a call to Lieutenant Edward Kennelly of the D.C. police; but, it being Sunday, Kennelly was not on duty. The D.C. police operator gave the sheriff the name of Stanislaw Szczygiel and suggested he telephone him. Sheriff Wallace said he'd made all the long-distance calls he cared to make, so Kennelly would have to call him back on Monday. In the meanwhile, he'd keep Wolfe in jail. What was more, if he didn't shut up back there, the sheriff would go back and club him.

Herschel Rinehart spent much of the weekend writing a long letter to his wife. In it he confessed that he'd had what he called a corrupt relationship with Vivian Taliafero, as a result of which he had paid blackmail to her for several months. Another result of it was that he was certain to be regarded as a suspect in the Taliafero murder. Much unsavory publicity was likely to appear. He begged his wife to forgive him. He sealed the seventh draft of the letter, meaning to take it to his bank Monday morning and lock it in his safe-deposit box. Then he set to work to draft a letter of resignation—which, too, he would lock away until it was needed.

Congressman Martin Dies was at home in Texas all that weekend. He had left Washington by train on Wednesday morning. He was untroubled by the news of the death of Vivian Taliafero. It did not occur to him that he could be suspected of killing her.

When she retired that Sunday evening, Mrs. Roosevelt took to bed with her a novel nearly eleven hundred pages long. Ordinarily she did not read the kind of fiction it represented, but since its publication a few weeks ago this book had become so important a bit of Americana that anyone who hadn't looked into it, at least, had to confess ignorance. In many circles, little else was discussed.

It was fascinating, it was boring; it was syrupy sweet, it was too frank and graphic; it was a package of propaganda, it was a reflection of true history. It was controversial, and it promised to set a long-time record on the best-seller list.

For an hour before she went to sleep, Mrs. Roosevelt read a few chapters of *Gone With the Wind*.

"The Alexandria boys are first-rate homicide investigators," Kennelly told Szczygiel on Monday morning. "And cooperative to a fault. I don't know if they would have been if the Secret Service had not been involved, but for whatever reason they have given us more than we asked for. A Lieutenant Hupp wants to meet with us sometime today. In the meantime, he's sent over some evidence. Like this—"

He handed Szczygiel a small glassine envelope, inside which Szczygiel could see a little tan-colored pill.

"What's that?"

"Sniff it," said Kennelly.

Szczygiel lifted the flap of the envelope and sniffed. "Shee!" he snorted. "What is it? Camphor . . ."

"A patent medicine called Campho-Lax. That little pill was found on the floor not far from Skaggs's body. The autopsy showed no sign that he'd taken any. He had no

Campho-Lax in his medicine cabinet. But guess who does take them? Guess who had a bottle of them in his possession when he was taken into custody Tuesday night? It was listed on the inventory of things we took off him before we locked him up.''

''Hausser.''

Kennelly nodded. ''Frederick Hausser.''

''Mrs. Roosevelt is going to tell you that's a very small clue,'' said Szczygiel. He glanced at the tiny pill and grinned. ''Forgive the pun. But, you know, it doesn't prove much. Millions of these pills are—''

Kennelly shrugged. ''Coincidence on coincidence,'' he said. ''By itself, nothing much. But Hausser is the same guy who had a visit from Vivian Taliafero minutes before she died.''

''Worth working on,'' said Szczygiel.

''Okay. Some more information. The autopsy establishes the time of Skaggs's death as Friday, probably in the morning. The neighbor lady said the house had been dark two nights. Why it was dark Thursday night, we don't know. It was dark Friday night because Skaggs was lying in there dead.''

''Suppose we find that Hausser spent the whole day Friday in his office.''

''Suppose the man who killed the woman isn't the same as the one who killed Skaggs,'' said Kennelly. ''Suppose in fact that several of these guys being blackmailed decided to get rid of both their tormentors.''

Szczygiel shook his head. ''They'd have gone after both of them at the same time. Anyway, if there'd been a plot like that, they wouldn't have left pictures of eight men in Skaggs's house. Don't you think they'd have grabbed and destroyed *all* the pictures, all the negatives?''

''Which brings us,'' said Kennelly, ''to a suspect whose picture is missing from the collection. Mr. Assistant Attorney General Wolfe. The Alabama state police picked him up. He's in the county jail in Gadsden, Alabama. And

Sheriff Buford Wallace has a question. Who pays for bringing him back to Washington? He has another question. Do we send somebody down to Alabama to bring Wolfe back, or does the sheriff send him back in custody of a deputy?''

"Tell him to send him back," said Szczygiel. "The Secret Service will pay the expense."

"Alabama," said Kennelly. "Where was he going? Mexico?"

"Ask the sheriff to get him back here as quickly as possible," said Szczygiel. "We'll pay train fare here and back."

In her office, Mrs. Roosevelt was busy dictating a memorandum to Postmaster General James A. Farley, who was officially the chairman of the 1936 campaign. She raised many questions:

> Who is responsible for studying news reports and suggesting answers to charges, etc.?
> Who is responsible for the planning of a radio campaign, making arrangements in the states for people to listen?
> Who is in charge of research? Have we a department with complete information concerning all activities of the New Deal, and also concerning Landon and his supporters?
> Who is handling news reels?
> How many people are now working on campaign speeches?
> Who is responsible for sending regular reports to friendly newspapers? By this I mean feature stories, pictures, mats, boiler plate, etc.

She was amused that morning by a newspaper story quoting Governor Landon as saying in a political speech—"Wherever I go in America, I find Americans." The newspaper had editorialized that—"With hard-hitting talk like that, the Governor is building a reputation for forthright courage."

The Republicans generally were not so cautious. Frank Knox told an audience in Pennsylvania—"Today no life insurance policy is secure; no savings account is safe." In a leaflet being distributed all across the country, the Republican National Committee said—"If the present Administration is not beaten in 1936, the American plan of government may be lost forever." The Hearst newspapers ran front-page editorials charging that, on orders from Moscow, the Communists were working to re-elect Roosevelt. In New York, Al Smith proclaimed that "Even a Communist with wire whiskers and a torch in his hand is welcome" in Roosevelt's Democratic Party.

When Stan Szczygiel stopped by to report to her what Kennelly had told him, she interrupted her work for a few minutes to discuss the murder mystery.

"I am very curious about something," she told Szczygiel. "Quite obviously—or, anyway, it seems quite obvious to *me*—the photographs, all the negatives as well as the prints, were kept in Miss Taliafero's cellar. The night she was killed, Mr. Skaggs—almost certainly it was Mr. Skaggs—went to her house and removed the photographs. He took them to *his* house. Now . . . How did the man who murdered Mr. Skaggs *know* that the pictures were in Mr. Skaggs's possession?"

"We've assumed he killed Joe Bob Skaggs to get the pictures from him," said Szczygiel.

"Precisely. Should we review that assumption?"

"I think what we have to do first is find out all we can about Joe Bob Skaggs," said Szczygiel. "I've asked for an F.B.I. check on him. I telephoned the chief of police in Biloxi this morning, but I can't say I got a lot of cooperation."

Mrs. Roosevelt reached for a box of file cards that she

kept in her desk. Opening the box, she flipped cards until she came to an entry for Biloxi. She scanned the card.

"Excuse me, Mr. Szczygiel. I'll have the White House operator put in a call for me."

Szczygiel waited as she spoke to the operator, then asked—"You know somebody way down there?"

She smiled. "I've traveled all over the country," she said. "I hope the newspaper editor in Biloxi will remember me."

Szczygiel laughed. "I hardly think anyone who's ever met you is likely to forget it."

After a couple of minutes the telephone rang, and the operator said she had Mr. Jennings Jackson on the line. Mrs. Roosevelt gestured to Szczygiel to pick up an extension earphone that lay on the desk, so he could listen.

"Mr. Jackson? This is Mrs. Roosevelt, calling from the White House. How are you this morning?"

"Well, Ah'm jus' fan, Miz Roosevelt, and honored to be talkin' to you."

"We met in Biloxi in 1934," she said.

"Actually, Ma'am, that was my father, since deceased. He spoke of the occasion often."

"Oh, I'm sorry to hear he has passed on. And you've taken over the newspaper?"

"Ah have, Ma'am. Ah have, and Ah expect to be endorsin' Mr. Roosevelt 'tween now and election day."

"We'll be grateful for that, Mr. Jackson," she said. "Send me the clipping, will you please?"

"Be honored to."

"Fine. This morning I'm calling about something else. Let me tell you that Mr. Stanlislaw Szczygiel is listening. He's an agent of the Secret Service. I imagine you know that two former residents of your city have been murdered in Washington this past week, one of them actually on the White House grounds. We'd like to ask for some information about Miss Vivian Taliafero and Mr. Joe Bob Skaggs."

"Ah knew 'em both personally, Ma'am. It's distressin' to learn of their deaths."

"May I speak to you confidentially, Mr. Jackson? I'd like to tell you something that you should not publish, or indeed even discuss, until the evidence is adduced that absolutely proves what I'm about to say."

"That sounds most mysterious."

"It's also most upsetting. What I'm about to tell you is almost certainly true. If by some chance there is another explanation of the facts, then we wouldn't want to slander the memory of these two people."

"Well, ah'll keep the secret, Miz Roosevelt."

The voice on the telephone line was somewhat distorted by distance, but it gave Mrs. Roosevelt the impression of a sober, sincere man, maybe forty to fifty years old; and if she remembered his father correctly, this man was probably dressed in a rumpled seersucker suit and was sitting at a roll-top desk, speaking on a candlestick telephone.

"Mr. Jackson," she said, "what can you tell me about Miss Taliafero's source of income?"

"Her daddy was a United States senator," said Jennings Jackson. "Ah *s'pose* she lived rat well off his pension."

"In fact she didn't. There was also a trust fund in a Biloxi bank. Was the family well off? I mean, would she have had a big inheritance?"

"Her daddy was a lawyer here for many years, and he might have made some pretty nice money if he hadn't been so interested in politics. He was a member of the state legislature, then ran for Congress and was beat, then ran for attorney general and was beat, and then ran for United States senator and was elected. I'd say he had a little money laid up when he died, but it wouldn't have been a fortune."

"Well, she lived as though she had a fortune," said Mrs. Roosevelt. "And what about Mr. Skaggs?"

"Poor as a church mouse, as the sayin' goes," said Jackson. "He was a nice young fella. Busted that leg in three or four places playin' football. Nevah did heal right. Crippled him for life. We were glad to find out how he was doin' well in the insurance business in Washin'ton.''

"I'm afraid he wasn't in the insurance business, Mr. Jackson. And Miss Taliafero didn't live on her father's senatorial pension. She seems to have engaged frequently in, uh . . . in illicit sexual affairs, which Mr. Skaggs photographed from behind a see-through mirror; and they earned their living by blackmail.''

For a long moment there was no sound from Mississippi, until Mrs. Roosevelt was afraid they had somehow lost the telephone connection.

"Mr. Jackson?"

"Are you reasonable sure of those facts, Ma'am?" asked Jackson somberly.

"More than reasonably sure, Mr. Jackson. We are all but certain. Miss Taliafero was murdered by one of her blackmail victims, almost certainly. And Mr. Skaggs was, too—again, almost certainly."

"Well . . . Ah guess ah can say that folks here wouldn't be *one hundred percent* surprised.''

"Oh-ho. Please continue, Mr. Jackson."

"Well . . . Ah don't want to slander folks, livin' or dead, but some things about Vivian and Joe Bob are—How to say it? Are the subject of rumor around here.''

"We are anxious to discover who killed the two of them, Mr. Jackson. We are also anxious to protect the names of the men they were blackmailing, which I may tell you includes members of both the Democratic and Republican Parties. Anything you feel you can tell us might be most helpful.''

"Well . . . To start with, the Skaggses are what some folks call poor white trash. Ah myself don't use that term, and if Ah did, Ah wouldn't apply it to that family. They jus' hardworkin' folks that nevah did much git ahead, if you know what Ah mean. But that wasn't good enough for Senator Taliafero. He didn't want no poor white trash hangin' 'round his daughter—and he *did* use the term. They were high school sweethearts so to speak, and that's one of the reasons the senator took Vivian to live in Washin'ton. She wanted to stay here and live with her aunt, but the senator wanted her as far from Joe Bob Skaggs as possible.''

"So he separated them," said Mrs. Roosevelt thoughtfully. "Did Mr. Skaggs then stay in Biloxi?"

"Yes, Ma'am. He tried to sell insurance, tried to sell used cars, tried to sell vacuum cleaners—but mostly what he did, he was the rack boy in a pool room. He didn't get around very well, walked with two canes. That didn't help him. But he was a proud young fellow. Spent whatever he could on clothes. Afternoons, evenin's, he'd rack pool for fifteen cents an hour, but if he was to come to your house to sell you a vacuum cleaner, of a morning, he'd be dressed like a gentleman—all in a suit, white shirt, a hat, shoes shined. And some way he attracted the girls. Senator Taliafero wasn't the only father that stepped between his daughter and Joe Bob Skaggs. Boy didn't have no prospects, you know—besides bein' a Skaggs.''

"Sounds like a sorry tale," said Mrs. Roosevelt.

"Yes, 'tis. Then the senator died, and first thing we know Joe Bob left town and went up to Washin'ton. We figured maybe he and Vivian was gettin' married then. But . . . But Ah don't know. Ah expect she understood by then why her father wouldn't let her marry Joe Bob. Ah expect she'd set her sights higher.''

"Mr. Jackson . . . You said people in Biloxi wouldn't be one hundred percent surprised to learn that Miss Taliafero and Mr. Skaggs were involved in an illicit activity. What did you mean by that?''

For another long moment there was silence from Mississippi, then Jackson sighed and said—"Well, there was always stories about Vivian. Her father wasn't home much. The aunt . . . Well, the aunt wasn't too bright, if you know what Ah mean. Fond of the bottle. The girl grew up pretty independent. Always had money. There were stories told around here that she . . . that she spent more money than anybody could account for; and there were stories about how she got it.''

"Specifically, Mr. Jackson?"

"Uh . . . Well, it was understood her father would kill any man that touched her. Ah mean, that's the way such a thing is looked at in this part of the country. And the story went 'round that some did touch her—and paid for the privilege.''

"Do you mean she sold herself in prostitution?"

"Ah mean she reminded one or two fellas about what would happen if she went to her father and confessed, as you might put it, that there had been a . . . relationship. The story was that one or two fellas gave her little bits of money from time to time, to keep her happy and quiet.''

"Gossip like that rarely has any foundation in truth,'' observed Mrs. Roosevelt.

"Ah never heard a story like that about anybody else,'' said Jackson.

"Did she ever come home?"

"Not since the senator died. Not once, that Ah know of.''

"No one from Mississippi has claimed her body."

"Ah don't reckon anybody will."

"And Mr. Skaggs?"

"They couldn't afford to ship him back."

"Would they want him if they could?"

"Ah doubt it. Like Ah said, they're hard workin' folks, honest, got a sense of pride. He never came home either. Not once, after he left here.''

"Anything else you can tell us, Mr. Jackson?"

"They were fond of the bottle, Vivian and Joe Bob. He could never get enough when he was around here. Couldn't afford it. He drank the stuff that was made in the woods, and the story was also told that he sometimes stole it. Nobody gonna be surprised he turned out bad. Most folks will be surprised to hear it of Vivian—but not everybody.''

* * *

Shortly after noon, Szczygiel arrived on Capitol Hill and went directly to the office of Senator Steven Valentine. Valentine was finishing a box lunch and sat in his shirtsleeves behind his desk. He offered Szczygiel a Coke, said he'd have one fetched from the cooler down the hall—and Szczygiel accepted.

"Sit down. Stan, isn't it? Let's make it Stan and Steve, okay? And you pronounce your name 'Siegel,' right?"

"Yes. Matter of self-defense. I've thought of changing it to Siegel."

Valentine took a moment to light a cigarette. He was a tall, husky man, forty-four years old, generally reputed to be handsome. He had worked for the Ford Motor Company until 1917, when he joined the army, was trained and sent to France. When he returned to Detroit in 1919 he was determined never again to work on the factory floor. He became a union organizer, then a politician. He had the gruff, direct manner of everything he had been: factory worker, infantry corporal, union organizer, and urban politician.

"I read the newspapers," said Valentine.

Szczygiel nodded. He had no response to that comment.

"I read the account of the death of Vivian Taliafero. Now I read of the death of Joe Bob Skaggs. Two murders. Not a coincidence. Right?"

"Not a coincidence," Szczygiel agreed.

"I asked a question or two this morning and find that the President, before he left, signed an executive order assigning the investigation into the Taliafero murder to the Secret Service."

"Because it occurred on the White House grounds," said Szczygiel.

Valentine smiled wryly. "Sure, Stan. Anyway, you seem to be in charge. So, I figure there's no point in putting off a meeting between us. My name has come up in the investigation. Right?"

"Right."

"I'm a suspect."

"Together with a dozen others," said Szczygiel.

"Sure. Just a dozen? Well . . . anyway, I'm one of them. We are all suspects for one reason, right?"

Szczygiel nodded. "One reason."

"Public disclosure could ruin any one of us," the senator said. "All of us, actually. How many people know the story?"

"Apart from the men on the list of suspects? Three or four."

"People who can be trusted?"

"Yes. Absolutely. If anything gets loose and is published, it won't be because of the people involved in the investigation."

Senator Valentine drew deeply on his cigarette. "I didn't kill either one of them, Stan," he said. "I'm not sorry they're dead, but I didn't kill them." He nodded. "That's easy to say, I know. But it's the truth."

"Can you account for your whereabouts Tuesday night and Friday morning?"

"Tuesday night and Friday morning? Well . . . Yes, as it happens, I can. On Friday morning I was in a meeting of the Railroad Retirement Subcommittee of the Senate Labor Committee. All morning. Tuesday night—Well, let's say I can prove where I was if I have to."

Szczygiel smiled. "One scandal or another," he said cynically. "But the one without a murder in it is far littler."

Valentine shrugged. "I'm caught between the devil and the deep blue sea. Given a choice, I'll take the deep blue sea."

"Why don't you give me the name?" Szczygiel asked. "You wouldn't be trusting me with anything as damaging as what I already know."

"No. It involves another name. I'll use that other name if I have to, but not until I have to."

"Okay. Another point, then. You say you understand the connection between the murders of Vivian Taliafero and Joe Bob Skaggs. Just what *was* that connection, as you see it?"

"Don't you know?"

"I think so, but I'd like to hear what you think."

The senator paused while his aide brought in the cold Coke he had ordered for Szczygiel. Then he said—"Skaggs was her photographer. And her collection agent. Vivian liked to play the lady, too refined to talk about money. Skaggs was a tough. He carried a gun, Stan."

"Didn't do him any good Friday morning."

"Which might suggest something," said Valentine. "You probably assume he was killed by one of the men he and Vivian were blackmailing. But if he let himself be beaten to death and never pulled his gun, maybe the attack came from somebody he trusted."

"There was no gun on him when we found him," said Szczygiel.

"Did he have the pictures . . . and the negatives?"

"Yes."

"And now you have them?"

"Yes."

"They could make you rich, Stan. They could even make you politically powerful."

"They could get me killed, too," said Szczygiel.

Valentine frowned hard. "What will happen to those pictures?" he asked. "I mean, after the mystery is solved and somebody hangs for the two murders?"

"Won't be up to me," said Szczygiel. "I assume they'll be destroyed."

"Are you sure you have them all? You *do* have mine?"

Szczygiel nodded.

"They're locked up someplace safe? With somebody trustworthy?"

Szczygiel grinned. "Steve, you wouldn't *believe* how trustworthy."

Detective Lieutenant Paul Hupp smoked a pipe. He wore a blue-white seersucker suit, which was a mass of wrinkles at the end of that hot July Monday. A stout man with a moon-round face, he filled his wooden swivel chair and seemed to have spread so comfortably in it that he had assumed its shape. He spoke with the soft southern accent of northern Virginia.

"An interesting new development in the Skaggs murder, gentlemen," he said to Stan Szczygiel and Ed Kennelly. "If you don't mind, though, I'll tell you some other things first, then come to the interesting new development."

Szczygiel nodded. "I'd like to make a quick point," he said. "Mrs. Roosevelt wanted to come over with us this evening. I discouraged her. I don't think I can emphasize enough that we want to keep her name out of this matter.

If we'd had any idea we were going to find a body Saturday afternoon, we would not have brought her with us."

"I've heard she likes to play detective," said Hupp.

"She does more than play at it," said Szczygiel. "She's a careful observer and a shrewd analyst of facts. When the body of Congressman Colmer was found inside the Oval Office, in 1934, it was taken for a suicide because the doors and windows were all locked from the inside. It was Mrs. Roosevelt who discovered how someone had shot him and left him inside a locked room."

"Well, the story is she can do anything."

"We keep looking for something that's beyond her," said Szczygiel.

"Anyway," said Hupp, settling even more comfortably into his chair, "let me fill you in on some things about the Skaggs murder. In the first place, we found a twenty-five caliber Browning automatic in his closet—what they call a Baby Browning. It was hanging in a well-worn shoulder holster. It looks as if he carried it. Nobody's fingerprints on it but his. Had been fired recently and not cleaned. The clip was short one shell."

"This afternoon somebody described him as Vivian Taliafero's collector," said Szczygiel. "Mentioned that he carried a gun."

"He was a gambler," said Hupp. "Well known around the bookie joints, pool rooms. He spent money, but nobody knows where he got it. No job. No business."

"We know where he got it," said Kennelly.

"Right," said Hupp. "The blackmail deal."

"When you searched the house, did you find any more pictures?" Szczygiel asked.

"No, no more pictures. Not even a camera. But money."

"Money?"

"Yes. Pretty close to a thousand dollars, hidden in some old shoes in his bedroom closet. Didn't find it the first search. Found it on the second, more thorough go-through.''

"That brings us to the new development," said Hupp. "I've got a girl back in the cells. Holding her for burglary. She broke into Skaggs's house last night. A neighbor saw her and called us.''

"What's the story?" asked Kennelly.

"Her fingerprints were all over the house," said Hupp. "I suppose she was Skaggs's girlfriend. She says she had his permission to enter the house any time, and she says she came to get some clothes that were hers. That could be true—there were a woman's clothes in his closet. I figure, though, she knew about the money and thought maybe we hadn't found it.''

"What's her name?" asked Szczygiel.

"Sally Partridge. Twenty-two years old, says she's from Alamance County, North Carolina. Want to talk to her?''

"Yes," said Szczygiel.

"I suggest we go back to the cells to talk to her," said Hupp. "Something about being behind bars makes most of 'em talk better sense.''

The Alexandria city jail had three cells for women, and that evening only one was occupied—by the distraught Sally Partridge. She was a blonde, slender, youthful, and quite pretty in a contrived way. She jumped up from her bunk and pressed against the bars of her cell door, as though she unconsciously entertained a notion that she could press through. She was dressed in a knee-length baggy gray dress—the uniform of the jail. The armpits were dark with her sweat.

"This is Mr. Stanislaw Szczygiel of the Secret Service and Lieutenant Edward Kennelly of the District of Columbia police. They want to talk to you about Skaggs.''

"I wisht I'd nevah met him," she sniffed.

"You have that in common with a great many people, Miss Partridge," said Szczygiel. "How long did you know Joe Bob Skaggs?''

"I didn't kill him," she said quickly. "I had every right to be in that house, and I ain't no burgular."

"That's between you and Lieutenant Hupp," said Szczygiel. "I want to talk to you about Skaggs."

Though her eyes were swollen from crying and she was without makeup, it was apparent that Sally Partridge thought she bore a resemblance to the movie star Jean Harlow and had gone to some trouble to enhance the image of herself as a Harlow look-alike. Her hair was bleached to the color of vanilla ice cream, cut short, and with heat and chemicals molded into deep waves. She had plucked her dark eyebrows into two fine arches.

"Secret Service . . ." she said cautiously. "Is that like G-men?"

"The chief job of the Secret Service is to protect the President," said Szczygiel.

"Well, what'd Joe Bob have to do with the President?"

"Vivian Taliafero was murdered on the White House grounds," said Szczygiel.

"Mind your own business and answer the gentleman's questions," snapped Hupp.

"Ain't I got no rights?"

"All the rights anybody's got who's caught in the act of burglary," said Hupp.

"I ain't no burgular!"

"Then why did you break the glass in the back door to get in? Why didn't you just call the police and tell us some clothes of yours were in Skaggs's house?"

"I nevah thought of doin' it that way."

"How long did you know Skaggs?" asked Szczygiel impatiently.

Sally Partridge glared at him for a moment, trying apparently to decide whether to be fearful or angry. "Six, eight months," she mumbled. She tightened her grip on the bars, and her knuckles turned white.

"You were his girlfriend."

"You could say that."

"How'd he make his living?"

"I never asked, and he never told me."

"Sally . . ." said Hupp quietly. "You know how many years you get for burglary in Virginia?"

She stared at Hupp for a moment, her resolution visibly faltering.

"Technically," he said, "the crime is called 'burglary of an inhabited dwelling house in the night season.' The penalty is life imprisonment."

She clapped her hands to her mouth, and her eyes widened with fear. *"Life!"* she whispered through her fingers. She shook her head. "Why, all I done was—You couldn't . . ."

"I surely don't want to, Sally. Now, you cooperate with these gentlemen. You cooperate, and maybe we can reduce the charge, or even drop it."

She turned toward Szczygiel. "He was a *crook!* Joe Bob was a dirty crook."

"How do you know?" asked Szczygiel.

"He . . . He asked me to git in their low-down business with them. That woman, she didn't want to go on doing it the way she done it. She wanted another girl to do the dirty part. Maybe me."

"Did you meet Vivian Taliafero?"

"I met her. Maybe I ain't nothin' but a waitress, but I'm more the lady than she was. She treated me like *dirt.*"

"Did you get in their business with them?"

Sally glanced from one of the men to another. "No. I never did. I might of." She nodded. "I just might of. But the Taliafero woman said I'd have to learn to be more of a lady first. Joe Bob, he was supposed to be teachin' me."

"How to pour tea, maybe?" asked Kennelly.

"Stuff like that. I already knew how to do the other part of the job."

"Was part of the money yours?" asked Szczygiel.

She lifted her chin. "He owed me."

Szczygiel ignored the appreciative glances of the other

two officers, who had watched him wait until the girl's guard was down from a conversational ploy, then drop on her a question she had not expected and had answered honestly.

"Why did he owe you?"

Sally Partridge dropped her head and sighed loudly. She knew she had lowered her guard and spoken ahead of her thoughts. "Hey . . ." she muttered. "Look. I ain't no burgular. I ain't done nothin' bad, 'cept maybe some *little* thing. Hey . . . My daddy finds out I'm in jail, I can't nevah go home again, not for the rest of my life! I'll do anything you guys want—jus' to get out of here. Okay? Okay? Whatta you want me to say?"

"It's really very simple," said Hupp coldly. "All you have to do is tell the truth."

She nodded. " 'Kay . . ."

"All right," said Szczygiel. "Why did Skaggs owe you money?"

"He promised to pay me for doin' something'," she said.

"What?"

Sally Partridge turned away from the bars of her cell for a moment. With her back to the three officers, she lowered her head and pondered for a moment. Then she turned abruptly—

"He had a *key!* We weren't no burgulars. He let us in the house with a key."

"Vivian Taliafero's house," said Kennelly.

"Yes. Sure. The way it was, I was supposed to come over to Joe Bob's house and meet him after work. Where I work is the Airline Bar, on Connecticut Avenue. Well, instead of that he shows up about nine and wants me to leave right then. Well, I couldn't. But he handed my boss, the bartender, a five-spot and said let me go and keep quiet. So off we went in Joe Bob's car. 'I ain't gonna kid you,' he said. 'Vivian's been killed tonight, and I didn't do it, but there's some stuff in her house that might make a lot of trouble for me if the cops get their hands on it, and I'll pay you two hundred bucks to come with me to her house and—' ''

"You believed him when he said he hadn't killed her?" asked Hupp.

"Why would he want to kill her? She was the only way he was makin' any money. Without her—"

"Okay, so you went to the house, and he let you both in with a key."

"Right, with a key."

"And you were in the house how long?"

"Twenty minutes, half hour," she said. "I guess."

"Did you find what you came for?"

"Yes sir. Pictures. I knew it was the pictures he wanted when he said there was stuff in the house that might make trouble for him if the cops found it. He picked up two dish towels in the kitchen and told me not to touch anything except with them, so as not to leave no fingerprints of mine. Then I went around where he told me, wipin' his prints off stuff."

"You didn't figure you were committing any crime," said Hupp dryly.

She closed her eyes. "Well, maybe . . . But it didn't make me no burgular or nothin'. He let us in with a *key!*"

"All right," said Szczygiel. "So you spent twenty minutes to half an hour wiping off fingerprints and gathering up—Well, gathering up evidence."

"What he was gatherin' up," she said, "was a fortune's worth of dirty pictures, what he and that Taliafero woman had used to make a livin'."

"Did he say anything to you about the murder?"

"Just that he swore he didn't do it. He said he didn't know who did. But I sort of got it from what he said that he maybe saw who killed her. He was real shaken up. He was scared."

"Were you scared?"

"Pretty quick I was. 'Cause somebody come!"

"Somebody—?"

"We was in the basement. We heard somebody walkin' upstairs. Joe Bob, he turned off the lights, and we waited in the dark. I figured it was the cops and was trouble. I don't know what he figured it was. Anyway, we waited— me scared half to death—and pretty soon the door opens at the top of the steps and a man starts down. And next thing I know—" She stopped and swallowed. "Next thing I know Joe Bob, he takes a shot at the fella!"

"He fired at the man?"

"He most surely did. Missed him, thank God. And the man, he run back up the steps and acrost the floor upstairs and out the front door."

"All right, Sally," said Szczygiel firmly. "A straight question. I want a straight answer. Who was the man on the stairs?"

She shook her head. "As God is my witness, Mister, I don't know."

"Would you know the man if you saw him? What if I show you some pictures?"

"Well . . . It was kinda dark. The man hadn't turned on the basement lights. You had to do that by pulling the strings. All the light was what came down from the hall. And he had on a hat. I don't know."

Szczygiel turned to Hupp. "Could you have an officer bring in my briefcase?"

Hupp stepped away from the cells for a moment to summon a uniformed policeman and give him the order.

"We didn't find any bullet holes in that basement," Kennelly said skeptically to Sally Partridge.

"It's a brick wall," she said. "There's a chipped place, if you look. And Joe Bob, he picked up the shell case that flew out of the pistol. He made me crawl around on the floor till I found the bullet. All I found, really, was a piece of it, all flat and busted up. I guess you could find other pieces of it, if you looked."

Stan Szczygiel had arranged for a photo lab technician

at the Bureau of Printing and Engraving to make a new set of prints from the Taliafero negatives, these showing only the faces of the men. They were a strange set of pictures. Absent the rest of the picture, the odd angles and strained expressions of the men were utterly inexplicable.

Sally Partridge frowned over these bizarre portraits of Senator Everett Cranshaw, Judge Beresford Kincaid, Admiral Richard Horan, Congressman Gordon Pierce, Burton Oleander, and Frederick Hausser. She squinted and seemed to strain to satisfy her interrogators by identifying one of them as the man she had seen on the stairs. Finally she shook her head.

"Don't know any of them?"

"No. I can't say any of them is the man. I can say one thing you might want to hear, though. None of them is impossible. It *could* be any one of them."

"If you break the case within twenty-four hours," said Mrs. Roosevelt, "then I suppose it should not be called a mystery. If, on the other hand, a week goes by, almost, and we still don't know who murdered Miss Taliafero, then it is a mystery. And is there not a rule, Mr. Szczygiel, Lieutenant Kennelly, that in solving mysteries, first impressions and hasty conclusions are almost invariably wrong?"

They had come to her office on the second floor of the White House to tell her what they had learned since she made her call to Biloxi earlier in the day. She had ordered iced tea and cookies, and they sat in the breeze from an oscillating fan.

Szczygiel smiled, and Kennelly grinned.

"That's not a rule?" she asked mock-innocently.

"I'll have to check the detective's handbook," Kennelly laughed. "But so far as I know, there are no rules."

"Seriously," she said, "let us not place too great emphasis on Senator Valentine's having told you Mr. Skaggs carried a gun and Miss Partridge's telling you he fired at someone.''

"Whoever he took a shot at on those cellar stairs knows he carried a gun," said Szczygiel. "Senator Valentine told me he carried a gun. Who else would have known it? He carried it hidden in a shoulder holster, and it's hard to think he pulled it out very often.''

"Maybe he pulled it often," said Kennelly. "He was a swaggering bum.''

Mrs. Roosevelt pointed at her chart of suspects. "We can remove the question mark beside Congressman Dies, in the second column," she said. "He was in Texas when Mr. Skaggs was killed.''

She rose and used a pen to write "Texas" over the question mark.

"I don't think Sally Partridge has told all she knows," said Szczygiel.

"She will," said Kennelly. "Hupp'll sweat her.''

"The question for which I should like to have an answer," said Mrs. Roosevelt, "is how did Mr. Skaggs learn so quickly of the death of Miss Taliafero? If Miss Partridge's account is correct, he hurried to pick her up and went to the house immediately. The woman couldn't have been dead more than an hour before he arrived there.''

"Followed by someone else—again, if Sally Partridge is telling the truth," said Szczygiel.

"What motive could Mr. Skaggs have had for killing Miss Taliafero?''

"We could speculate on that for an hour and not come up with the answer," said Kennelly. "A falling-out between two crooks. A falling-out between lovers. We don't know they weren't still lovers, the way they'd been in Mississippi.''

"He went to get the photographs," said Mrs. Roosevelt. "That's clear enough. He went to get them and did get them. And that, incidentally, shows that Miss Partridge has told the truth, at least in part. She told you they went to the house to get the photographs—which she couldn't have known unless that was in fact what they went to get. So she *was* with Mr. Skaggs that night.''

"A wee bit fanciful, Ma'am," said Szczygiel.

"Also," said Mrs. Roosevelt, "she did not kill Mr. Skaggs. If she did that on Friday morning, why would she not have taken what she wanted from his house at that time? Why would she return on Sunday night? I venture to guess she didn't learn of his death until Sunday."

"I'll add a guess of my own," said Kennelly. "She says he'd promised to pay her two hundred dollars and she came to get it. We've guessed she really came to get his whole stash. Better than that, I bet she came to see if she couldn't pick up the pictures. She knows they were worth a fortune—her words."

Mrs. Roosevelt's thoughts were not following this string of surmises; they had turned to something else. "How did the murderer enter and leave the grounds of the White House after dark?" she asked. "I understood the premises were closed at sunset."

"The premises *are* closed, Ma'am," said Szczygiel. "But only officially. It is still entirely possible to enter the grounds and wander about. A trespasser is not likely to encounter a policeman or a Secret Service agent until he attempts to enter the House itself. We've suggested repeatedly that the White House should be better protected, but more protection would require more officers, which in turn would require a bigger appropriation."

"Besides," she said, "everyone is reluctant to abandon the old tradition that the White House grounds are a sort of public park to be enjoyed by the people of Washington."

"And that the House itself is a public building," added Szczygiel. "When I first came to work here, it was still just that; and anyone could wander in. We've closed it gradually, and many people resent it."

"The fact that the murder occurred in the White House

Rose Garden does not limit the list of suspects, then,'' she said.

"It does not, Mrs. Roosevelt," said Szczygiel. "Unfortunately, it does not."

"Then we had better begin eliminating question marks," she said, glancing at the chart. "We know that Mr. Dies didn't kill Mr. Skaggs but not that he didn't kill Miss Taliafero. Not much progress, hmm, gentlemen?"

"Actually, we've learned a lot," said Szczygiel. "But I do agree we must set to work matching what we know against our list of suspects."

10

Mrs. Roosevelt stood at her mirror, looking critically at herself. She had no time for primping and little patience with it. She did, though, want to make a good appearance this evening, if only out of respect for the people whose dinner she was attending. The National Association of Manufacturers contained few admirers of the New Deal or of the Roosevelts personally. Furthermore, they were annoyed that it was *Mrs.* Roosevelt and not the President who was attending their dinner. In fact, there had even been some huffing that the President had chosen this week for his vacation, just to avoid attending their dinner. So, she did want to make a respectable appearance, to give them no reason to believe she was slighting them. Otherwise she would not have dressed formally on so hot and muggy an evening.

Her dress was of green silk with a pattern of white leaves and flowers. She wore a single strand of pearls at her throat and another on her wrist. The organization had sent her a large orchid, which—though it did not match her chosen ensemble—she wore pinned to her shoulder.

A White House limousine carried her to the Mayflower Hotel, and she was escorted to the dining room by two agents of the Secret Service—Baines and Deconcini. A reception was taking place just outside the dining room, and there she was met by Whitson Wilson, president of the Association.

"Ah, Mrs. Roosevelt!" he cried, hurrying across the room toward her. "A pleasure! An honor!"

She smiled and extended her hand—for the moment overlooking the fact that not a week before he had called her husband "an errand boy of the Communist conspiracy."

He was a bald man, with a ruddy pate and a fringe of white hair all around, wearing a pince-nez on a black ribbon—with, of course, white tie. He was reputed to be worth $110,000,000.

"Well . . ." he said. "To whom shall I introduce you first?"

"I see many people to whom I need not be introduced," she said. "I see many people I know well."

Indeed she did. Secretary of the Interior Harold Ickes was there—prickly and curmudgeonly as always. Although he had been a Republican, he was as loyal and supportive as any man in the Administration, Mrs. Roosevelt knew; and she was glad to see him. Harry Hopkins was there. She was glad to see him; yet, his appearance tugged at her heart, since he was there, really, because Louis Howe was gone. The third representative of the Administration was Secretary of Trade Herschel Rinehart. She returned his smile from across the room, but she could not help but remember where his fingerprints had been found.

She, Ickes, and Rinehart would represent the Democratic Party at the speakers' table.

She was pleased to see, also, the men who would sit

there as representatives of the Republican Party. First among them was Governor Alfred Landon, the Republican candidate for President. Wilson escorted her directly to him and broke through the knot of men around him.

"Governor, allow me to present the First Lady."

Landon turned toward her and extended his hand. His smile was so warm and friendly that she had no doubt it was genuine. "You won't remember, Mrs. Roosevelt, but we have met briefly before," he said.

"You were one of the Midwestern governors who came to the White House in 1933 to meet with the President about drought relief," she said. "We met in the East Room, and I asked you if you rode horses."

"Mrs. Roosevelt!"

"It would be very pleasant," she said, "if we could go riding together in Rock Creek Park." She paused and smiled. "Say, in the spring of 1937?"

Governor Landon laughed. "When I will be unemployed and you will still live in the White House!"

"Or I shall be unemployed and *you* will live in the White House," she said.

"Either way," he said, "I hope we will be friends."

"I've no doubt of it, Governor. Why not, after all?"

"And—" He turned and nodded toward the man standing somewhat expectantly, somewhat uneasily beside him. "You know Mr. Hoover, of course."

She extended her hand. "Mr. President," she said to Herbert Hoover. "How very nice to see you again."

Hoover bowed. "It's always a pleasure to see you, Mrs. Roosevelt."

"I understand you are to be our speaker tonight," she said.

"Yes. Since the President could not be here this evening, it was thought better not to have the Governor speak. I am to say something non-partisan."

"Oh, Mr. Hoover, I hope not," she said. "I hope you speak your mind. Whether I am able to agree with you or not, I am sure that whatever you have to say will be instructive and thought-provoking.''

Herbert Hoover blushed. "I shall try to make it so," he said.

Wilson was beckoning others to meet her.

Among those who came forward to shake her hand and say a word was Henry Ford. An emaciated, somewhat vacant-eyed old man, he shuffled across the room and seized her hand in a tight grip. "I do hope your husband understands the awful threat of the Zionist conspiracy," he said.

"My husband is very pleased with his Ford car," she replied.

John Hay Whitney hurried over to see her and say a few words. They would talk more later, he said. Will Kellogg, founder of the breakfast-food company, shook her hand gravely. Alfred Sloan, president of General Motors, was animated and personable, as was the industrialist Henry Kaiser.

Then—unfortunately, in her judgment—there were some representatives of the Roosevelt-hating far right. When Burton Oleander oozed his way up to her to offer a limp handshake, she was almost glad she had seen the grotesque obscene photograph of him that had been taken by Joe Bob Skaggs. It seemed appropriate to the man.

At the head table she was seated between Whitson Wilson and Chief Justice Charles Evans Hughes.

The bald, white-bearded Hughes, who was seventy-four that year, was a stately figure obviously nearing the end of a distinguished career. He had been Governor of New York, then Associate Justice of the Supreme Court, from which position he resigned to be the Republican candidate for President in 1916; after which he had been Secretary of State under Harding and Coolidge; and finally, in 1930, he had become Chief Justice of the United States. He was a formidable man with a formidable, studied dignity.

"I remember well," said Hughes gravely, "that pleasant evening when we dined—you and your husband, my wife and I, and Holmes. Do you recall?''

"Absolutely, Mr. Chief Justice," she said. "During the war. Mr. Justice Holmes was an awesome figure to a young wife newly introduced to Washington society."

"My dear lady," said Hughes. "There is no such thing as society in *Washington*. The pretense is sometimes amusing, but the reality is absent."

"Spoken like a true New Yorker," she said.

"If we must have our capitol city in this jerkwater town," he said, "I should think we New Yorkers could detach ourselves from the pretense."

"Mr. Hughes—"

"Alabamans," said the Chief Justice. "Arkansans, Ohioans, Nebraskans, Dakotans, Coloradans, Californians . . . All pretending to be civilized. My dear Mrs. Roosevelt. It is distressing to have to live among such yahoos."

"I observe, Mr. Chief Justice," she said, "that you have decided not to be a candidate for high elective office another time."

Hughes guffawed, attracting the attention of others at the head table and people at the tables below, who wondered what Mrs. Roosevelt could have said to him.

To the other side of the president of the Association, Alf Landon leaned forward and asked—"What did she say to you, Mr. Chief Justice?"

"Mrs. Roosevelt speaks with Confucian wisdom," said Charles Evans Hughes. "It never comes off so well when repeated by others."

Landon smiled and returned to conversation with the man to his left, Alfred Sloan.

"I have heard," said Charles Evans Hughes, "that an assistant attorney general has been arrested in Alabama, apparently as a fugitive from justice."

"That is true," said Mrs. Roosevelt. "Mr. William Wolfe."

"A suspect in the murder of Vivian Taliafero?"

"Yes. His abrupt departure from Washington may be the chief evidence against him, but he is being returned from Alabama."

"That woman—"

"Do you know something about Miss Taliafero?" asked Mrs. Roosevelt.

"Oliver Wendell Holmes used to visit her house," said the Chief Justice. "I went with him a few times myself, since he enjoyed it so much. He held court there. He presided like Voltaire presiding over a Paris salon in the eighteenth century. The dear old man never suspected anything about that woman."

"What did he not suspect, Mr. Chief Justice?" asked Mrs. Roosevelt.

Visibly flustered, the Chief Justice smiled weakly. "I'm sorry to have mentioned it," he said, "but I should suppose her death by murder was no great surprise."

"It was to me," said Mrs. Roosevelt.

"Yes. Yes. I should hope so. And perhaps we should abandon so delicate a subject."

"To the contrary," she said. "I have taken a personal interest in the investigation into this murder—and also the murder of Miss Taliafero's friend Mr. Joe Bob Skaggs— and I should be most grateful if you would tell me anything you know about Miss Taliafero."

"Well . . ." said the Chief Justice awkwardly. He paused to twist the end of his white mustache. "Miss Taliafero was something of a . . . femme fatale." He chuckled nervously. "There was always a certain amount of talk about her."

"About her and whom?"

"Well . . . It would perhaps be improper of me to—"

"Mr. Chief Justice," said Mrs. Roosevelt. "The investigating officers are looking at the names of ten suspects, all of them prominent men. I have seen their list, and am unlikely to be surprised—either if you mention one of those names or add another to the list. I am beyond being surprised in this case. Or shocked. I have already been both. Emphatically.''

The Chief Justice's smile, beneath his white mustache, was obscured and cryptic, yet boyish. Above his white beard, his cheeks reddened. He was of a generation that did not discuss anything titillating with ladies. Their sensibilities were not able to take such jolts. Certain things were discussed by men over cigars and whiskey, never in the presence of ladies.

"I know about the activities that took place upstairs above Miss Taliafero's parlor," said Mrs. Roosevelt.

The Chief Justice stared at her for a moment. "Then I need not discuss the matter further," he said.

"Except for one thing," she said. "It is very likely that one of the gentlemen who went upstairs is the murderer, not only of Miss Taliafero but probably also of Mr. Skaggs. The . . . *private* activities that took place in Miss Taliafero's bedroom have become a matter of public concern."

"You understand, I hope," said the Chief Justice, "that visiting Miss Taliafero in her public capacity was nothing extraordinary. Indeed, I may say that conversations between me and other judges in her parlor were productive of some important new attitudes I took toward some cases. Why, Holmes and I talked about—''

"That is entirely understood," she said. "There was no impropriety in your being there, Mr. Chief Justice. I have no thought that there was and no intention of so suggesting. But—''

"But you want to know if I can testify to any *impropriety.*''

"Not testify, sir," she said. "Just tell me. I will guard your confidence. If you know anything."

"I should be distressed if too much emphasis were to be laid on what I am about to tell you," said the Chief Justice. "The words I am about to repeat may have had their origin in the bottle and nowhere else. I should not repeat them except for what you have told me, that culpability for the murder of two people is yet to be established.''

"I should not want to hear gossip, except for that circumstance," she said.

"I met with a group of senators about two months ago," said Charles Evans Hughes. "The subject of discussion was the judiciary appropriation. After we met, I repaired to the Caliber Club with several senators. We drank and nibbled on the hors d'oeuvres for some time, and shortly all were gone except myself and Senator Everett Cranshaw. The senator had consumed a good deal of Scotch by then, plus some champagne. Somehow the conversation moved to Miss Vivian Taliafero. For a few minutes it was a rather ordinary conversation; then he became emotional. The woman was a *demon*, he said. He expounded on that thought for a minute or so, and then he said she was going to destroy many careers if she were not stopped, and he said he hoped some man would have the courage to put a stop to her."

"Oh . . . 'Put a stop to her.' What do you suppose he meant by that?"

The Chief Justice shrugged. "What could he have meant?"

"But was he more specific?"

"He said the world would be better off without her."

Mrs. Roosevelt was anxious to leave as soon as she tactfully could after the dinner and speeches. It was the custom of the National Association of Manufacturers for the official dinner to be followed by a number of unofficial gatherings in hotel suites, where cigars would be smoked, much liquor would be drunk, and the gentlemen would enjoy a variety of forms of entertainment, ranging from high-stakes games of cards to licentious performances. She noticed Governor Landon hurrying from the hall, anxious to be away before it became awkward for him to decline an invitation. Similarly, Chief Justice Hughes worked his way toward the door, smiling and accepting greetings, but determinedly progressing toward his goal to leave.

Mrs. Roosevelt had no fear she would be invited to any of the later parties. She simply wanted to go back to the White House to return to a few details of work she felt she should dispense with before she retired. But she was to be delayed—

Herschel Rinehart, Secretary of Trade, hurried across the room toward her, just as her Secret Service guard had returned to her side.

"Ah, Mrs. Roosevelt! I'm sorry we didn't have a chance to talk before now."

Herschel Rinehart was the picture of an American businessman in the fourth decade of the twentieth century, which he had been before he joined the Administration. His curly dark hair had retreated off his forehead. He wore round, gold-rimmed eyeglasses. For this dinner he wore white tie, but he was known in Washington for the quality and conservative image of his tailoring. He had earned his fortune in the wholesale grocery trade and had learned in that business the respect for the disadvantaged of America that had oriented him to Democratic politics and encouraged him to accept a cabinet position in the New Deal.

"Why, yes, Mr. Rinehart," she said. "I too was sorry we were seated so far apart."

He glanced around. "A word, Mrs. Roosevelt?"

She nodded to her two Secret Service agents—a long-understood nod, meaning, stand back a few paces and save my privacy if you can.

"I understand," he said, "that Assistant Attorney General Wolfe is being returned to Washington as a prisoner and will be charged with the murder of Vivian Taliafero."

"He is being returned in the custody of an Alabama sheriff. I am not certain he will be charged with anything."

The man could not conceal his disappointment; obviously he had hoped to hear Wolfe would be charged.

"I understand, too," he said, "that you have taken a personal interest in the matter."

"When someone is murdered in the White House Rose Garden," she said, "it calls in question the safety of all who live and work there. I have to be interested."

"Well, then—" he said. He glanced around again, to be sure no one was listening. "Maybe I can give you some information that will be helpful in solving the case."

"I would be grateful."

"I couldn't testify to what I am about to say. I don't have this information from personal knowledge. But I can tell you there was some kind of personal relationship between Bill Wolfe and Vivian Taliafero. Some kind of . . . personal relationship."

"How do you know that?" Mrs. Roosevelt asked bluntly.

"I knew both of them," said Rinehart. "I liked Vivian, really. She was a bright, vivacious woman. I was her guest often, at her soirées. For a year or more. Bill Wolfe was almost always there when I was. We struck up an acquaintanceship, then a friendship. He spoke very frankly to me about Vivian."

"Saying what?"

"Well . . . You know, neither of them were married. They developed a strong personal attachment. Why shouldn't they have? But, as he told it, she was a demanding woman. She wanted him to marry her. Immediately. She insisted he must."

"Why?" asked Mrs. Roosevelt.

"He had, uh . . . compromised her honor."

"Really, Mr. Rinehart! The evidence adduced since the death of Miss Taliafero rather clearly suggests that there was no honor to be compromised."

Rinehart's jaw fell. He had never heard the First Lady

speak that way, had never heard *of* the First Lady speaking that way. "Surely—" he muttered.

"A very large number of photographs were found," she said. "Miss Taliafero was not a virtuous woman."

"Photographs . . ."

"Photographs."

"Were found by whom?"

"Were found by the Secret Service and the District police, who are cooperating in the investigation."

"And where are those photographs now?" asked Rinehart. His face had collapsed, become slack and pallid. "I mean, uh . . . who has them?"

"They are under lock and key in the White House," she said.

"You've seen them?"

"Unfortunately, yes. I wish I hadn't."

Rinehart trembled. He wiped the sweat from his upper lip with a broad stroke of his hand. "Do you want my resignation?" he sighed.

"I don't. Of course, the President knows nothing of this matter. And, as you know, it hasn't been made public. Maybe it need not be. That will depend on the outcome of the investigation into the murders of Miss Taliafero and Mr. Skaggs."

"I . . . Is it possible to speak with you somewhere else? Could we—"

"Would you like to come to the White House with me?" she asked.

Stan Szczygiel was available to sit down with Mrs. Roosevelt and Herschel Rinehart. He had been sipping gin with Missy in her third-floor suite, and she came to the First Lady's office with him. It was impossible for Mrs. Roosevelt to overlook the fact that both of them showed the effects of happily imbibing during the past two hours. Szczygiel's red nose was redder than usual, and he sat down and began to pick at his fingernails nervously. Missy was flushed and a little too ready to laugh. Both of them were embarrassed, but neither was so embarrassed as not to come when Mrs. Roosevelt called.

Shortly after they came in, the night butler arrived carrying a pitcher of lemonade and a small platter of tuna-salad sandwiches. It was George, and he glanced at Missy and lifted his eyebrows almost imperceptibly. Missy broke into a sustained giggle—the reason for which was totally obscure to Mrs. Roosevelt and made her attribute it strictly to drink.

"Please have a sandwich or two," she said to Missy—causing Missy to giggle all the more.

Rinehart sat staring, astounded. He had heard that Missy LeHand had a close personal relationship with both the Roosevelts, but he had no idea the President's secretary would allow the First Lady to see her tipsy—or that Mrs. Roosevelt would for a moment tolerate it.

Mrs. Roosevelt smiled and said, "Mr. Rinehart had something rather serious to discuss with us. It *is,* though, long after working hours, and I've no right to demand that the two of you be here."

"I'm sorry," said Missy, her giggle slowly trailing off. "We've been relaxing a bit."

"Well . . . Feel free to leave if you want to. I thought you might want to hear what Mr. Rinehart has to tell us."

Missy nodded solemnly and reached for a sandwich. Szczygiel had already taken one and was munching determinedly, as if a quick ingestion of bread, tuna fish, and mayonnaise would counteract the gin he had thoroughly enjoyed.

"I've explained to Mr. Rinehart that both of you have been closely involved in the investigation and that it is entirely appropriate that you should hear what he has to tell us. So, I'm going to ask him now to tell us what he knows about Miss Taliafero."

It was an odd scene: Mrs. Roosevelt sitting at her desk, in her green-and-white silk dress, her pearls, and the orchid that had held up surprisingly well all evening; Rinehart in white tie, slumped on a straight upholstered chair and looking miserable; Szczygiel in a wilted gray suit, now wolfing sandwiches; Missy in a white summer dress, nibbling on one of the hated tuna-salad sandwiches and trying to hold herself solemn and attentive.

Rinehart began. "I started going to see Vivian Taliafero about a year ago," he said. "I was introduced to her by Judge Kincaid. At first I just went to her soirées. I enjoyed the company. She was a marvelous hostess and attracted some distinguished people, who sat around in her parlor and talked. After . . . oh, I guess it was after about three months, Judge Kincaid suggested to me one evening that it cost Vivian a lot of money to provide food and drink for so many guests and that occasionally some of the men who came regularly gave her a little money to help defray the costs. I thought that was fair, and that evening I gave him a hundred dollars in cash, to give to her. Uh . . . I have to tell you that later, when the relationship between Vivian and me was different, she told me the Judge had turned over only fifty dollars in my name. He had given her the other fifty dollars as a contribution from himself."

"Swell fellow, the Judge," remarked Stan Szczygiel.

Rinehart nodded. "I guess more than a few of her guests gave her money to help her sustain the salon, if that is what it should be called."

"I can think of another name," said Missy.

"So can I," said Rinehart bitterly. "Anyway, maybe a month later—maybe a month, maybe six weeks—Judge Kincaid suggested to me that another hundred would be appropriate. I said, 'Hey, look, a hundred a month is a bit much.' I gave him twenty dollars. He turned over all of that to Vivian, as she told me later.

"After that, I handed over a twenty-dollar bill from time to time. Each time, I gave it to Judge Kincaid. I wasn't sure just how to hand it to Vivian. I mean, I was naive enough to think she would be embarrassed."

"I can certainly understand your thought," said Mrs. Roosevelt. "Even if it does turn out to have been naive."

"We stood around in her parlor, drinking expensive champagne, eating fine food. It was to our immense advantage that she made her home available to us that way. Well . . . The relationship changed. I—There is no circumspect way to say this. Vivian, whom I had seen and talked with many, many times over the months, gradually became more friendly. She would touch my hand as we talked. She kissed my cheek when I came to the house and when I left. And eventually—"

"Yes," said Mrs. Roosevelt. "We know. When did you learn that you had been photographed?"

Rinehart pursed his lips and blew a loud sigh. "Within a week," he said. "Skaggs—that slimy worm—came to me with the pictures."

"You *saw* the pictures of you with Miss Taliafero?" asked Mrs. Roosevelt. Her thought was that *she* hadn't seen them. Pictures of Herschel Rinehart were missing from the set. "You saw photographs of you—? Well, we need not describe what kind of photographs they may have been."

"Yes. I saw them."

"Mr. Skaggs brought them to you. Had you known him before?"

"Not really. I had seen him at her house. Briefly. I took him for a servant, maybe the dishwasher."

Mrs. Roosevelt sighed and turned to Szczygiel. "Do you have any questions, Mr. Szczygiel?"

Szczygiel nodded emphatically. "How much did you pay her?" he asked.

"A hundred dollars a month."

"Cash?"

"Yes. *My* payments were in cash."

Szczygiel smiled ironically. " 'Your' payments. That implies you know there were other payments."

"She was blackmailing others," said Rinehart. "In fact,

I was given to understand I could skip half my payments if I introduced her to another victim who would end up paying as much as I did.''

"A regular business, complete with Washington's Birthday sales," laughed Missy.

"A great many men had motive to kill her," said Rinehart.

"We know that," said Szczygiel. "But who *did* kill her? Where were you last Tuesday night?"

"I was at home."

"Witnesses?"

He shook his head. "My wife plays bridge on Tuesday evenings."

"Friday morning?"

"Friday morning? I . . . was in my office, I suppose. I'd have to check my calendar."

"All right," said Szczygiel. "You paid Vivian Taliafero and Joe Bob Skaggs a hundred a month to keep your photos secret. I suppose your wife didn't know about these payments."

"No one knew. That is . . . Well, Judge Kincaid knew. I mean . . . after all, he had played procurer, in effect."

"When was the last time you were in Vivian Taliafero's bedroom?" asked Szczygiel.

Rinehart frowned and glanced from Szczygiel's eyes to Mrs. Roosevelt's, then to Missy's. "Once they had me on the hook," he said, "she made it very plain I was no longer welcome there."

"I believe, Mr. Rinehart, we should tell you some things you may not know," said Mrs. Roosevelt. "In the first place, photographs of you were not among those found in the Taliafero-Skaggs collection. We—"

"You've tricked me!"

"Not really," she said calmly. "The absence of photographs is in this instance more incriminating than their presence. The photographs were found in Mr. Skaggs's house, the day after he was murdered. Certain ones were conspicuously missing—yours among them.''

"Why missing? Why did you *expect* to find pictures of me there?"

"Because your fingerprints were found in Miss Taliafero's bathroom," said Mrs. Roosevelt. "Her *private* bathroom, upstairs.''

Rinehart, who had risen angrily in his chair as if he were about to leap up, sank back and closed his eyes. "So from this you conclude that I murdered Vivian," he said.

"Not necessarily," said Mrs. Roosevelt. "There may be another explanation. We would like to hear what explanation you have to offer."

Rinehart crossed his arms on his knees and leaned forward. "I am a wealthy man," he said despondently. "Vivian knew that. I said I gave her a hundred dollars a month. That is true. I did. Regularly. But sometimes she asked for more. Sometimes . . . She talked about marriage. She said if I could get a divorce—'' He shrugged. "I gave her more."

"You went upstairs?"

"We talked upstairs. She allowed me . . . intimacy. I wouldn't go in her bedroom. I knew about the mirror by then. I took her in the bathroom.''

"Where we found your fingerprints," said Szczygiel.

"Where you found my fingerprints.''

Mrs. Roosevelt frowned as she poured herself a glass of lemonade. "You had ample motive to kill her," she said gravely.

Rinehart shook his head. "I gave her maybe four thousand dollars all told. That's not much to me, Mrs. Roosevelt. It's a small fortune to many people, but it's not to me. In all modesty. I was talking to her about settling a substantial piece of money on her, in return for the photographs and negatives. She said she was interested. In a short time I might have bought her off, once and for all."

"Suggesting that you didn't kill her," said Missy.

"Not for four thousand dollars. Not for forty thousand dollars. That's what I was talking to her about—forty thousand."

"Let's see now," said Szczygiel. "She was black-mailing you and had taken you for a substantial sum of money—and you were talking about ten times more. The photographs she had would have ruined your marriage and career. You have no firm alibi for last Tuesday evening." He shook his head. "That doesn't look so good, Mr. Rinehart."

"Your case has a fatal flaw, Mr. Szczygiel," said Rinehart bitterly. "She wasn't killed to stop the black-mail. Anyone who wanted to kill her for that reason would have killed her at home, where she had the photographs, not in the White House Rose Garden. Besides, whoever killed her didn't *get* the photographs. *You* got them."

"Except yours, Mr. Rinehart," said Mrs. Roosevelt. "Yours are missing from the collection."

Rinehart frowned and nodded emphatically. "Exactly," he said. "You told me a while ago that the absence of my photographs from the collection was more incriminating than their presence would have been. I'd have had to be a fool to kill Vivian, then kill Skaggs, and take only my own photographs."

"Unless you supposed we didn't know you were one of Vivian Taliafero's victims," said Missy.

"Others knew that," he said. "Judge Kincaid knew it. Bill Wolfe knew it. I wish it had been a more closely guarded secret than it was."

"Who killed Miss Taliafero?" asked Mrs. Roosevelt bluntly.

"I don't know," said Rinehart. "I really don't know."

"You were prepared earlier to accuse Mr. Wolfe, I thought. You said she was pressing him to marry her."

"That's not the truth," said Rinehart sadly. "This whole thing has become—"

"Yes, it has," she interrupted. "So, do you have anything more to tell us, that is the truth?"

He nodded. "It involves me more deeply. I wish—Well, never mind what I wish. Do you mind if I smoke?"

"If it will make you more comfortable," she said.

Rinehart's hands shook as he lit a cigarette. "Bill Wolfe called me Tuesday evening," he said. "He told me Vivian Taliafero was dead, that she'd been murdered. When the police got to her house, he said, they'd almost certainly find the photographs—his, mine, a lot of others. We had an hour maybe, to go to the house and find the pictures. He wanted me to go with him."

"Mr. Rinehart—"

"I refused. I wouldn't go. He got mad and hung up."

"At what hour was that?" asked Mrs. Roosevelt.

"I don't know exactly. Sometime after nine. I'd heard the nine o'clock news on the radio and was getting ready for bed. My wife was out playing bridge, as I said. I usually lie in bed and read until she comes home, and I was undressing and—"

"Did he say he was going to the Taliafero house whether you went with him or not?"

Rinehart shook his head. "He just hung up."

"Did he call others with the same request?" asked Mrs. Roosevelt.

"I don't know."

"So," said Szczygiel. "Learning that Vivian Taliafero had been murdered, you finished your interrupted undressing and went to bed?"

"As a matter of fact, no," said Rinehart. "I got on the phone and tried to warn others I knew were in hazard of serious embarrassment."

"Who did you tell?"

"The only man I reached was Burt Oleander. I tried to reach Steve Valentine and Judge Kincaid, but neither of them answered his phone. I didn't see anything odd in that. It was only a little after nine. If they had been out to dinner, they wouldn't have reached home by that hour."

A week has passed since the body of Washington so-
cialite Vivian Taliafero was found in the White House
Rose Garden, and still there has been no arrest. Investigation of the murder has been assigned by presidential
order to the Secret Service, an organization ill-equipped,
either by training or experience, to investigate mysterious deaths. While the President vacations off the Atlantic coast, Mrs. Roosevelt is supervising the detective
work, according to White House sources. It seems the
incompetent are being led by an officious intermeddler.
We hope someone will turn the whole matter over to the
F.B.I. where it should have been assigned in the first
place.

Mrs. Roosevelt put the newspaper aside. An abashed
Stan Szczygiel was drinking coffee as though there were
nourishment in it, even though he was drinking it black.

" 'Officious intermeddler,' " she said. "If the President receives this newspaper aboard the yacht, he will have *such* a laugh. As I am having, in fact. I am laughing, Mr. Szczygiel. Do you know why? Because so far this snooping anti-New Deal, anti-Roosevelt newspaper has failed to discover—as have all the rest of them, for that matter—the colossal scandal that lies behind the Taliafero murder."

"If they knew anything of that, we'd have to call in a regiment of troops to guard the White House from reporters," said Szczygiel unhappily.

"Tell me, Mr. Szczygiel," she said. "Do you think it was Mr. Wolfe at whom Mr. Skaggs fired a shot Tuesday night? Was *he* the mysterious man on the cellar stairs?"

"He makes as good a candidate as any."

"Don't you find it suggestive that the two sets of photographs conspicuously missing from the set are Mr. Wolfe's and Mr. Rinehart's?"

"Suggestive, but—"

"Think of it this way," she said, her enthusiasm growing. "If in fact Mr. Wolfe went to the Taliafero house and did not find the pictures, then maybe he went to the Skaggs house, killed Mr. Skaggs, stole his own photographs—and, while he was at it, stole Mr. Rinehart's too, because Mr. Rinehart was the only one who knew he was going to try to enter the Taliafero house and steal the photographs."

"Well, we'll have a chance to interrogate Wolfe this evening," said Szczygiel. "He's coming in on a train from Alabama, about six."

He was. In a coach on a Southern train that was at that hour chugging up through Virginia, a forlorn William Wolfe sat in handcuffs, leg irons, and a black-and-white-striped Alabama convict's suit—with, incongruously, the brown-and-white wing-tip shoes he had been wearing when he was arrested. He hadn't shaved since he left his Georgia tourist cabin, and in a sense he was glad for that—at least no one would recognize him. He was excruciatingly conscious of the curious stares of people wandering up and down the aisle of the car.

He'd been taken off the train last night in Statesville, North Carolina, so Sheriff Buford Wallace, traveling with great delight on a federal expense account, could spend his evening in a restaurant, eating a fried-chicken dinner, and the night in what he called a "fust-class hotel," while Wolfe spent the night in a squalid little jail, where he and the only other prisoner ate a dinner of grits, greens, and some sort of greasy meat he could not even identify, then slept curled up on the brick floor.

"What that feller done, Sheriff?" a dozen inquisitive people had asked.

"They say he murdered a woman up at Washin'ton. Mebbe another feller, too. I'm takin' him up on a federal warrant."

"Ugly-lookin' brute, ain't he?"

Actually, of course, he was not returning to Washington on a federal warrant. He could have insisted on all kinds of procedures—a hearing before an Alabama court, and so on—but his chief wish had been to be out of Alabama, out of an Alabama jail, and he would have endured worse than he was enduring here to accomplish that.

Duty required Stan Szczygiel to interview Judge Beresford Kincaid once again—though he would rather have taunted a bear in his den.

The judge, on the telephone, rumbled that he would meet with Mr. Szczygiel for lunch at the Caliber Club. Szczygiel was there, at 12:30, and was ushered immediately to the judge's table, to wait for the arrival of the great man.

"Mr. Szczygiel. Good to see you—I hope."

Judge Kincaid was sixty-eight years old, though he did not really show that many years. His white hair lay in strands across his flushed pate. His face was a pan of loose flesh: brows that rose and fell like two pump handles, eyes that opened and closed like envelopes squeezed at the ends, a mobile mouth that exaggerated all his expressions.

"Mr. Szczygiel. I see you have a drink. What is that? A martini? If it is, I will have one myself. I understand the President mixes them five to one. Three to one is the classic martini. Three measures of gin to one of vermouth. I am utterly at a loss to understand how anyone could ask for a chunk of lemon peel in a martini. Ughh! What an aberration! The thought of it is enough to make one vomit."

"I have a strong inclination to straight gin," said Szczygiel. "It was difficult to obtain during Prohibition, and I could not bring myself to profane it with an Italian herbal wine. Straight, Your Honor. The only way to drink gin!"

Judge Kincaid grinned and summoned a waiter with a raised finger. "Straight it is," he said. The waiter approached. "A gin like Mr. Szczygiel's. And another for him."

"Thank you, sir. Thank you very much, indeed."

"Well," said the judge. "You asked to see me. I surmise you want to accuse me of the murder of Vivian Taliafero."

Stan Szczygiel leaned back in his chair and regarded Judge Kincaid calmly. The judge wore a Phi Beta Kappa key on his expanded vest.

"No, sir," he said. "I do have another charge against you."

"Do you really? Can you prove it?"

"I shouldn't want to have to—on the basis of the evidence at hand," said Szczygiel. "It has to do with your collecting money for Miss Taliafero—and maybe not turning every cent of it over to her."

Judge Kincaid tipped his head to one side, thrust out his lower lip, and regarded Szczygiel with a confident little smile. "Who will testify to something like that?" he asked.

"Oh, I think two gentlemen might," said Szczygiel, intentionally exaggerating the number who would so testify, to see what reaction he got.

The judge ran his hand across the lower side of his chin. "Let's assume every word you've heard is true and that you can prove it," he said. "So what?"

Szczygiel shrugged. "Conduct inappropriate to a judge of the federal courts," he said. "Nothing much. The newspapers will take more interest than a prosecutor will."

Judge Kincaid raised his eyebrows. "Are you suggesting the allegations you are making will be handed to a newspaper?"

"Not if we can avoid it," said Szczygiel. "Mrs. Roosevelt is most anxious that should not happen."

"I believe I begin to understand."

"If you can help us identify the killer," said Szczygiel somberly, "you may help us make it possible to settle the matter quietly, protecting the names of the many men involved. The longer the case drags out, the greater the pressure to tell all."

"Oh, God forbid you should tell all," said the judge.

Stan Szczygiel was uncertain in his evaluation of this man. Was his flippancy founded in confidence or in defiance?

"Would you mind accounting for your whereabouts last Tuesday evening and last Friday morning?" he asked.

"Friday morning is easy enough," said the judge. "I was on the bench, hearing motions. Tuesday night . . . I had dinner at the Army-Navy Club with Dick Horan— *Admiral* Richard Horan. We were finished at, say, eight-thirty or nine. I caught a taxi and went home."

"Directly home?"

"Yes, directly home. I see your point. If I left the Army-Navy Club at eight-thirty or nine, I had time to go by the

White House and strangle Vivian Taliafero in the Rose Garden.''

''What time did you arrive home?''

''Oh, nine-fifteen, nine-thirty.''

''Was your wife there?''

''No. She and her artist friends were making the final arrangements for a sidewalk art show they held in Alexandria on Saturday and Sunday. It was probably ten before she came in.''

''You live only about three blocks from the Taliafero house, right?''

''That's right. It was very convenient,'' said the judge in a voice thinned by sneering irony. ''Sometimes I strolled over for a visit in the middle of an evening.''

''When we first talked, Judge, I told you I *surmised* there were photographs of you. You know what I mean.''

The judge lit a cigarette. He nodded.

''What I surmised has proven true. We have the pictures.''

The judge's chin and brows rose, and his body stiffened. He glanced up and accepted the gin now put before him by the waiter, but his eyes remained closely focused on Stan Szczygiel.

''Mine and others, I suppose.''

''Yes.''

The judge shrugged. ''It doesn't prove I killed her.''

''No. And everyone involved in the investigation—Mrs. Roosevelt especially—would like to settle the case without the necessity of the pictures becoming public knowledge.''

''You say Mrs. Roosevelt is personally involved in the investigation?''

''Totally.''

''The case could develop interesting constitutional implications,'' said Judge Kincaid. Then he smiled bitterly and added—''To be decided by another judge, after the scandal has driven me off the bench.''

"Everyone wants to avoid anything like that," said Szczygiel. "Except for the man who murdered Vivian Taliafero, none of the men involved with her impresses me as deserving to be driven out of public life."

Judge Kincaid stroked his chin between his thumb and fingers. "I think I know who killed her," he said. "In fact, I'm pretty damned sure of it."

"Who?"

"Well . . . I can tell you this: She was afraid of Joe Bob Skaggs."

"How do you know?"

"She told me she was. She was paying him a percentage of whatever she took in. He wanted more."

"So, he killed her to get more?"

"To get the whole kit and caboodle," said the judge. "With Vivian dead, the photos and all the money they were worth belonged to him."

"Makes sense," said Szczygiel. "Except for one little thing. Who killed Skaggs, and why?"

"Think about it," said the judge. He took a drag on his cigarette, then raised his glass of gin. "Vivian is killed. No suspect in sight. What would the cops do first? What would anyone expect? They'd run to the house. Wouldn't they? If you were Skaggs and killed her, isn't that what you'd expect?"

Szczygiel nodded.

"But Skaggs doesn't move too fast, so he can't be sure of the race to the house. So what does he do? He sends his girl to raid the house and pick up the photos. And he's got a girlfriend, incidentally: a bimbo named Sally Partridge who hung around the house and . . . Well, the cute little Sally was a part of the whole deal. Let's say maybe he telephones her from somewhere downtown. Sally Partridge moves in, picks up the photos, and meets Skaggs at home in Alexandria. Simple. Those photographs were worth a fortune."

"Then who killed Skaggs?" asked Szczygiel.

"Sally Partridge, who else? She saw the value of what she'd stolen from the Taliafero house, Skaggs was paying her a pittance for carrying off a burglary, so they argued about it—She was strong enough to beat him to death with some kind of weapon, while he stumbled around on one good leg, desperately trying to escape her."

"But she was arrested as a burglar in Skaggs's house Sunday night," said Szczygiel. "If she killed Skaggs on Friday, why didn't she take the photographs with her when she left the house? Why did she come back on Sunday?"

Judge Kincaid sighed and shook his head. "Inter-rupted . . ." he suggested. "A person—a woman espe-cially—who's committed a murder will panic and flee at the first noise. Maybe she was somehow frightened off. By the mail delivery, say. So she came back to get what she'd come for."

The newspapers might call Secret Service personnel in-experienced in criminal investigation, but Szczygiel at least knew when to fall silent and let the suspect ponder, then talk. He stared for a long moment into his fresh gin, then took a sip, then waited patiently for the judge to repair the gaps in his story.

"I only know this," said Judge Kincaid. "Vivian was afraid of Skaggs. She said to me . . . She said, if anything bad happens to me, it will be because of Skaggs. The man was the lowest of the low, you understand, Stan. A slimy little criminal."

Szczygiel found Missy in the swimming pool, stroking back and forth alone. He took a swimsuit from the closet in the Executive Wing and joined her in the cool water, taking refuge from the oppressive heat.

"Let's elevate Judge Beresford Kincaid a step or two higher on the list of suspects," he said when he had swum two laps back and forth in the pool. "He's not a very smooth liar."

"None of them are," said Missy. "They are uniformly

frightened. And why wouldn't they be? Frankly, Stan, I wouldn't take inexpert lying as much in the way of evidence."

Szczygiel bobbed in the water. "Here comes Mrs. Roosevelt," he said.

She'd had the same idea as Missy's. Clad in a white terry-cloth robe over her swim suit, she strode along the colonnade in flapping beach shoes, and she grinned happily when she saw Missy and Stan in the water.

"I've had a wire from the President," she said as she slipped off the robe and lowered herself into the water. "He's having a marvelous holiday, enjoying himself immensely. The word of our investigation has reached him. He asks if my role is Holmes or Watson. I wired him back, Mr. Szczygiel, and told him I am Watson, you are Holmes, and Missy is perhaps one of the Baker Street Irregulars."

"A mudlark?" asked Missy uncertainly.

"No, no, my dear," said Mrs. Roosevelt. "Holmes's irregulars were by no means mudlarks. Mudlarks were the urchins who eked out a wretched living on the tidal flats of the Thames. The irregulars were Baker Street children who were always ready to run errands for a few pence, so served Holmes when he needed them. Different sorts entirely."

Missy climbed out of the pool, then ran her hands down across her body to smooth the wrinkles out of her bathing suit. "Oh, thank God," she laughed.

Mrs. Roosevelt swam the length of the pool, conscious that her swimming was not as strong or expert as Missy's or her husband's, still confident and comfortable in the water. The water, though it was not cold, was refreshing.

"Stan has raised Judge Kincaid to a higher place on the list of suspects," said Missy.

"Indeed?"

"He is an inexpert architect of lies," said Szczygiel.

"A key," said Mrs. Roosevelt, "may be the testimony

of Mr. Wolfe. We will see him here this evening. I've made some arrangements.''

"Wash yer ass, buddy,'' a jail guard barked at the naked William Wolfe, who stood under a shower head in the communal shower of the Alexandria jail, wary of the torrent of water, hot or cold, that was about to issue from the threatening pipe.

He had no idea what was going on. He and Sheriff Wallace had left the train at Alexandria, instead of Washington; and they had been rushed in a car to the Alexandria jail. Maybe it was a boon. A hundred reporters undoubtedly awaited him in Washington, to photograph him and shriek questions at him as he was led through the station in his awful striped clothes and chains. He had been dreading that.

Now a flood of warm water rushed over him, and he gratefully rubbed a bar of white soap over his head, then his face, then his entire body. A few minutes later, a guard stared at him as he soaped his face and scraped off his ugly accumulation of beard with a razor that was none too sharp but was effective. Then they gave him blue-denim pants and a blue shirt, handcuffed him again, and took him in a car across the Potomac.

"It was Mrs. Roosevelt who arranged for you to be taken off the train outside the city,'' said Lieutenant Kennelly to Wolfe. "She didn't want you to be humiliated.''

"I guess I should be grateful to her,'' said Wolfe.

"Yeah, I think you should be. It was her orders that you be taken off the train somewhere outside Washington, given a chance to bathe and shave, and be given some clean clothes—then that you be sneaked in the back door here. The newspaper guys know you're in the District jail, but they won't get to see you.''

Wolfe was thoroughly subdued. He sat facing Kennelly across a small square table in an interrogation room in

D.C. police headquarters. He wore the ill-fitting, worn blue denims that had been handed him at the Alexandria jail—and still the brown-and-white wing-tip shoes. Kennelly had offered him a cigarette, and he was smoking gratefully—though without the wobbling holder he usually affected.

"Mrs. Roosevelt will be coming here to talk to you," said Kennelly. "It'll be to your advantage to talk nice to her and tell her the truth—and to keep your mouth shut afterward that you ever saw her."

"What am I charged with?" asked Wolfe.

"Murder. What did you suppose?"

"I didn't kill her," said Wolfe despondently.

"Maybe not. But you killed Skaggs."

"*Skaggs?* This is the first I heard he was dead!"

"Sure. Well, okay. Just sit still. Finish that cigarette before the lady gets here."

Mrs. Roosevelt arrived a few minutes later, with Stan Szczygiel. She introduced herself to Wolfe and shook his hand. Then she sat down in the armchair Kennelly had dragged in for her.

Wolfe averted his eyes from Szczygiel's. He remembered all too painfully the hard left Szczygiel had driven into his gut on Friday afternoon. Could it have been only Friday afternoon?

"We may as well start with what is probably the most important question, Mr. Wolfe," said Mrs. Roosevelt. "Why did you . . . ? I guess the phrase is 'take it on the lam.' Why did you take it on the lam?"

Wolfe sighed. "Because I was stupid. Szczygiel there had accused me of murdering Vivian Taliafero. He told me my fingerprints had been found on her bed. And . . . Well, I knew it would look bad for me. Besides the fingerprints, there had to be some pictures around. Photographs. You probably know what I mean."

"Indeed we do."

"I had another reason," said Wolfe sullenly. "I guessed

that I was the likeliest fall guy. A lot of men had reason to want Vivian Taliafero dead, but the rest of them were important, prominent—a senator, a cabinet officer, a judge, and so on. Why not settle the case the easiest way, by pinning it on a mere assistant attorney general?"

"You are not paying a very high compliment to Mr. Szczygiel or Lieutenant Kennelly," said Mrs. Roosevelt.

"I didn't know them," he said.

"You speak of motive for killing Miss Taliafero. You say prominent men had reason to want her dead. What motive, what reason, do you have in mind, Mr. Wolfe?"

"You know . . ."

"Yes. I think we do," said Mrs. Roosevelt. "But suppose you tell us."

Wolfe glanced at Szczygiel and Kennelly. "She was blackmailing us," he said.

"But why murder her on the grounds of the White House, then?" asked Mrs. Roosevelt. "She wouldn't have been carrying the obscene photographs with her."

Wolfe shook his head. "I don't understand it," he said. "I didn't understand it from the beginning—I mean, from the moment I heard she'd been killed. It was a stupid thing to do."

"Until you caught up with Joe Bob Skaggs and got the pictures," said Kennelly.

Wolfe spoke to Mrs. Roosevelt, in whom he detected a degree of sympathy, readiness to withhold judgment, reluctance to condemn. "Until a few minutes ago I didn't even know Skaggs was dead. When was he killed anyway?"

"Friday morning," said Kennelly.

"Ah . . . Well, then," said Wolfe, his chin rising, "it couldn't have been me. I was arguing a motion before the United States District Court on Friday morning. I went to the Justice Department a little after eight to pick up my papers, then took a cab to the court, and I was in the courtroom until almost noon. You can check it out."

"We'll do that," said Kennelly. "So where were you Tuesday night when the Taliafero woman was strangled?"

"I was at home. Alone, unfortunately. I live in a boarding house. Though there are always people around, I . . . I have to admit I could have gone out a back way and returned the same way, and probably no one would have seen me. But it's like you say—*Why* would I kill her? What good could it have done me? The blackmail pictures were at her house."

"Did you go out at all that night?" Szczygiel asked.

"No."

"Did you make any telephone calls?"

Wolfe frowned as if trying to remember, then shook his head.

"What about Secretary Rinehart?" asked Mrs. Roosevelt.

Wolfe started. "All right. Yes. I called Rinehart."

"Tell us what you said to him."

"He told you, I suppose."

"*You* tell us."

"I . . . told him I'd heard that Vivian had been killed. I said the police would be searching her house before the night was over and when they did they'd find the pictures. I said to him, we ought to go there. The two of us. We ought to go and get the pictures, before the police find them. I argued to him that it was a two-man job, one to search the house, one to watch for the police. But he wouldn't go with me. He . . . wouldn't go with me."

"So you went by yourself," said Kennelly.

Wolfe shook his head emphatically. "No. I tried to call Judge Kincaid, but I didn't get an answer on his telephone. I didn't dare call anyone else, and I *wouldn't* go by myself. I figured about the time I got up to her second floor, where I guessed she probably had the pictures in her extra bedroom, the police would come in through the front and back doors. Without someone to watch and warn me, so I could get out in time, I wouldn't—Well . . ."

"What time did you call Judge Kincaid?" asked Szczygiel.

"Right after I called Rinehart. What time did he say it was? Before ten."

"I should like to have the answer to a question, Mr. Wolfe," said Mrs. Roosevelt. "You telephoned Mr. Rinehart and told him Miss Taliafero had been murdered. And he confirms that. But how did you know Miss Taliafero was dead? You say you were at home all evening. If so, how did you find out that Miss Taliafero had been killed?"

Wolfe frowned skeptically, as if he found her question disingenuous, as if he supposed she already knew the answer. His voice was thin as he answered—"Fritz Hausser told me. He called and told me she had been murdered on the White House grounds and that some of us ought to rush to the house as fast as possible and see if we couldn't get our hands on the pictures."

"How did you respond?" asked Mrs. Roosevelt.

"I told him I'd meet him there and we'd go in together. But he said he didn't think he could. He said he expected to be arrested at any minute. She'd been in his office just before she went out and got killed, he said. She had a check of his in her purse. He figured he'd be the chief suspect, at least at first, and he was expecting the Secret Service or police to break in on him at any moment."

"What if Frederick Hausser denies he called you?" asked Szczygiel.

Wolfe threw up his hands. "What if all of them deny everything?" he muttered. "I'm in jail. They're all out, meeting together, comparing stories . . . probably deciding to let it all fall on Wolfe's head. Why not? Nobody's going to get too excited about that."

"There is another piece of evidence that points to your guilt," said Mrs. Roosevelt. "In all fairness to you, you should know what it is. The photographs, you see, have been found. They are in a safe at the White House. We have obscene photographs of Miss Taliafero with seven men. But you are not one of them. Your fingerprints were found on her bedpost, and you've admitted she was blackmailing you; but no photograph of you is among those found in Mr. Skaggs's house after he was murdered. Have you an explanation for that?''

He shook his head, and his eyes fell. ''No . . . I haven't,'' he mumbled.

''We told you we found pictures of seven men,'' said Szczygiel. ''Who would you guess they were?''

''Well . . . Rinehart. Hausser. Judge Kincaid. Senator Valentine. Burton Oleander.'' He paused and counted on his fingers the number of names he had mentioned. ''Uh, Alex Bushnell.'' He shook his head. ''That's six. I don't know who else.''

''You knew Alex Bushnell?'' asked Mrs. Roosevelt.

''Yes. Vivian and Skaggs killed him, the same as if they'd shot him. Vivian used him to prove to the rest of us that she really would do what she'd threatened.''

''You think she deserved to die, then,'' said Kennelly.

Wolfe's nostrils flared. ''Five or six times over,'' he sneered.

12

"We can strike another question mark from our chart," said Mrs. Roosevelt. "I inquired of two friends on Capitol Hill and learned that Congressman Dies was at dinner with friends on Tuesday evening. They were together until almost midnight. Whatever may have been his relationship with Miss Taliafero, he didn't kill her."

"We didn't find pictures of him, either," said Szczygiel. "Maybe when he welcomed Hausser to 'the club' he meant something entirely different from the group of blackmail victims."

"I don't propose to ask him," she said. "And I think you need not, either."

"I'm glad to get one suspect off the chart, anyway," said Szczygiel. "If only we could get another one or two off."

"I'm going to strike off another question mark," she said. "On Friday morning, when Mr. Skaggs was killed,

Mr. Hausser was in the Executive Wing. I went there and talked to him myself.''

"Well, I don't know," said Szczygiel. "I asked around the Executive Wing. People remember seeing him Friday morning. No one's willing to say he was there all morning.''

"It is not physically impossible that he should have gone over to Alexandria and returned, either before or after I was in his office; but I think you will agree it is highly unlikely. Don't you agree?''

"Highly unlikely," Szczygiel conceded.

"I'm going to strike his question mark," she said. "We can restore it if we want to.''

She stood at the chart and used her pen to make the two new entries. The chart then looked like this:

Suspect	Where Tues. Night	Where at Death Skaggs
Cranshaw	White House	?
Kincaid	?	In court
Valentine	?	Senate committee
Hausser	Executive Wing	Executive Wing
Horan	?	?
Pierce	?	?
Oleander	?	?
Wolfe	?	In court
Rinehart	?	?
Dies	At dinner	Texas

Szczygiel stood and stared thoughtfully. "We're making good progress on eliminating suspects in the Skaggs murder," he said. "But not in the Taliafero murder. Cranshaw and Hausser were on the White House grounds that night. Judge Kincaid and Admiral Horan were at the Army-Navy Club, and either one of them could have come over to the White House and strangled Vivian Taliafero.''

"Or could they?" asked Mrs. Roosevelt, suddenly

skeptical. "No. Think about it. Neither of them could have come here to murder Miss Taliafero *unless he knew she was going to be here*. And who knew that? Mr. Hausser, of course. Who else?"

"Anyone *he* told. Anyone *she* told," said Szczygiel.

"Plus of course Mr. Skaggs," added Mrs. Roosevelt. "He might have known. He might even have followed her here."

The telephone rang. Mrs. Roosevelt took the call. It was from Lieutenant Kennelly at D.C. police headquarters. She listened, thanked him warmly, and hung up.

"Interesting," she said to Szczygiel. "A part of Mr. Wolfe's story is confirmed. He had no telephone in his boarding-house room. The telephone is in the hall downstairs. A man did call him about nine on Tuesday evening, one of the other boarders says. Then Mr. Wolfe placed two calls of his own. She says she remembers very well because she wanted to make a call and was annoyed that Mr. Wolfe received one call and placed two without giving up the telephone."

"So he called Rinehart, which Rinehart admits; and he called Kincaid, but Kincaid didn't answer—though he says he was at home."

Mrs. Roosevelt looked at the chart. "Congressman Gordon Pierce," she mused. "Admiral Richard Horan. And . . . unfortunately, Mr. Burton Oleander."

An hour later Stanislaw Szczygiel strolled through the colonade with Representative Gordon Pierce. They were on their way from the Executive Wing to the White House proper. Pierce had entered the grounds through the southwest gate, had come to the Executive Wing to ask who was in charge of the Taliafero investigation, and had waited for Szczygiel. It was coincidence. Szczygiel had not called him. Neither had Mrs. Roosevelt.

"I decided it might be just as well if I came in and talked the situation over," he said. "Though I see you have Wolfe under arrest and will apparently charge him with the murder, I know you must have found pictures of me. I thought I might at least be able to ask what is to be done with those pictures.''

Szczygiel had checked Pierce's credentials and had learned that he was regarded as one of the most promising young members of the House of Representatives. He was forty years old but looked as though he might be twenty-five. His hair was light and thin, letting the skin of his pate show through, shiny and ruddy. His blue eyes were lively and expressive. He had a narrow mouth, full lips, a cleft chin.

There was also something oddly interesting about Representative Gordon Pierce. His father had been seventy years old when he was born; and *his* father had been in his seventies when *he* was born, meaning that Gordon's grandfather was born in the middle of the eighteenth century. Gordon's grandfather had served in the Revolutionary Army, under General Nathanael Greene; and Gordon's father, who had lost a leg as a boy and could not serve in the Union Army during the Civil War, had instead served three terms in Congress in the 1860s and had witnessed both inaugurations of Abraham Lincoln.

"Pictures . . ." Szczygiel mused. The image in his mind was of the congressman with Vivian Taliafero. "Yes, your picture is among the ones we picked up," he said. He stopped with that comment, to let Pierce worry a moment.

"Well . . . uh . . . What's to become of these pictures? I mean—"

"Let's hope we can destroy them," said Szczygiel.

"Which will depend on . . . ?"

"An arrest and conviction," said the Secret Service man bluntly.

"Am I a suspect?"

"Every man whose picture we found is a suspect. Some of them have alibis for Friday morning, when Skaggs was killed. So far none of them have any for Tuesday night, when the woman was.''

"But you have Wolfe in jail.''

"Wolfe ran away. Also, he lied. But if we had in jail every man who's lied to us, we'd have quite a collection.''

"I have no alibi,'' said Pierce. "My wife and children are at home in Pennsylvania, as they are every summer, when I let them go home to escape the Washington climate. I was alone Tuesday evening and so went to a movie. I saw *Mutiny on the Bounty*—Clark Gable, Charles Laughton. Friday morning I left home about eight and drove to the Poconos. I hold a party for my closest political friends every summer, and I was on my way to the Poconos, to the mountain cabin where the party is held.'' He paused and shrugged. "There is no point in my telling you I could not have driven over to Alexandria and murdered Skaggs, then gone on to Pennsylvania.''

Szczygiel glanced at him and smiled wryly. "Well, I doubt you did,'' he said. "If you had, why wouldn't you have grabbed your pictures? We might never have known of the relationship between you and Vivian Taliafero, except that we found your pictures.''

Pierce turned down the corners of his mouth. "It's kind of you to say so, but I'm afraid you would have found out about me and Vivian. Some of the other men—suspects, I suppose they are—knew about it. Personally, I'm going to name them, and I imagine they will name me, if they haven't already.''

They had reached the entry door into the White House itself and now entered the long center hall of the ground floor.

"If you wonder where I'm taking you,'' said Szczygiel, "it is to see Mrs. Roosevelt.''

"Why on earth Mrs. Roosevelt?''

"She is personally involved in the investigation.''

"My God! Has she . . . ?''

"Seen the pictures? She *has* the pictures. In her safe.''

Pierce stopped. "I can't see her. I can't face her, if she's seen—"

"If it will make you feel any better, she only glanced at the pictures for an instant, then looked away. We then had a set made with faces only."

"That makes no difference. I can't face—"

"I don't think you have much choice, Congressman."

"I am pleased to have met you, Mr. Barrow," said Mrs. Roosevelt to the tall, muscular Negro who smiled shyly and nodded. "I hope the pictures turn out handsomely."

She had just been photographed with this man, shaking his huge, hard hand. Mary McLeod Bethune had told her he was something of a legend, in Detroit at least if not nationwide, and it would be valuable to the 1936 campaign if pictures of him being received at the White House could be published in Negro newspapers.

Her response had been that she had heard his name and was reluctant to exploit it—but if he really wanted to come to the White House, she would be more than pleased to meet him.

They had sat on a couch in the Red Room, chatting for a few minutes. Tea had been served, but he had been so obviously uncomfortable with the little cups and saucers that she had suggested they move upstairs to her office where they could be more informally comfortable and have some lemonade, which was more appropriate to this hot morning.

"Well, Ah'm jus' . . . honored, Miz Roosevelt," he said. "Ah never thought . . . Ah never thought—"

"You'd sit down, stretch out your legs, and be comfortable in the White House? Neither did I, Mr. Barrow. Neither did I."

"Ah greatly 'preciate it," he said.

"We'll, I'm pleased to have met you, and I wish you great good luck in the ring. I'll be watching the newspapers for stories about you."

"Ah'm gonna win th' *championship.*"

"I have no doubt of it, Mr. Barrow. And I will be proud of you. Now . . . Unfortunately, I have a congressman to see."

The big man stood. The photographer caught a final shot of him shaking hands with Mrs. Roosevelt. His manager and backers slipped up to have the honor of shaking her hand, too. All these pictures would appear in a score of newspapers during the next few months. To the few who said the meeting had been inappropriate, she would reply that she would always cherish the experience of meeting Mr. Joe Louis Barrow—Joe Louis.

"I fully understand how you feel, and let's not speak of it further," she said to Representative Gordon Pierce. "You are terribly embarrassed. So am I. I am embarrassed. But together we may be able to contribute something toward bringing a murderer to justice, and—"

"The murderer could be me," said Pierce dejectedly.

"If it is you, Mr. Pierce, you could do your country a certain service by confessing now. It could save the reputations of some men whose reputations are valuable."

Pierce shook his head. "I didn't kill her," he said.

"Or Skaggs?" asked Szczygiel.

"Not Skaggs, either."

"Well then, Mr. Pierce," said Mrs. Roosevelt. "What can you contribute to the solution of the mystery?"

"Save one, I may have been the last of Vivian Taliafero's victims," said Pierce. "I was with her . . . only four months ago. She made a total fool of me! She—"

"She seems to have had something of a talent for making fools of men," Mrs. Roosevelt observed.

"I . . . I can't, in all propriety, go into that," he said. "She had a . . . How can I say it? A practiced guile. She was utterly amoral. That . . . Well, that has its appeal, to many men. Besides, she was utterly ruthless. There was something behind that, Mrs. Roosevelt. Bitterness. She had a quarrel with the world.''

"If you were her penultimate victim, then who was the last?" asked the First Lady.

"Wolfe. I think she began blackmailing Wolfe within the two weeks before her death."

"Which makes Wolfe the prime suspect once again," said Szczygiel.

"And you were blackmailed how long, Mr. Pierce?" asked Mrs. Roosevelt.

"Four months, about."

"During which time you saw some of the other men, I imagine," said Szczygiel.

"Well . . . Some of them."

"I'm sorry to have to ask you this, Mr. Pierce, but we really do need the names of the men you know who were victimized by these people."

Pierce exchanged glances with Szczygiel. He wasn't sorry to be asked. He had already said he was going to name every name, as he supposed the other suspects were doing.

"Besides me and Wolfe," he said. "Well . . . I saw a lot of men at her house. As for those who went upstairs—and that's how you might define the victims: the ones who went upstairs—I know that Senator Steve Valentine did . . . and Burt Oleander. And Hersch Rinehart."

"Any others?" asked Szczygiel.

"How many suspects are there?" asked Pierce.

"Nine," said Mrs. Roosevelt. "If we count the fact that Mr. Skaggs may have killed her, ten."

"If you take Sally Partridge into account, eleven," said Szczygiel.

"Sally Partridge?" asked Pierce. "Is she—"

"She's in jail in Alexandria, on a charge of burglary of Skaggs's house," said Szczygiel. "And of course she may have killed Skaggs."

"She had reason," said Pierce. "She had reason to kill either one of them."

"I believe you must amplify on that comment," said Mrs. Roosevelt.

"I suppose she says she's a waitress," said Pierce. "She probably says she works at the Airline Bar. Ask the management how many days a week she works. I'll be surprised if it's two. She had her share of the Taliafero-Skaggs business."

"Well, just what was her role, Mr. Pierce?"

"Number-two girl," said Pierce. "Stand-in for Vivian. Errand-runner. Collection agent."

"Stand-in?" asked Szczygiel sharply.

"Vivian didn't blackmail every man," said Pierce. "Sometimes she just provided a . . . service. For money."

"And Sally Partridge was the service?" asked Szczygiel.

Pierce nodded. *"And . . . "* Suddenly his eyes focused as if on something unseen, something in the remote distance. "And, say! I may have an alibi for Tuesday night after all! Or . . . " And his enthusiasm disappeared as quickly as it had appeared. "Oh . . . well, never mind."

"A penny for your thoughts, Mr. Pierce," said Mrs. Roosevelt.

He sighed. "I did talk to someone on the telephone Tuesday evening, who could maybe have testified that I did in fact go to the movies that night. But . . . It was too early. I called him before seven, and—But . . . Wait a minute! I called Steve Valentine and asked him if he wanted to have a drink with me after the picture, because we needed to talk about the Susquehanna Watershed Bill. He sort of laughed, and I asked him what was funny. And . . . "

"What was funny, Congressman?" asked Szczygiel.

Pierce shook his head and sighed. "This is a dirty thing to do," he muttered. "In any other circumstances, I wouldn't do this. But . . . *damn!* I'm suspected of murder!''

Mrs. Roosevelt's eyes passed significantly over Szczygiel's.

"Okay . . .'' said Pierce. "My family's out of town for the summer. Steve's is out of town. He told me he couldn't see me for a drink after the movie because he . . . Well, he said he had a date. He knew I understood who he meant. I mean, he was into the Taliafero-Skaggs net two ways. He was seeing Sally Partridge. Regularly. Paying her, of course. Paying Vivian, actually. But the night when Vivian was killed, Steve was with Sally. Or at least he said he was going to be. He was going to pick her up after she finished her work at the Airline Bar.''

"Interesting,'' said Szczygiel.

"Well, it gives *him* an alibi, if she'll back him up. It doesn't do much for me.''

"You don't know what a wretched *hole* this place is,'' Sally Partridge complained angrily to Szczygiel and Kennelly. She gripped the bars of her cell in the Alexandria jail. "You *know* I ain't no burgular! There's some smart girls, that know the law, come in and out of this place, and they told me I had every right to go in that house. You *know* I had every right to be in that house. You said you'd get me out of here if I told you the truth. Well, dammit, I *told* you the truth!''

"Not all of it,'' said Kennelly. "Anyway, you're not in our custody. You're in Lieutenant Hupp's.''

"Hupp . . .'' she said forlornly to the pipe-smoking Alexandria police detective, who puffed contemplatively and regarded her with detached calm and no sympathy. "Mr. Hupp . . . it's damn hot in here.''

"Tuesday night,'' said Szczygiel. "Somebody told us you had a date Tuesday night.''

"I already told you where I was Tuesday night.''

"You told us where you went *after* Vivian Taliafero was

murdered. Somebody told us who you were with *at the time* when she was killed. You may have an alibi that gets you free of any suspicion that you killed her, and you may be able to offer an alibi to someone else. Who would that be, Sally? Anybody we know?''

"I . . . I'm not sure what you're talkin' about.''

Lieutenant Hupp knocked his pipe on the bars of her cell and let the ash fall on the concrete floor just outside. "You're gonna be in here a long time, Sally, if you don't answer the gentlemen's questions,'' he said.

"Ain't I entitled to see a lawyer?''

"Oh, sure. You want to see a lawyer? We'll get one in here to talk to you this afternoon. Sure, you been here forty-eight hours; you're entitled to see a lawyer. We, uh— We haven't put the burglary charge on the books yet. We'll do that, and then you can talk to your lawyer about how he's going to defend you in court.''

"I ain't no burgular!"

"You can tell your jury that,'' said Hupp, raising his eyebrows high and beginning to poke in the bowl of his pipe with a small, spoon-shaped tool.

She closed her eyes and went slack against the bars. "I ain't . . . I don't like it in here! I ain't no . . . burgular. I ain't done nothin'.''

Szczygiel could sympathize with the girl. There was a kind of simple-minded innocence in the trouble she had taken to try to make herself look like Jean Harlow. She was pretty. She was at *such* a disadvantage. It was unfair to use her miserable situation as pressure for her interrogation. But he had no choice but to press her—

"Your story Monday was that Skaggs came to the Airline Bar and handed your boss a five-spot to let you leave work early, so you could go to Vivian's house with him and help him collect the photographs. Right?''

She nodded weakly. "I guess . . .''

"Well, is that what you said or isn't it?'' Kennelly demanded angrily. He felt no sympathy for her. He was annoyed with himself for not having called the manager of the Airline Bar and checked her story. The fact was, he had not taken Sally very seriously. "If it was the truth, you'd know what you said."

Szczygiel raised a hand to restrain Kennelly. "Where were you Tuesday night when Joe Bob Skaggs called you and said he wanted you to go with him to Vivian's house?" he asked.

"I was home," she said. "I got the upstairs of a house. I was home."

"Not at the Airline Bar, then," said Szczygiel quietly, feigning patience. "This is a new story. Is this one the truth?"

She nodded. "I was home."

"Alone?"

She shook her head.

"Who was with you, Sally?"

"A boyfriend of mine."

"What's his name?"

"You really want to know? I mean, don't you know already, since you know so much?"

"What's his name, Sally?"

"Steve."

"Steve what?"

"Steve Valentine. The senator."

The Alexandria police dropped the burglary charge against Sally Partridge, on condition that she offer no legal resistance to being taken across the river and lodged in the District jail. Kennelly told her he would hold her as a material witness and file no criminal charges against her, if she did not try to get herself released. Early in the evening a matron brought her back to Washington.

"Let me get this straight," she said, when she was behind the bars of a bigger cell and was the beneficiary of a rattling fan that moved the hot, wet air in the women's jail. "You're gonna let me go entirely when this is all some way settled."

"Unless it turns out that you killed Skaggs," said Kennelly.

She turned and paced the bounds of her new cell. "I never been in jail before in my life," she said. "Now in one week I'm in two of them. Hey, I'm just . . . I ain't done nothin', really. I mean, maybe I ain't no angel, but—"

"You want to get out of here," said Kennelly sternly, "you keep your mouth shut. You talk to *nobody* about what happened. Or about the questions you're gonna be asked. And don't get it in your mind that I haven't got enough on you to send you away for a long, long time. I don't know whether or not you were a burglar in the Skaggs house; but I do know you were one in the Taliafero house."

"Hey, I ain't no burgular!"

"Maybe. At the very least you're a prostitute."

"Hey! Don't charge me with *that!* It ever got back to my family that—"

"Just talk to me and talk to Szczygiel when he comes, and otherwise keep your mouth *shut,"* said Kennelly.

"Szczygiel . . . The G-man . . ."

"Yeah. G-man. He's having dinner with somebody. Then he's got some more questions for you."

Stan Szczygiel had eaten dinner with Mrs. Roosevelt and told her what Sally Partridge had said. Mrs. Roosevelt considered the girl's story, bolstered of course by what Congressman Gordon Pierce had said, evidence enough to write on her chart, so eliminating another question mark. This made Senator Steven Valentine the only suspect clearly unable to have murdered Vivian Taliafero— provided what Gordon Pierce and Sally Partridge said was true.

Szczygiel arrived at the jail about eight. Kennelly had gone out, so he talked to Sally alone. She was sitting on her bunk, with her feet up and her hands clasped around her knees.

"Comfortable?" he asked dryly.

"There ain't no comfortable," she muttered.

"Tell me why you were seeing Senator Valentine," said Szczygiel.

"You know why. Why play games, G-man? You know why. He was a nice-enough guy, but it was the usual arrangement."

"I'm going to name some names, Sally. I want to know which ones you know. And, like you said, let's don't play games. You can get yourself in more trouble—or out of part of what you're in."

"Maybe I didn't know the names," she said. "Maybe they lied to me about what their names were."

"Maybe. But let's go down the list, and you tell me what these names mean to you. Okay?"

She shrugged.

"Cranshaw."

"The senator? One of the guys. Heavy drinker. Hot temper. He knocked Joe Bob sprawlin' one day. That wasn't so nice, was it? I mean, Joe Bob bein' crippled and all. Anyway . . . Maybe it never happened, but that's what Joe Bob told me he did."

"Kincaid."

"The judge? Yeah, I know who he is. Big cheese. Very important fella."

"How? What do you know about him?"

"Well . . . He was around. That's all. I know he was around. He never touched me, if that's what you want to know."

"Hausser."

"Little guy that works at the White House. Crazy as a bedbug. Vivian and Joe Bob, they laughed at him all the time. And I never—You know."

"Horan."

"Never heard the name."

"Pierce."

She smiled. "I know the congressman well—if you know what I mean. Gutless. Scared of his shadow."

"Oleander."

"Burt Oleander. Sure. I know him pretty well, too. Another big cheese."

Szczygiel shook his head and leaned against the bars. "When we showed you the pictures of these men, you said you didn't know any of them."

"Well, what would *you* do?" she asked. She tipped her head and regarded Szczygiel with the beginning of a small, sly smile. Maybe she had sensed his incipient sympathy for her and wondered if she could play on it. With her blue eyes she tried to project the image of innocence, but cunning was all too evident in their lift and purposeful steadiness. "Hey, I was *behind bars,* Mister. Still am, too. I was scared and confused. I didn't know what to say to you guys. I didn't know what to do."

"All right. Wolfe."

She shook her head.

"Rinehart."

"I heard the name. Never saw the man."

"One of the men I just named accuses *you* of killing Skaggs," said Szczygiel. It was true. It was what Judge Kincaid had said over lunch at the Caliber Club yesterday. "Which one do you suppose said that?"

Sally Partridge scrambled off her bunk and stumbled to the bars. *"Which?"* she demanded.

"You tell me."

"Whichever is the lyingest SOB of them all!"

"Which one of them has something against you, Sally?"

She heaved a loud sigh. "Well, all of them. All of them that hated Vivian and Joe Bob could hate me."

"You were in it up to your neck, weren't you?"

The corners of her mouth turned sharply down. "Hey," she said. "The deal was that I got out of here unless I killed Joe Bob. Wasn't that the deal? Hey! *Wasn't* it?"

"Right," said Szczygiel. "That's the deal."

"Hey," she said. "Think of somethin', G-man. Think about how neat it would be if everybody decided Joe Bob killed Vivian and then I killed Joe Bob. I . . . I'm scared of that! That gets everybody off the hook . . . except nobody. Except the nobody in the deal. Me."

Szczygiel nodded. "The idea occurred to me, too, Sally. It's not going to happen that way. So, tell me—Which one of them do you think accused you?"

She leaned against the steel bars, her eyes closed tight, drawing a deep breath through clenched teeth. "There's two crooks in this deal, Mister," she said. "You know, some of those men—most of those men—were just . . . well, just guys that wanted what men want. But there's two sleazy crooks in the deal."

"I'm listening," said Szczygiel crisply.

"Burt Oleander," she grunted. "And Berry Kincaid. Besides them, Senator Cranshaw could have murdered somebody. What with his temper, he could have killed Vivian or Joe Bob, just on general principles."

"Okay. But that doesn't say why somebody murdered them."

Sally shook her head. "Who'd want to kill Vivian Taliafero? Who wouldn't? That's the question. Who wouldn't? Not me. Why would I want to kill her? But anybody else . . . including Joe Bob."

"And Joe Bob, then?"

She shook her head and looked at him with a smile that asked how he could be so innocent. Her cheek touched a bar. "Hey, Mister . . . Whatta ya think? Joe Bob was on the phone from Tuesday night till . . . Well, till he was done in, I suppose—telling all those guys he had their pictures and they weren't to stop payin'. Nothin' was changed, he was tellin' 'em. And there wasn't a one of 'em didn't want him dead."

"Which one of them, Sally?" asked Szczygiel. "Which one killed Vivian and Joe Bob?"

She cocked her head to one side and studied Szczygiel's face through the bars, with that communicative little smile she had shown him before.

"Look at it this way," she said. "Berry Kincaid, he's a crook. Money sticks to his fingers. Burt Oleander, he's got too much to worry very much about what Vivian and Joe Bob were taking from him. Berry, he must have been making it up some way. Like, I know he introduced new suckers to Vivian—and you can bet he got paid for it. Burt, he'd just figure how to take some other sucker for whatever Vivian cost him. So I'd say, look for the guy who couldn't afford it."

"Meaning—?"

"Well . . . Take Cranshaw. Ev Cranshaw. Serious-minded New England type of guy. I doubt he's on the take as a senator. So if Vivian was getting fifty a month from him, or a hundred—You see my point."

"I see your point."

"Besides which . . . Besides which, who else had the temper to use his fists on a cripple? Hey, G-man! Maybe you're lookin' for a guy who didn't use good sense when he strangled Vivian. And that guy might be one that doesn't always use good sense."

Szczygiel smiled. "I think I've just heard what's called native intelligence at work. Too bad you got yourself crosswise with the law, Sally. You might have made a halfway-decent detective."

She sighed loudly and closed her fists around the bars of her cell. "Get me out, G-man. Get me out of here. You promised. You did promise, remember."

13

"I've searched for an alternative, Senator," said Mrs. Roosevelt. "I regret that I haven't found any. I really don't see how we can avoid asking you some questions. Because . . . Well, because of your close personal relationship with the President, and because, frankly, I have always thought highly of you myself, I thought it might be best, and not inappropriate, if I asked you to meet with me and talk about the matter in private. Of course, I couldn't exclude Mr. Szczygiel from such a meeting."

"I understand," said Senator Everett Cranshaw. "I understand that I'm a suspect. That's inevitable, I guess, in the circumstances. It's embarrassing, of course. I know what you've learned. It's distressing."

Looking at the tall handsome senator, it was difficult for Mrs. Roosevelt to believe the Sally Partridge story that he drank too much, had a hot temper, and had struck the crippled Joe Bob Skaggs. He had a long, solemn face, with a sharp nose, a long jaw, a wide mouth with thin white lips. His abundant light-brown hair was combed—one might have said slicked—from side to side across his head. His smile came easily and often, but it was a reserved smile, with something introspective about it, suggesting that its origin was in some private thought he was not communicating.

"Fortunately," he went on, "I have a perfect alibi for the Tuesday evening of last week. As you will recall, I was with the President that evening. After you left and Missy came in, I sat with the President for quite some time. I guess I was later in leaving than most cocktail-hour guests."

"What time did you leave, Senator?" asked Szczygiel.

"I am not precisely sure," said Senator Cranshaw. "Let us say a quarter to nine. Surely no earlier."

"How did you leave, Senator?" asked Szczygiel.

"South Portico," he said. "I walked over to the Willard Hotel for coffee. I'd drunk a little more than I intended and decided some strong black coffee would be a good idea. As a matter of fact, I ran into Burton Oleander in the dining room and sat down and had coffee with him."

"And Friday morning, if you don't mind?"

"I was with Secretary Rinehart. I had a ten o'clock appointment. Discussion of the lumber-import bill."

Mrs. Roosevelt regarded Senator Cranshaw gravely, her hands pressed together and held to her slightly pursed-out lips. "So, actually, all we can say about your possible involvement in the case, Senator, is that you had a motive. It is to your advantage, is it not, that Miss Taliafero and Mr. Skaggs are no longer among the living?"

"I wouldn't be surprised," he said, "if you could find people who will report that I expressed myself more than once to the effect that the world would be better without either of those two loathsome wretches."

"I believe we have heard something to that effect," she said.

"I won't say I'm sorry they're dead. I'm of course deeply concerned to know what becomes of the photographs."

"Yours is not flattering, Senator," said Szczygiel sardonically.

"You have me at a disadvantage, Szczygiel," said the Senator.

Mrs. Roosevelt tried to suppress a smile but could not. "When the case is closed," she said, "I hope we can hold a small private gathering at which time we pour a half pint of gasoline over all the prints and negatives, in a garbage can, and toss in a match."

Stan Szczygiel had a luncheon date with Missy LeHand. With the Boss out of town, Missy had time to relax a little—though she had campaign work to do, and plenty of it. Missy was dedicated to the President and gave him her every waking hour, practically, when he needed her. But she was only thirty-eight years old, blithe of spirit; and, although she missed Franklin Roosevelt when he was away, still she could not help but welcome respite from the heavy demands of her job.

Stan was a pleasant man, twenty-four years her senior, unthreatening and undemanding. He enjoyed her company for the same reason she enjoyed his: that nothing but a pleasant, casual relationship could possibly ever develop. Both were Catholics. Stan was deeply devoted to the memory of his late wife. Missy's world revolved around her job and the Boss—and also around her family. She enjoyed lighthearted company, good conversation with spirited men, but she backed away from a serious relationship with any of them. A lunch with Stan Szczygiel was her idea of a good time.

His idea was to get out of central Washington, to get away from the heat and dust. He took an inconspicuous dark-blue Chevrolet from the Secret Service motor pool and drove out to Silver Spring, where they sat on a terrace like the lovers they were not and ordered food and drink as though their companionship were far more intimate than it was.

In fact, their conversation turned very quickly to the murders.

"Tell me something," he said. "Would you call Mrs. Roosevelt naive?"

Missy's attention was at the moment focused on retrieving the olive out of her martini, and she frowned over that little task as she answered—"In a sense, she is. I mean, she can be naive in her evaluations of people. She always wants to believe the best of them. She's a shrewd judge of character, and it would be difficult to deceive her; but she always proceeds from an assumption that a person is honest and well motivated."

"She scratched two question marks off her chart this morning," said Szczygiel. "Senator Cranshaw told her he was with Secretary Rinehart. She was skeptical enough to call Rinehart and ask, and Rinehart confirmed that he and Cranshaw met and discussed some bill on Friday morning. So, she concludes that each of them is the other's alibi." He shook his head. "*I'm* not so sure."

"You think they're both lying?"

"Well . . . The Taliafero murder is more than a week old. The Skaggs murder will be a week old tomorrow. Some smart, powerful men are suspects. They're smart enough to manufacture alibis for themselves."

Missy sipped from her glass. Her eyes were fixed on distant Maryland hillsides, where the sun drew a blue haze up from expanses of evergreens. No one could have guessed that she was pondering the solution to a murder mystery—that is, a real one, a live one, involving people she knew.

"Are you suggesting Cranshaw and Rinehart killed Taliafero and Skaggs?" she asked.

"No," he said. "Even the men who didn't commit the murders are anxious to escape the suspicion."

"They more than anyone else," said Missy thought-fully.

Szczygiel nodded, and for a moment he was silent as he watched a pair of young women cross the terrace, following a waiter to their table. He enjoyed seeing how their lightweight summer skirts swished around their long young legs.

Then he said—"I'm beginning to think there's something to be learned by taking a closer look at the times when things happened Tuesday night."

"The problem is, we don't know exactly when Vivian Taliafero died," said Missy.

"Fritz Hausser says she left his office around eight-thirty. For the moment, let's assume that's true. For the moment it's difficult to see why he would lie about that—particularly since he couldn't have known when he said it that we wouldn't find another witness who would tell us *exactly* when she left."

"Okay, so let's assume that's right," said Missy.

Szczygiel drew a corner of his lower lip in between his teeth, and he frowned. The combination gave him a grotesque but thoughtful expression.

"Senator Cranshaw told Mrs. Roosevelt and me this morning that he had a perfect alibi in the murder of Vivian Taliafero, which was that he was with you and the President for cocktails at the time she was murdered. Is that true?"

Missy raised her chin and pondered. "What time did he leave . . . ? I—"

"He said he stayed longer than the usual cocktail-hour guest. Does that help?"

She smiled. "He stayed long enough to get pretty disgustingly tight," she said.

"Tight?"

"Drunk."

"Oh—"

"So, anyway, what time did he stagger out the door?" she mused. "You know, I honestly can't tell you."

"I know exactly what time it was when I called the private quarters to tell the President a body had been found in the Rose Garden," said Szczygiel. "It was nine-ten."

"How long before that had they found the body?" asked Missy.

"Ten minutes," he said. "Fifteen at the most. I was the duty officer in the Secret Service office that evening. They called me. By the time I got there, they had set up lights and were making photographs."

"So, we can guess they found the body at nine o'clock?"

"They don't keep a log," said Szczygiel. "They just opened their notes and wrote it down that the officer had found a body about nine."

"Next question," said Missy. "How long had she been dead?"

"The best guess is that she'd been dead at least half an hour when she was found. I—I have to admit to you that I wouldn't know. I'm a Secret Service agent, not a detective. I don't know how fast bodies cool, how they change color, when they begin to turn stiff—all that gruesome stuff. The medical examiner fixes the time of death as 'mid-evening, Tuesday, July fourteenth, 1936.' And that's as far as he goes."

"Half an hour . . ."

"Well, I can put a limit on it. The sun set about eight on July fourteenth. The uniformed policemen who make rounds of the premises are certain she was not lying there when there was sunlight enough for them to see her. Say twilight ended by eight-thirty. She could have been there a few minutes earlier, when the twilight was weak."

"Anyway," said Missy, "the Executive Wing casts a shadow over the Rose Garden in the evening."

"Right," said Szczygiel. "But, you see, Hausser's statement comes out pretty good, when you think about the light. If she left his office at eight-thirty or so, she left just as it became too dark for a patrolling officer to see her in the Rose Garden. She went out into the colonnade, on her way to the South Portico and exit, and there she encountered—''

"Or maybe Hausser went out with her and led her into the Rose Garden."

"Possible. Not to be eliminated as a possibility. Anyway, I think we are safe in saying she was killed between eight-thirty and eight-forty-five. So, if Senator Cranshaw was with you and the president until eight-forty-five, he is a much less likely suspect. If he left before that time, he becomes a distinct possibility. Particularly—''

"Particularly if he is lying about what time he left," she said.

"That's what I had in mind," said Szczygiel. He signaled the waiter to bring them another round of drinks. "So can we figure out what time the senator actually left the second floor?"

Missy nodded. "After Cranshaw left, I called for Arthur Prettyman, the Boss's valet, and Arthur came in and helped the President undress and bathe and get into bed. I went up to my apartment, bathed, and dressed in a nightgown and robe. Then I came back down. Arthur had already called the kitchen to order the President's dinner, and mine. The dinners were brought up shortly—two trays. The President eats dinner in bed usually. I eat from the little table there in his bedroom. We put on some records and listened to music. By the time you called, at nine-ten, we had finished our dinner."

"Suppose the senator did leave at eight-forty-five—''

She shook her head. "Cutting our time awfully short. The President needs help to undress and bathe. The braces have to be removed. He—Well, it takes fifteen to twenty minutes at the very least before he gets into bed. Our dinners are very simple. I don't suppose we take more than fifteen or twenty minutes to eat."

"The time is critical," said Szczygiel. "I called you at

nine-ten. I'm sure of that. Fifteen minutes before that was eight-fifty-five, and fifteen minutes before *that* was eight-forty. We can't argue with the senator's eight-forty-five if he actually left the second floor at eight-forty.''

Missy stared into her martini, biting her lips, reviewing in her mind the casual events of the evening of Tuesday, July 14. Abruptly she brightened.

''I know how to find out something more about the time,'' she said. ''We were playing records on the new RCA phonograph that changes the records automatically. And I know what we listened to. All I have to do is check the time it takes those records to play, and I'll know how much time passed while the Boss and I were eating dinner.''

''Great!''

''I can tell you one thing already,'' she said. ''We played Gershwin's 'Rhapsody in Blue' first. That takes a good fifteen minutes. Afterward, we were playing something the President likes very much, the choral movement of Beethoven's Ninth. When you called, it had been playing for a few minutes; I'm not sure how long.

''If you listened to it again, could you identify the point where I called?''

''Probably.''

''With any certainty?''

''Yes, I think so,'' she said. ''And to the time of the music, you have to add some more time. The new record player drops the records automatically, but you still have to get them out of the cabinet and put them on. Also, I had to put the 'Rhapsody' records back in their album after they were played, then take out the Ninth records. I—''

''Missy,'' he said. ''I think the only thing to do is go back to the President's bedroom and duplicate what you did. With a stopwatch.''

Missy felt bound to stop by Mrs. Roosevelt's office and tell her what they would be doing. The First Lady was curious and interested, and shortly after Missy and Szczy-giel arrived in the family quarters Mrs. Roosevelt came up the hall and said she wanted to watch.

"I shall remain silent," she said. "I understand you must try to duplicate what you did last Tuesday evening, so that any pause for explanation or comment would make the test inaccurate."

"All right," said Missy. "Now. When I arrived, the President was in bed, propped up on his pillows and ready for his dinner tray. I came in. You can start the stopwatch now, Stan."

There was nothing awkward about what followed. Mrs. Roosevelt was perfectly well aware—and perfectly content—that Missy kept the President company while he ate his dinner and usually ate hers at the same time. Her own busy schedule allowed the First Lady to take her dinner with the President only rarely. She appreciated Missy's keeping him company at the dinner hour. She knew they joked and gossiped and listened to music in a way she simply hadn't the time to do. She understood also that the President really preferred Missy's company at dinner, since Missy would never raise any serious subject—which she herself could never resist doing. Missy never had a project to bring to the President's attention at dinner. He liked that.

"I walked in," said Missy, "and we said a few words— I'm not sure about what—and he said he'd like to hear some music while we had our dinner. I went to the cabinet and opened it. He said, 'Let's hear "Rhapsody in Blue." ' I took the album out—"

She removed the album of records from the cabinet, switched on the new RCA machine, and stacked the records on the changing mechanism. She pressed a switch, and the turntable began to spin. After a moment to allow the tubes in the machine to warm up, she turned a little handle, and the mechanism moved slowly and released a record to fall on the rotating turntable. Then the arm swung very slowly to the edge of the record and lowered the needle into the groove. The opening notes of "Rhapsody in Blue" sounded through the room.

Stan Szczygiel frowned over the stopwatch. Missy had so far used two minutes and forty seconds. Now, while the records played, they had to wait. And they could talk.

"This test will not *prove* that Senator Cranshaw strangled Miss Taliafero," said Mrs. Roosevelt.

"It may prove he was lying this morning," said Missy.

"It may prove he was too drunk to know what time he left," said Szczygiel.

"Oh, Mr. Szczygiel! Do you think . . . ?"

"I'm sorry," said Missy briskly. "He was in pretty poor shape."

Mrs. Roosevelt shook her head. "Franklin's martini cocktails . . ." she murmured.

"He enjoys them," said Missy.

The First Lady nodded. "Of course. And he's entitled to his small pleasures."

They waited, glancing at the stopwatch from time to time. Mrs. Roosevelt stepped next door to the President's second-floor study, to place a telephone call. She returned before the "Rhapsody" was finished.

"Rhapsody in Blue" played for a little more than sixteen minutes. With the time Missy had used before the music began, nineteen minutes had elapsed.

"Now," said Missy. "We hadn't finished eating, and I asked the President if he'd like to hear something more. He said he would and suggested the choral movement from Beethoven's Ninth. I took the 'Rhapsody' records off and put them back in their album. Then I went to the cabinet—"

She did what she described. The symphony, of course, filled a large album with twelve-inch records, and as she took some of them out she explained that she had to identify the choral-movement disks before she could put them on the player. She carried the selected records to the machine, and the machine began to play them.

Returning the "Rhapsody" to the cabinet and starting the symphony had taken almost four minutes.

Mrs. Roosevelt looked at the big records and said, "This will take some considerable time. How much time has elapsed, Mr. Szczygiel?"

"Twenty-three minutes," he said. "Which takes us back to eight-forty-seven."

Missy listened intently. The President's fondness for this music had given her some familiarity with it. She had heard it three or four times. She followed it, nodding, frowning. Then—

"Okay. Okay, stop the watch. That's it. That's about it."

Mrs. Roosevelt bent over to see how much more time had passed. About six minutes.

"That brings the time Tuesday evening back to . . . eight-forty-one," she said.

"Now take into consideration," said Missy, "the time it took for Arthur to help the President through his bath and into bed. I *know* that's more than ten minutes. I'd rather think it was fifteen."

"If so," said Mrs. Roosevelt, "we are back to eight-twenty-six. Are we saying, then, that Senator Cranshaw left you and the President no later than eight-twenty-six?"

Missy sighed and nodded. "I myself went upstairs, bathed and changed, and came back down. I can hardly have taken much less than a quarter of an hour."

"So what have we proved?" asked Mrs. Roosevelt.

"Not that Senator Cranshaw killed Vivian Taliafero," said Missy. "But we have proved that the senator was not still sitting with the President, drinking martinis, when the murder took place. He had left."

"He told you and me this morning that he had an alibi," said Szczygiel to Mrs. Roosevelt. "The perfect alibi—he was with the President when the woman was killed. Well, his alibi doesn't hold up.''

"Perhaps because he misjudged the time," said Mrs. Roosevelt pensively. "But . . . perhaps because he was lying.''

14

"I felt some obligation to advise you about it, Ma'am," said Judge Beresford Kincaid to Mrs. Roosevelt. "Strictly speaking, I shouldn't be speaking to you on the subject. As a matter of respect and, if you will allow me, friendship—"

"I am grateful to you for coming to see me, Judge Kincaid," she said.

It was less than an hour after she watched Szczygiel time Missy's re-enactment of her dinner with the President on the night when Vivian Taliafero was murdered. She had returned to her office to dictate some memoranda and letters, only to learn that three people had asked for appointments—the last of whom was Beresford Kincaid, Judge of the United States Circuit Court of Appeals, Second Circuit. Even a First Lady, even a President for that matter, accorded a degree of respect to a circuit judge; and she had made time to meet him when he arrived at the White House at 4:45.

"Uh . . . Since the President appointed me, I do feel a strong affinity for him . . . and you."

"It is kind of you to say so."

"Well, uh . . . As I said, strictly speaking it is inappropriate for me to bring to your attention a legal matter that may come before my court, but—"

"Please, Judge Kincaid," she interrupted. "I would not want you to do anything unethical."

"Oh, oh . . . of course," he said. "Uh . . . and it's not unethical. No. Not at all. It's just a bit awkward."

She smiled, nodded, and waited for him to go on. His appearance and manner brought to her mind the actor Lionel Barrymore. That Barrymore had a special facility for speaking innocent words in an innocent tone, yet suggesting something corrupt underneath. Maybe the suggestion was in the way his brows rose and fell, his eyes opened wide and returned to a heavy-lidded introspection. It was not easy to trust the man, not easy to believe he was telling the truth. She wondered how he could have become a judge.

"Well . . ." he said. "It seems an action at law may be filed." He paused and nodded, as if to suggest what he had just said was weighty with significance. "Question of law, question of constitutionality . . . The question is, Did the President have the power to issue an executive order assigning responsibility for the investigation of the Taliafero murder to the Secret Service? It's outside their statutory—"

"I quite understand," she said.

"Did you anticipate the question?" he asked.

"The President did," she said. "He had the law thoroughly researched before he issued the order."

God would forgive her, she was sure.

"Oh . . . And the President felt sure his order was—"

"Within his constitutional and statutory prerogatives," she said with a neat smile.

Judge Kincaid released a noisy sigh. "Well . . . Others are not so sure. Others feel the investigation is entirely within the defined authority of the Federal Bureau of Investigation."

"Mr. Hoover," said Mrs. Roosevelt firmly, "works for the President, who assigns him his duties. The President is satisfied with what Mr. Hoover is doing to eradicate gangsterism and wants him to concentrate on that duty."

"If the President orders J. Edgar Hoover not to—"

"If the President," she said firmly, through a brittle smile, "orders Mr. Hoover not to go to the tracks and bet on horses—and he does—the President may elect to dismiss him from his position."

The judge fluttered his hands before him. "Of course, of course," he said. "But the Secret Service—Well . . . I didn't come to debate the question, Ma'am. I came to tell you that there may be a lawsuit filed to annul the President's order assigning jurisdiction to the Secret Service."

"Who would want to do that?" she asked ingenuously.

"You, uh . . . You have to expect a certain amount of— How to put this? I, uh—"

"Who, Judge Kincaid?"

He drew a long, deep breath, inflating and stiffening, his mouth open to take in the air. "Uh—Well—Mr. Burton Oleander. His attorneys advise him—"

"What is his interest?" she interrupted.

"He was a friend of Miss Taliafero," said the judge.

"Indeed he was," she said. "I think it not an exaggeration to describe him as an *intimate* friend."

"Well, he wants her murderer brought to justice," said the judge weakly.

"Does he *really?*"

"Oh, ma'am, I assure you he does. He knows his own reputation is to some extent at hazard."

"Then advise him not to interfere in the investigation," she said with cold finality.

"I thought you would want to know," said Burton Oleander to Stanlislaw Szczygiel. "The President was wrong. We will not tolerate it."

" 'We'? Who is 'we'?" asked Szczygiel insouciantly.

Oleander had asked him to sit down at the bar in the Caliber Club, over early-evening cocktails. Szczygiel, to Oleander's open surprise, was drinking straight gin on the rocks. Oleander sipped Scotch.

"Frank Roosevelt seems to think he has become the only political power in Washington," rumbled Oleander. He was a heavy man, conspicuously accustomed to having his words heeded. "But he isn't. He is a temporary aberration, who will be sent back to his mama's estate on the Hudson in November. A one-term President, Szczygiel. Don't give him too much loyalty. Have you read the polls?"

Szczygiel shrugged. "I came to the Secret Service not long after the assassination of William McKinley," he said. "They beefed up the Service then, and I was lucky enough to get a job, guarding Theodore Roosevelt against idiots like Czolgosz. Maybe it was the 'z's' in my name that got me hired. Anyway, I've been around a long time and am not long from retirement, and my loyalty is to the office, not to the man."

"Do you consider yourself qualified to investigate a murder?" Oleander asked bluntly.

"No, I suppose I'm not. But I've been given that responsibility."

"By a wholly unlawful executive order," said Oleander.

"Who says it's unlawful?"

"I do."

Szczygiel looked at Oleander and smiled mockingly. "Unfortunately for you, the President's authority is higher than yours," he said. "Until I get better orders, I follow the President's."

"And his wife's," said Oleander.

Szczygiel shrugged. "I suspect you know better, Mr. Oleander."

"You and Mrs. Roosevelt could be heading yourselves into deep trouble. You had poor Bill Wolfe shanghaied in Alabama and hauled back to Washington in chains. You're holding him in jail, without a shadow of legal authority. You'll be lucky if he doesn't sue you. Does Mrs. Roosevelt understand how far off base she is?"

"Mrs. Roosevelt is a shrewd and capable woman," said Szczygiel.

"I'm surprised at how slavishly you follow her. Don't you know that four months from now Roosevelt is going to be swept out of office by a landslide?"

Szczygiel lifted his glass and rattled the ice cubes—a signal to the bartender to pour more gin over his melting ice.

"What do you want, really, Brother Oleander?" he asked.

Burton Oleander chuckled under his breath, shaking his heavy body. He turned down the corners of his mouth. His jowls quivered. He was wearing a white linen suit, complete with white vest; and, though the evening was Washington-hot, his clothes were crisp and sharp-pressed.

"Brother Szczygiel," he said, the words coming through the final rumbles of his laugh, "what I want is for you to back away from any suggestion that I had anything to do with the murder of Vivian Taliafero or Joe Bob Skaggs."

Szczygiel shook his head. "I'm not aware of having suggested that you did," he said.

"Well, I understand my name has come up," said Oleander.

"A lot of names have come up," said Szczygiel. "Would you like to tell me where you were on the evening of Tuesday, July fourteenth and the morning of Friday, July seventeenth?''

"Ah-hah! You see? It sounds like a police interrogation."

"It's what we ask all the suspects," said Szczygiel calmly.

" 'Suspect!' You call me a *suspect*, Mr. Szczygiel?''

"You are one of the suspects, Mr. Oleander.''

Oleander glanced around the bar. He lowered his voice. "That's why a lawsuit is going to be filed to have the President's silly executive order—"

"Before Judge Kincaid?" Szczygiel asked.

"I—"

"Judge Kincaid will have to stand aside if any such case is filed in *his* court," said Szczygiel.

"Why?"

Now the Secret Service man glanced around to see if anyone was watching or listening. He reached inside his jacket and took out a small envelope. It contained a photograph, and he handed it to Oleander.

The picture was of Oleander in bed with Vivian Taliafero. Oleander stared at it for a moment. His face flushed, and he slapped it down on the bar.

"I have another one just like it, of Judge Kincaid," said Szczygiel.

"You are subjecting us to *blackmail*," muttered Oleander.

"Blackmail is what the case is all about," said Szczygiel. "Vivian Taliafero had quite a collection of photographs like these. Prominent men. She was murdered. Then her house was entered and the collection stolen. Or . . . apparently that's what happened. Last Friday, Skaggs was murdered. The photographs were in *his* house. Maybe they'd been there all along. He was the woman's confederate.''

"Are you asking me to prove I didn't kill her?"

"No. If we want to make a case against you, we have

to prove you *did*. On the other hand, you can take yourself off the suspects list by proving where you were last Tuesday night and last Friday morning.''

"To hell with that," said Oleander.

"Have it your way," said Szczygiel.

Oleander watched Szczygiel return the photograph to the inside pocket of his tan double-breasted jacket. "You're serving a rotten administration," he groused. "The Roosevelts would do anything to discredit me."

Szczygiel raised his newly replenished glass of gin. He sipped and waited, curious to see what tack the fat man would take next.

"I'll still be in Washington when they're gone," said Oleander.

Szczygiel nodded. He couldn't argue with that. This kind—lobbyists, manipulators—had always been around, always would be.

"You'll be retiring soon, I suppose," said Oleander. He raised his Scotch to his lips. "When? Next year?"

"In 1939," said Szczygiel.

"A man with your experience can always make his retirement more comfortable," said Oleander. "I mean, for example, my organization could become interested in putting you on our payroll, say as an adviser. You might even think of taking early retirement."

"I don't know what I could do for your organization," said Szczygiel with bland mock-innocence.

"The Coal-Fired Utilities Association pays good money for services rendered."

"But what services could I possibly render you?"

Oleander tipped back and drained his glass. "You could, for example, deliver to me all negatives and prints of that photo," he said brusquely.

"For how much money?" asked Szczygiel.

"Say five thousand dollars."

"One of the other men involved offered Vivian Taliafero

forty thousand dollars for the negatives and prints of *his* pictures."

"I don't believe that," said Oleander. "I'm not bidding anywhere near that high."

"I'm not soliciting a bribe, Mr. Oleander," said Szczygiel. "Are you offering one?"

"I am more interested in reputations," said Oleander, "than in the murder of two worthless people who deserved what happened to them."

"So where were you last Tuesday night?"

Oleander thrust his lower lip forward and curled it down, though somehow his upper lip at the same time curled up, fashioning the caricature of a cynical smile. "Would you mind telling me what hour, exactly, you want me to account for?"

"Let's say eight to nine."

"Well . . . Unfortunately, I have no alibi for that hour. I dined alone in the Willard Hotel dining room. Senator Cranshaw came in about nine and joined me at my table for a brandy and coffee. Until he arrived, I was alone."

"Your waiter?"

Oleander shrugged. "I wouldn't remember him. Why should he remember me?"

"All right. What about Friday morning?"

"It's an indignity to have to account for my time, like a common felon. But, very well, I was in my office all morning. You can check with my employees."

"You say Senator Cranshaw arrived at nine?"

"Nine? Oh—Yes, nine. About that."

"A little under the weather, was he?"

"Under the weather . . . ? Why, no. Not at all."

"How many drinks did he have with you?"

"Why . . . He had just one. It was a double, a double brandy, with coffee. What's the point of this cross-examination?"

Szczygiel lifted one shoulder—a half shrug. "Someone said he was pretty drunk that evening."

Oleander shook his head. "No . . . I don't recall his being drunk. I don't recall that."

"Okay," said Szczygiel with a faint smile. "Maybe someone was wrong."

"We can't continue to hold him without bail, Ma'am," said Lieutenant Kennelly to Mrs. Roosevelt. "Either I charge Wolfe with murder, or I let him go. I can't do anything else."

"I appreciate your calling, Lieutenant," she said. "I realize it is an extraordinary procedure for you to feel obligated to call *me*—"

"I'm very happy to do it, Mrs. Roosevelt," said Kennelly. "You do see my position."

"Entirely."

She had stepped outside a meeting of western Democratic state chairmen to take his call. They were in town to plan campaign strategy for their section of the country and had not concealed their annoyance that the President was off sailing and was not in Washington to meet with them.

"We can lay the murder charge on him," said Kennelly.

"In your judgment, Lieutenant, is there sufficient evidence to charge Mr. Wolfe with murder?"

"No, Ma'am. We're holding him on suspicion, and that's all. We can charge unlawful flight to avoid prosecution, but that's bailable, and I have the impression that the lawyer who's here to offer bail is ready to put up big money if he has to."

"And what is that man's name again?" she asked.

"James Townley," said Kennelly. "The firm is Townley, Thorndike."

"What's the connection?" she asked. "Why does this Mr. Townley suddenly appear, after Mr. Wolfe has been in custody almost a week?"

"He won't say. He says he doesn't have to tell us—which is right."

"He didn't by any chance offer to bail out Miss Partridge, too?"

"No, Ma'am. Just Wolfe."

"I think you have no choice, Lieutenant. Mr. Wolfe has already been held in custody as long as good conscience allows."

"I'm concerned about just one thing," said Kennelly. "Who's Townley? And why is he bailing out Wolfe? When I went back to the cells to talk to Wolfe, he didn't seem to know him. In fact, I don't think he ever heard of James Townley."

"Is he willing to be bailed out by Mr. Townley?"

"Oh, sure. He'd accept bail from Adolf Hitler."

"Then I think you must release him, Lieutenant. It's not my decision to make, of course; and you must use your own judgment. But I really see no alternative to letting him out."

"So, fine," said Sally Partridge. "I'm locked in, and everybody else is out. It's real handy, isn't it? Stick it all on Sally. She's nobody."

Mrs. Roosevelt had asked Missy to go to the D.C. jail and talk to Sally Partridge—that evening if possible. She had one or two questions for her, and she thought the unfortunate girl should know that Wolfe had been released. It might move her to say something more—maybe in anger.

Szczygiel had arrived back at the White House just as Missy was leaving. They went to police headquarters together.

Kennelly had not introduced Missy. Sally Partridge had assumed Missy was a policewoman, and he had not seen fit to disabuse her. She didn't know the First Lady was taking a personal interest in the murders, and it was just as well she didn't know.

Missy had a question that Mrs. Roosevelt had prompted her to ask—"Sally. On the night when Vivian Taliafero was killed, you were with Senator Valentine. Isn't that what you said?''

"Yes. That's what I said."

"And Joe Bob Skaggs interrupted your little party with the senator and demanded you go with him to the Taliafero house."

"Right."

"How did Skaggs contact you, Sally? You don't have a telephone."

"Well, I—"

Szczygiel slapped his fist into his palm. "Dammit, you said he *called* you!"

Sally Partridge shook her head solemnly. "I nevah said that. *You* said he called, and I let it go at that."

"Well—"

"Did you make notes of what we said, Mister G-man?"

Szczygiel glanced at Missy, then calmed. "How *did* he contact you?"

"He came to the house."

"And saw Valentine? And Valentine saw him?" Missy asked.

"Yes to both questions," said Sally, nodding. She rested her hands on a cross-brace and clasped them outside the bars. "Sure. The next question is, did they know each other? The answer is yes."

"Did Skaggs tell Valentine Vivian was dead?" asked Missy.

"Well—He told me. Steve heard it."

"How did Skaggs know Vivian was dead?" asked Missy. Mrs. Roosevelt had anticipated these answers and had prescribed this line of questions. "Did he tell you?"

"Not then he didn't. Everybody was all excited. I asked him later. He told me to mind my own business."

"Meaning he killed her himself," said Szczygiel.

"*Him?* Vivian would've knocked him sprawling, if he hadn't used his gun on her."

Szczygiel smiled at that answer. "All right, then," he

said. "So Senator Valentine knew Vivian was dead. Now, let's get it all straight. Did Skaggs say Vivian was *murdered*? Did Valentine hear him say she was murdered?"

Sally nodded. "Yes to both questions," she said.

"How did Senator Valentine react to the news that Vivian Taliafero had been murdered?" asked Missy.

"He was upset. He was *really* upset."

"Why? Could you tell?"

" 'Cause of the pictures, naturally," said Sally. "He saw the same problem Joe Bob did—that a lot of people were in big trouble if the cops got their hands on those pictures. 'Course . . . Actually, it didn't work out that way, did it? Sally's in jail. Just Sally."

Szczygiel put his foot on the lower cross-brace of the barred cell. "I want to hear exactly what Skaggs said to Valentine and what Valentine said to Skaggs. And if you want out of here, no playin' around."

Sally heaved a loud sigh. "Okay. I'm with Steve. Big loud knock on the door. I goes to the door. 'Vivian's dead!' he yells. 'Murdered!' he says. Steve comes out of the bedroom. 'Murdered?' asks Steve. 'Murdered,' says Joe Bob. I—"

"Joe Bob wasn't surprised to see Steve there, I suppose," said Szczygiel.

"No. Anyway, Joe Bob says, 'We got to get over to the house and grab the pictures and negatives, before the cops get there.' Steve says, 'Yeah! Before the cops get there!' Joe Bob says, 'Don't you worry about it, buddy. It's me and Sally is goin' to get the pictures.' 'I'll go,' says Steve. 'You will like hell,' says Joe Bob. Steve, he sort of stares at Joe Bob for a minute, but Joe Bob stares him down— likely because he knows Joe Bob has a gun inside his coat. So we left. We left him standin' there with his teeth in his mouth."

"You think Steve Valentine's stupid?" Missy asked. "Or spineless?"

"No to both questions."

"So what do you figure he did?"

Sally frowned at Szczygiel. "Steve's not the man Joe Bob took a shot at," she said. "Not unless he went home and changed his clothes before he showed up at Vivian's house. I might not have been able to see the face in that light, but I wouldn't have missed that cream-white suit."

"So he . . . ?"

"I figure he went to a phone somewhere and started calling the other guys. They were all in deep trouble. I figure he started warning them. I mean—" She shrugged. "That's what I'd have done if I was him."

"Do you *know* he made any calls?" asked Szczygiel.

"I don't know for sure. It's just my guess."

Szczygiel pondered for a moment, then said—"Sally . . . If we let you out of here, where would you go?"

"I suppose my place is still mine. The rent's paid up for July."

"I'm going to ask Kennelly to let you go," he said. "You're right about it's not being fair to keep you in jail when every other suspect is running around. But I warn you, girl, if you take off, we'll catch you if it takes a hundred years, and you'll do ten years if you do a day."

15

Mrs. Roosevelt's desk faced her office wall—faced a mirror on that wall, actually. On the desk and on the wall to either side of the mirror she kept family pictures, plus a picture of the late Louis McHenry Howe. Like the President, she enjoyed ship models, and a handsome model of a square-rigged ship sat on a table beside the desk—partially hidden by framed photographs. The desk was small. To her left she kept a stack of leather-covered document boxes. To her right she kept a Dictaphone, so she could dictate letters when her secretary was not available. A couple of extra Bakelite cylinders for the Dictaphone sat on end beside the machine. A small vase of flowers sat in the center. This morning the rest of the desktop was covered by newspapers. She had not yet finished scanning the news.

Her chair did not swivel. It was a simple wooden armchair, not upholstered, with a cane bottom. When she wanted to talk to guests in her office, she stood and turned the chair around.

As she had done this morning—

Secretary of the Navy Claude Swanson nervously smoothed his mustache with the knuckle of the index finger of his right hand and struggled to say what he had come to say.

"The admiral here," he said, "has offered to resign his commission. For conduct unbecoming an officer of the United States Navy."

"Offered? Has he actually resigned?"

"No, not yet. We thought we should talk to you first."

"Well, you don't submit your resignation to the First Lady, Admiral," she said crisply. "What is more, I don't tell you whether or not you should resign. I would only be meddling."

"Unofficially," said Swanson. "We wondered if we might talk unofficially. I know of your interest in the Taliafero murder investigation. I might tell you also that I am most reluctant to lose the services of a fine officer."

"I know almost nothing of the admiral's record," she said. "Other than that he has engaged in conduct unbecoming et cetera. What navy regulations and traditions require, I do not know."

"I would like to avoid his having to resign," said Swanson flatly.

"Then he shouldn't," she said. "At least not for now. That's my strictly unofficial suggestion. It is quite unclear how the murder investigation is going to develop. I would make no precipitate decisions. We're not making them in the investigation, so why should you make one, Admiral, while the matter remains entirely up in the air?"

She had hardly ever seen a more miserable-looking, more chastened man than Vice Admiral Richard Horan. He sat with his white cap on his lap, his fists clenching and unclenching. His face was flushed. His white summer uniform was limp from his sweat.

"Admiral Horan," Swanson continued, "knows that you have seen the incriminating photographs. He—"

"How do you know I've seen them, Admiral?" she interrupted.

Horan's lips fluttered. "Well, I . . . Uh, someone called me and told me."

"Who called you and told you?"

Admiral Horan glanced uneasily at the Secretary of the Navy. "I'm not sure I should say."

"I think you'd better," said Swanson curtly.

The admiral had a reputation for being a handsome man, and something of a lady-killer, as Mrs. Roosevelt had heard; but all he looked like now was a man driven into a corner and pummeled, like a boxer about to go down for the count.

"Mrs. Roosevelt—" He stopped and seemed to gain resolution. "I suppose I had better. I was telephoned by Judge Kincaid."

"When?"

"Yesterday. He told me you had seen the pictures, as had others—Secret Service agents, probably D.C. police detectives—and that it was probably only a matter of time before the whole affair became public."

"It would be desirable, I think you will agree, if the matter did not become public at all," she said. "That may require some cooperation on the part of the several men involved."

"Mrs. Roosevelt," said the admiral soberly, "I will cooperate in any way I can. I'll tell you everything that happened to me."

"Frankly, Admiral Horan, the stories are distressingly alike. All I'd be interested to know, for the moment, is why Judge Kincaid should have been the one to telephone you."

The admiral's already-flushed face reddened. "It was the judge who lured me into the Taliafero snare," he said. "Judge Kincaid is a very cordial, sociable sort of fellow.

We . . . share certain interests. We are friends. Or—Well, I thought we were. Now that I understand better, I—''

Mrs. Roosevelt nodded and interrupted him. ''You know about the photographs. How many men do you suppose appear in them? And who?''

''You're asking me to—''

''Yes. Didn't you adhere to an honor code at Annapolis? Aren't naval officers bound by one? I know little boys don't tattle, but grown-up men *do*. It is not honorable to conceal misconduct, perhaps even a crime as serious as murder.''

''I don't know who killed those people, Mrs. Roosevelt.''

''Horan—'' grumbled the Secretary of the Navy. ''Answer the lady's questions.''

Horan exhaled loudly through a wide-open mouth. ''Very well. Besides Judge Kincaid, I am sure that Secretary Rinehart was being blackmailed by Vivian Taliafero. And Burton Oleander. And Senator Valentine. And Senator Cranshaw. There were others, I think, but I don't know who they were.''

''Besides Judge Kincaid, has any of them talked to you about the murders?'' she asked.

''No.''

''When did you first learn that Miss Taliafero had been murdered?''

''Within an hour after it happened, I suppose. I was having dinner with Judge Kincaid at the Army-Navy Club. The judge was called away to the telephone and came back saying that Vivian had been killed.''

''Who had called to tell him?''

''Senator Valentine.''

''And how did Senator Valentine know?''

''The judge didn't say. I'm afraid you'll have to ask him—or, better yet, Senator Valentine.''

''I am most certainly going to do that,'' said Mrs. Roosevelt.

* * *

Steve Valentine's habitual optimism allowed him to put troubles away in compartments of his mind and ignore them until he was compelled to focus on them. It had been noticed of him during the several stages of his career that he could walk with a light step—could even swagger— while carrying troubles that would have hunched the shoulders of another man. So it was that on the morning of Friday, July 24, 1936, "the Senator from the U.A.W.," as he was called in Republican newspapers, strode up the walk and into the White House to keep an appointment with Mrs. Roosevelt: outwardly, at least, easy of mind, though he knew his summons from the First Lady was to discuss a very heavy topic.

At the same time, Sally Partridge entered the White House in a very different mood—awed, awed and afraid. She was in the custody of Lieutenant Edward Kennelly. At least, custody was how she saw it. This morning he'd told her she was free to leave the jail, but then he'd said she had to go to the White House. He'd sent her home in a police car, with a policewoman to watch her and with instructions to bathe and dress properly for a visit to the White House. *The White House!* Anyway, she did look a little like Jean Harlow . . .

Senator Steve Valentine was wearing a light-gray double-breasted suit and a snappy straw hat. Sally Partridge had picked out the best dress she had, but she wasn't sure how the White House would look at a form-fitting rose-colored silk that was maybe modest enough, except that it clung to her breasts and hips and displayed them as much almost as if they weren't covered at all. Well, it was the best she had; it was all she could do; and if they didn't like it at the White House, they'd have to manage somehow to live with it.

The woman who met them in the colonnade between the White House proper and the Executive Wing was the woman who'd come to the jail last night. Kennelly introduced her as Miss Marguerite LeHand. My God! Sally had heard the name. She was the secretary to President Roosevelt!

"It will be a few minutes before you're called, Sally," said Miss LeHand. "Suppose I show you around the White House a little. Have you ever been here before?"

"Sit down, Steve," said Mrs. Roosevelt. "You know Mr. Szczygiel, I believe."

Valentine shook hands with Stan Szczygiel.

They were meeting in the President's study, the oval room directly above the Blue Room, overlooking the South Portico and the Ellipse. It was furnished to F.D.R.'s taste, with ship models and ship prints predominating. It was here that the President liked to lie on a couch and read and dictate. The phones were within reach of his couch. On a sunny July morning the sun swept in through the easternmost of the three windows on the arcing south wall and crossed the room, making dramatic contrasts of bright light and deep shadow.

Mrs. Roosevelt had ordered tea and coffee brought on a tray—together with a modest supply of small pastries. Senator Valentine had already accepted her offer of coffee, and she was pouring as she invited him to be seated.

"Do you know why I've asked you to come by this morning?" she asked him.

"I've got a pretty good idea," he said. "Having Stan Szczygiel here makes your purpose less than subtle—though I anticipated the reason anyway."

She handed him his coffee and offered the plate of pastries. She was not surprised that he accepted one. People who had come up from his background—industrial worker, soldier, union organizer—instinctively accepted food whenever it was offered.

"I am going to ask you two straightforward questions, Steve," she said as she handed the plate to Szczygiel. "Did you kill Miss Vivian Taliafero or Mr. Joe Bob

Skaggs? From what I've learned of them, I could hardly blame you if you did—*but did you?*''

"Eleanor," he said, "I don't fault you for asking. And I'm glad to be able to tell you, the answer is no."

"Then I must ask, do you know who did?"

"No. Honest to God, Eleanor, I don't know."

She smiled, but her smile was not characteristic of her; it was not real but forced. "I'm pleased to know it, Steve. Frankly, I believe you. But I think you can help us find out who committed these crimes. I'm going to ask Mr. Szczygiel to put some questions to you. Please answer frankly—even if the answers are embarrassing. There is a major difference between being embarrassed and being an accessory to murder."

Valentine frowned at Szczygiel. "All right . . . It sounds ominous: 'accessory to murder.' ''

Szczygiel shrugged. "I doubt you are, Senator. But you could become an accessory, if you're not careful. Okay? I, too, have really just one or two questions for you. Let's start with this one—When I interviewed you Monday, you said you could provide a witness who could testify about where you were last Tuesday night when Vivian Taliafero was murdered. The time is now, Senator, to name that witness."

Valentine grinned. "Well . . . The truth is, Stan, Eleanor, I tried to make it easy on myself by talking about an alibi witness I could produce if—"

"Steve!" Mrs. Roosevelt protested.

"I—"

"Well, let's just see if your witness can be produced," she said.

The First Lady rose and went to the door of the study. She stepped out into the hall. Missy was to her left, standing in the door of the West Sitting Hall, waiting for her signal. Mrs. Roosevelt nodded, and Missy turned to Sally Partridge and summoned the frightened young woman to come out of the Sitting Hall.

"Mrs. Roosevelt! Oh, God!"

"You are Sally Partridge."

Miss Partridge tried to curtsy. "Oh, Mrs. Roosevelt!" she breathed.

"Miss Partridge . . . I'm sorry you've had to spend some time in jail. Come now and help us do something toward solving the mystery surrounding the deaths of Miss Vivian Taliafero and Mr. Joe Bob Skaggs. If you can help us, you will be doing something important toward showing us *you* didn't do it. Anyway, I'm sure you're interested in seeing justice done, as much as we are."

"Mrs.—But why *you?*"

"I don't like to see innocent people accused, Miss Partridge," said the First Lady. "And . . . And, though you are not exactly an *innocent,* I don't think you are guilty of murder, or of being an accessory to murder, and I don't want to see you charged."

"Mrs. Roosevelt . . ."

"Come into the President's study. There's someone there whom I think you know quite well."

She led the trembling young woman into the oval study.

"Steve!"

"Sally!"

"Your alibi witness, Steve," said Mrs. Roosevelt, unable to conceal her amusement.

Senator Steven Valentine rose and walked toward Sally Partridge. He extended his hands toward her, and she raised hers to meet them. They clasped hands and stood at arm's length.

"All right," said Valentine, turning toward Mrs. Roosevelt. "I was with Sally when Vivian was killed. Wasn't I, sweetheart?"

Sally Partridge nodded emphatically. "He was with me."

"You aren't sweethearts," said Szczygiel gruffly.

Valentine's frown was sad, almost tragic. "No . . . I guess the relationship was not that innocent. But—I can vouch for where she was when Vivian was killed, and she can vouch for me.''

Sally nodded again. "Steve was with me," she said.

"We've heard you were, Senator," said Szczygiel. "But you were interrupted. And—''

"Joe Bob—" said Sally.

"No," said Szczygiel brusquely. "Let the senator tell us.''

"Skaggs came to Sally's house," said Valentine. "He came to tell Sally that Vivian was dead and—''

"Did he say who killed her?" Mrs. Roosevelt interrupted.

"No," said Valentine. "From the way he talked to Sally, I got the impression he didn't mean to say he'd killed her himself. But he wanted Sally to go—''

"Yes, we know," Szczygiel interjected. "He wanted her to go to the Taliafero house to search for the photographs. You wanted to go, but he—''

"He had a gun inside his jacket," said Valentine. "And he was nutty enough to use it. I didn't argue.''

"Continue your narrative, Steve," said Mrs. Roosevelt, suggesting by a glance at Szczygiel that they should not interrupt so much.

"Well . . ." said Valentine. "He demanded—I mean, *demanded*—that Sally go with him. So—She went.''

"And what did you do, Steve?" asked Mrs. Roosevelt.

Valentine shrugged. "I . . . I went home.''

"And what did you do when you reached your home?" she asked.

"I went to bed," he said.

Mrs. Roosevelt shook her head gravely. "No, Steve," she said. "We know you made some telephone calls. Tell us about those.''

"Oh . . . Well, yes, I did make a couple of calls. You understand, the news of Vivian's death was a shock, and it created a terrible problem. So, yes, I made a couple of calls, to tell some friends that—''

"Who?" asked Szczygiel.

"Well, uh—Judge Kincaid, first. You know—"

"We know in what respects the judge was involved in the Taliafero schemes," said Mrs. Roosevelt. "Where did you reach him, and what did you tell him?"

"I reached him at the Army-Navy Club," said Valentine. "I knew he was at dinner there. I had intended to have dinner with him there myself, with Admiral Richard Horan also. The appointment had stood for a week. We were going to talk—to be altogether frank—about what we could do about the Taliafero blackmail, which was getting entirely out of hand. But—"

"You had a better offer," interjected Sally.

"A better opportunity," said Valentine. "I called the judge and begged off. But I knew where he was, and when the terrible news came—"

"Terrible because you knew what could happen to the photographs," said Szczygiel.

"Terrible for that reason," said Valentine. "Her death—Hell, Szczygiel, I couldn't have cared less. Forgive me, Eleanor. Why should I have been distressed to hear that Vivian Taliafero was dead?"

"You telephoned Judge Kincaid," said Mrs. Roosevelt.

"Yes. He was having dinner with Horan, he said. I told him exactly what had happened. I said I guessed Skaggs had killed Vivian. I doubt that now. I don't think the little bastard could have done it."

"Very well," said Mrs. Roosevelt. "To be entirely candid, Steve, so far you've told us nothing we didn't already know. Now tell us what happened next. Did you telephone anyone else?"

"Yes, in fact," said Senator Valentine. "Yes, I did. I knew one more man who needed to know, tout de suite. Burt Oleander. I knew Skaggs was going to pick up pictures of Burt, and I called him and—"

"*Where did you reach him?*" asked Mrs. Roosevelt.

Valentine frowned. "Uh . . ." He shrugged. "At home,

of course. It was, uh, after nine. I supposed he would be at home, so—''

"Game's over, Senator," said Szczygiel. "Let's get this one down *damned straight*, okay? Not straight, you're an accessory to murder. We want to know exactly what time it was when you called Kincaid, exactly what time it was when you called Oleander. Where do you live, Senator? Did you really have time to go home before you telephoned Kincaid?''

Valentine stood and walked around the room. He looked at Sally Partridge as if he thought he could find solace from her, if not a suggestion as to how to answer the question. He sighed loudly.

Then he shrugged. "I didn't go home," he muttered. "I ran from Sally's house to the nearest telephone, in a neighborhood bar. I—''

"Steve," said Mrs. Roosevelt. "What time was it when you reached Mr. Oleander on the telephone?''

He looked up at the ceiling. "Oh . . . Nine o'clock. Could have been nine-ten, no later than nine-fifteen.''

"You reached Mr. Oleander at home?''

"Yes.''

"And he lives . . . ?''

"Burning Tree," said Valentine. "It was a toll call. I had to get change from the bartender, to feed the telephone.''

"You're telling us," Szczygiel interrupted, "that Burt Oleander was in Burning Tree, Maryland at . . . Well, at nine-fifteen, latest?''

Valentine nodded. "I spoke to his home. His wife answered and called him to the telephone.''

Mrs. Roosevelt walked through the colonnade with Szczygiel and Missy. They were on their way to the swimming pool, where they had agreed they could spare thirty minutes for a swim that would temporarily relieve the heat of a Washington summer. Senator Steven Valentine had—

most uncomfortably—left the White House. Sally Partridge had left too, expecting to be returned to jail and surprised and pleased when the police car dropped her at her house. Mrs. Roosevelt wore a white robe over her swimsuit, as did Missy. Szczygiel expected to take his swimming clothes from the Executive Wing closet.

"Well . . ." said Mrs. Roosevelt. "I guess we know who killed Miss Taliafero." She shook her head. "Most distressing. I wish it were not so. But it's clear enough, isn't it?"

"Uh . . . I guess I've missed something," said Missy.

"I'm afraid I have, too," said Szczygiel.

"Oh, no. It has become entirely apparent," said Mrs. Roosevelt. "I am not yet sure who killed Mr. Skaggs, but I am more than reasonably certain who killed Miss Taliafero. Don't you see?"

16

A secretary came from the Executive Wing. "I'm sorry," she said. "But there's a Lieutenant Kennelly of the D.C. police on the line. He wants to speak to you, Mr. Szczygiel. I told him you were in the swimming pool, but he says it's urgent."

Szczygiel climbed out of the pool, dried himself a little with a towel, and hurried into the Executive Wing—a little self-conscious about going there covered only by a swimsuit and a towel wrapped around him, and still wet—but he took the call in the office of the Press Secretary.

"Stan? Ed. Listen, I thought you'd want to know right off. Wolfe's took a powder."

"What?"

"Gone. On the lam again."

"How do you know?"

"I figured he might," said Kennelly. "So I had a couple of the boys checking on him from time to time. When we let him out last night, he went back to the boarding house where he lived before he took off for Alabama. Apparently they let him have his old room again, 'cause he stayed there last night. Well . . . He stayed there part of the night. Made some phone calls and went to his room. They supposed he'd gone to bed. One of the boys stopped by this morning to check, and Wolfe was gone. Left in the middle of the night, a witness says. Just walked out, got in a car that was waiting for him on the street, and took a powder.''

"Maybe he went to work," Szczygiel suggested.

"Not if he works at the Department of Justice, he didn't. He hasn't been there."

"Where else have you checked?"

"The usual. Hospitals. Hotels. The railroad and bus stations. He's gone."

"Jumped bail," said Szczygiel.

"It looks like it. I've informed the lawyer who posted the bail, that fellow Townley. He's not too happy. It cost him five thousand dollars."

"No," said Szczygiel. "It cost some client of his five thousand dollars."

"Yeah. Well, I can make a guess who that is. I had a man checking into the firm, to find out what he could about who they represent. The name of the law firm is Townley, Thorndike. One of their big clients is the Coal-Fired Utilities Association. In other words, one of their big clients is Burt Oleander."

"You think Oleander put up the bail for Wolfe?"

"It'd be hard to say, if he won't tell us. He put it up in cash—one-hundred-dollar bills, fifty of them."

"Of course he won't tell us."

"No, I suppose he won't."

"But Mr. Oleander might," said Mrs. Roosevelt. Szczygiel had returned to the pool with his report. The

First Lady was still in the water, and she listened gravely, then offered the suggestion that he call Burton Oleander.

"I think Mr. Oleander has some reason for cooperating," she said.

"The pictures—"

"No, not the pictures. He's lied to us, interfered in a criminal investigation."

"I'm afraid I haven't caught the lie," said Missy. "I guess I'm overlooking something."

"Perhaps," said Mrs. Roosevelt. "Of course, it could be that Mr. Oleander is telling the truth and Senator Valentine and Secretary Rinehart are lying. Either way, there's lying."

"About . . . ?"

"Mr. Oleander says he was dining at the Willard Hotel when Senator Cranshaw came in and joined him for brandy and coffee. And he says that happened at almost exactly nine o'clock last Tuesday evening. But Senator Valentine and Secretary Rinehart both say they reached Mr. Oleander by telephone no later than a quarter past nine. They also say they reached him at home. Now, Mr. Oleander lives in Burning Tree; and there is absolutely no way he could have had brandy and coffee with Senator Cranshaw at nine, then received calls at home at nine-fifteen. How much time would it take to drive from downtown Washington out to the Burning Tree area? Nearly an hour, I should think."

"Right!" exclaimed Missy. "Ah-hah! So . . . How are you going to resolve that discrepancy?"

"I see no choice but to confront Mr. Oleander," said Mrs. Roosevelt.

The First Lady was mildly surprised, not only that Burton Oleander agreed to come to the White House to meet with her, but also that he said he would come immediately.

He was not only the president of the Coal-Fired Utilities Association; he was also president and largest stockholder of the Mingo Valley Electric Company. He had fought bitterly against the President's effort to secure passage of the Utilities Holding Company Act; and when it was passed, he had vowed it would be repealed in 1937, by a Republican Congress at the behest of a Republican President. He was active in the Liberty League. He was a vehement Roosevelt-hater.

When he said he could come immediately, she suggested he join her and Szczygiel for a light, informal lunch. She had it set up in the private dining room, the room where she had dined with Mary McLeod Bethune on the evening of the Taliafero murder. Mrs. Nesbitt sent up from the kitchen a platter of chicken salad, surrounded by carrot sticks, radishes, and slices of tomato. She sent also a big pitcher of iced tea.

"Well," said Mrs. Roosevelt to Oleander. "I am most grateful to you for breaking into your busy schedule and meeting my request."

"The pleasure is mine," Oleander rumbled. "To be altogether frank with you, I haven't been invited to the White House since 1932."

She smiled and did not give voice to her thought—that she and the President numbered their critics among those they entertained at the White House but that so violent a critic as he could hardly expect to be invited to break bread.

Oleander was wearing a light-blue suit, tailored expertly to drape smoothly over his expansive belly. Mrs. Roosevelt had put on a loose white cotton summer dress. They sat down at the table, she and Oleander at the ends, Szczygiel between them.

"My good friend Wendell Willkie is in town," said Oleander conversationally. "I'll be having dinner with him this evening. I believe you know him."

"Yes, I do," said Mrs. Roosevelt.

Willkie, the president of Commonwealth and Southern, had been a more moderate opponent of the Utilities Holding Company Act. It was rumored that he had political ambitions.

"You'd fault me for lack of candor if I told you I am an admirer of the President," said Oleander. "But Wendell is."

"He and the President exchanged amusing letters last year," said Mrs. Roosevelt. "Mr. Willkie wrote saying he was rather upset about a remark the President was rumored to have made. The President wrote back, saying, 'You should pay as little attention to rumors of intemperate remarks I am supposed to have made as I pay to rumors of intemperate remarks you are supposed to have made.' "

Oleander laughed. She handed him a plate she had filled with chicken salad and vegetables, then began to serve Szczygiel.

"Well, Mrs. Roosevelt. I am afraid you have asked me here to talk about something not very pleasant."

"I am afraid that is true."

"I will answer any question I can."

"Thank you. First, then, would you mind telling us if you are the person who posted bail for Mr. Wolfe?"

Oleander's smile disappeared and his face stiffened, but he nodded and said, "Yes, I did. I sent my attorney to arrange for Bill Wolfe to be released on bail. I felt very badly that he was being held in jail. Frankly, I can't imagine there was any case against him."

"Do you know where he is now?" she asked.

"Why, no. No. I don't know."

"Neither does anyone else," said Szczygiel. "He left his boarding house in the middle of the night and hasn't been seen since."

"Are you suggesting he's skipped bail?" asked Oleander.

"It is too early to reach that conclusion with finality," said Mrs. Roosevelt, "but if you have any idea where he can be contacted, we would appreciate knowing."

"I've no idea," said Oleander. "If he's skipped bail, he's cost me five thousand dollars."

"A condition of his bail," said Szczygiel, "is that he is not to leave the District of Columbia. He was picked up by a car, mysteriously, in the middle of the night and has apparently disappeared. I am more interested in knowing why than in knowing where he is."

"I'd like to know both," said Oleander. "I thought getting him out of jail was a big favor, big enough that he might feel obligated to meet the terms of his bail and not cost me my money. Why would he . . . ?" He stopped and shook his head angrily. "That's a lot of money."

"It doesn't look good for him, does it?" said Mrs. Roosevelt.

"Well, I . . . I have to say it doesn't. And I'm sorry, too. I befriended that young man when he came to Washington."

"If you hear from him—"

"I'll let you know. I'll let the police know."

"We would appreciate that," said Mrs. Roosevelt. "Now, if you don't mind, I would like to try to clear up some confusion that has arisen around another point in the investigation."

Oleander began to eat, apparently with satisfaction, and his mouth was full, so he nodded.

"You live, I believe, at Burning Tree," she said.

"A little north of there, actually. I have a country place. Used to be a horse farm."

"How long does it take you to get home from the center of the city?"

"Oh . . . Depends on the traffic. Depends on the time of day."

"At best, Mr. Oleander. What's the best time you can make?"

He pondered for a moment. "Usually it takes an hour. Sometimes a few minutes more. I do enjoy a country place, even if it's inconvenient."

"Well then, Mr. Oleander, there is a discrepancy between your account of last Tuesday evening and the accounts of two other witnesses."

"Oh, really?"

"Yes. To begin with, how did you learn of the death of Miss Vivian Taliafero?"

"I received a telephone call. Actually, now that I think of it, I received two calls. Senator Steve Valentine called me. And Secretary Herschel Rinehart."

"When?"

Oleander could not hide his reaction, his quick, involuntary frown, an abrupt pursing of his lips. He scratched his eyebrow. "Well," he said, "I can't say exactly. It was shortly after I got home that night."

"All right. You came home from where?"

"From the Willard Hotel. I had dinner there."

"And were joined after dinner by Senator Cranshaw," she said.

"Yes. For coffee and a brandy."

"And the senator arrived at . . . ?"

"Nine o'clock."

"He had coffee and brandy with you. He must have been with you at least a quarter of an hour."

"Well, uh . . . Not really. At any rate, not more than that. I was about ready to pay my check and leave when he arrived, and he was anxious to go on home."

"What is the earliest that you could have left the Willard Hotel, Mr. Oleander?"

He turned down the corners of his mouth and shrugged. "A quarter past nine, I suppose. Maybe ten past."

She nodded. "All right. You say you require at least an hour to drive home. You couldn't have been home before 10:15, could you? More likely, later."

Oleander fully understood the purpose behind this line of questions, and he could not conceal his dislike for it. "I suppose you are going to tell me Valentine and Rinehart say they called me earlier than that."

"Yes," said Mrs. Roosevelt gravely. "An hour earlier than that."

Oleander's face was flushed now, and his eyes seemed to retreat beneath his heavy lids. "It seems very dramatic, I suppose," he said. "But the discrepancy can be resolved. I wasn't staring at my watch all that evening. Senator Cranshaw may have arrived at the Willard earlier than I said. And I doubt Valentine and Rinehart can be absolutely precise about their times, either. If you're trying to hang something on this, Mrs. Roosevelt, I'm afraid you're only going to succeed in embarrassing yourself."

Szczygiel spoke. "We can check the time it takes to drive from the Willard to your home," he said.

"I don't want to amend that," said Oleander. "It's an hour, give or take ten minutes."

"Then—"

"Well, the key to it may be very simply that I was wrong about the time when Senator Cranshaw joined me at the Willard. Maybe it was only eight-thirty."

Mrs. Roosevelt shook her head firmly. "Senator Cranshaw says he was with the President until eight-forty-five."

"Does the President confirm that?"

"Well. The President is away."

Burton Oleander broadened as he let his shoulders slump and his bulk settled. "Well . . ." he said. "All this hairsplitting about times will be satisfactorily explained—if in fact it must be explained. I find no profit in chewing on it."

"That is probably right," said Mrs. Roosevelt with a smile. "Perhaps we should change the subject. What is your forecast for the November vote?"

"A country place," said Szczygiel. "A remote country place. What would you like to bet we find Wolfe there? I wonder if we shouldn't ask the Maryland police to stop by the Oleander horse farm and have a look."

"From a practical point of view, that may not be a good

idea," said Mrs. Roosevelt. "I doubt he's there, to begin with."

They remained in the private dining room, talking for a few minutes after Oleander had left.

"What's difficult for me to comprehend," she said, returning to a thought Szczygiel had interrupted, "is *why* Mr. Oleander would lie. If he thinks of himself as a suspect in the Taliafero murder, isn't it in his best interest to confirm that Senator Valentine and Secretary Rinehart telephoned him at home a little after nine? That provides him a perfect alibi, since he couldn't have murdered Miss Taliafero at eight-thirty and have been home by a few minutes after nine."

"Are you still satisfied you know who killed the woman?" asked Szczygiel.

"I am fairly confident I do," she said. "But Mr. Oleander's lying does not fit with my theory. That confuses everything."

"Why don't you tell me who you think did it?"

Mrs. Roosevelt smiled mischievously. "Oh, Mr. Szczygiel," she said. "I'd rather you reach an independent conclusion. I don't want to influence you to accept my analysis."

"I feel I don't have enough facts yet," said Szczygiel.

"Perhaps I've skipped ahead," she said. "Let's get more facts. They will confirm my theory or shoot it down entirely."

"You don't think it was Wolfe, do you?"

"No. I really don't. But I have no explanation for his disappearance. Or for Mr. Oleander's having bailed him out of jail."

"He lied about that, too."

"Mr. Oleander is in deep trouble," said Mrs. Roosevelt.

William Wolfe's disappearance lasted less than twelve hours. He was found about noon, in the Tidal Basin, by a family from Missouri whose visit to the Jefferson Memorial was spoiled when their eight-year-old son, who wanted to throw pebbles in the water, spotted the body lying beneath the surface.

The body was not identified for more than two hours, not until fingerprints were taken and matched at the F.B.I. central file. Until then, the body was described as "Caucasian male, approx. 40 yrs., well dressed, no identifying papers. Apparent cause death: drowned." The inventory of possessions read: "Suit double-breasted, black, shirt white, underwear, socks, shoes brown and white, $11 bills, $1.15 change, key, package Chesterfield cigs., amber cig. holder."

When the body was at last identified, Lieutenant Kennelly was notified, and he called Stan Szczygiel, who carried the word immediately to Mrs. Roosevelt. By then there was an autopsy report—

Cause of death, drowning. Approximate time of death, 2:45 A.M., July 24, 1936. Body bears no mark or other suggestion of violence. Subject not under influence of alcohol at time of death. Subject was alive when submerged. Tentative conclusion: suicide.

"Too bloody convenient," said Missy. "How very nice for the rest of them. Pin the murders on Wolfe. He's dead. He can't complain."

"You could only pin one of them on him," said Mrs. Roosevelt, pointing at her chart, which she had just uncovered. "Mr. Wolfe was pleading a case in court on the Friday morning when Mr. Skaggs was murdered. That's been confirmed, hasn't it, Mr. Szczygiel?"

"Yes. Wolfe didn't kill Skaggs."

"But on Tuesday evening," said Mrs. Roosevelt, "he remained at home in his boarding house and did not go out—he said. So he had no alibi for that evening. It is not impossible for him to have killed Miss Taliafero."

* * *

"Coincidence," said Kennelly to Szczygiel. "There is just no end of coincidences in this case."

"Meaning, of course, that you don't believe it," said Szczygiel.

"I'll let you judge for yourself," said Kennelly.

Mrs. Tanner was a woman of indeterminate age, maybe forty-five, maybe fifty-five. She was also a woman of indeterminate complexion and hair color, the one being hidden under a heavy application of rouge and powder, the other under a henna rinse that had stained her hair a flaming red. She did not smoke cigarettes, she had told Kennelly with some pride; but she did chew gum, and her jaws worked vigorously as she faced Szczygiel, tipped her head, and let him see that she was making a judgment of him as much as he was making one of her.

He made a judgment. It was based partly on her clothes. She wore a shiny white loose blouse and a pair of white slacks with grotesquely wide bell bottoms. She was the keeper of the boarding house where Wolfe had lodged, Kennelly said. He had checked that; she really was.

"I keep hearin' about Wolfe," she said once she was prompted by Kennelly to repeat her story to Szczygiel. "Now I hear he's dead. Like I said to the guys who came to the house to ask questions this morning, he left in the wee hours of the night. I keep a respectable house, Mr. Szczygiel. My guests are at liberty to come and go when they please, but there are some limits."

"Anyway—"

"Well, anyway, I hear the question is, did Wolfe have anything to do with the death of the Taliafero woman? So I can tell you, anyway, that Wolfe wasn't home the night it happened. He wasn't home *all* night. That is, he wasn't home when I went to bed. I never heard him come in."

"It is very good of you to come in and give us this information at this particular time, Mrs. Tanner," said Szczygiel dryly.

"Well . . . Now that Wolfe's been murdered and all—"

"Murdered?"

"Well, uh . . . *wasn't* he? I mean, you said you found the man drowned. I mean, he's hardly a likely fellow to have drowned, unless he was dead drunk when he went in the water. You've seen the room he rented from me, haven't you? All those swimming trophies! I—'Scuse me. I talk too much."

17

Mrs. Roosevelt studied her chart, frowning, shaking her head. "I should dislike having to add another column," she said. "For 2:45 A.M."

She had returned from a dinner of the Women's Conference on Economic Justice and now sat in her office on the second floor of the White House, still wearing her white dinner dress, her white gloves tossed on her desk. Agent Stan Szczygiel regarded her gravely. Lieutenant Ed Kennelly nodded his agreement that he, too, would not want to have to account for the whereabouts of the remaining suspects in the early hours of the morning. Missy LeHand used her right index finger to trace an invisible design on the palm of her right hand.

"I would guess," said Kennelly, "that none of the gentlemen whose names are on your chart is the murderer of William Wolfe. The evidence suggests to me that he was killed by at least *two* men, working together. I don't see how any one man could have done it."

"Please expand on that idea, Lieutenant Kennelly."

"The coroner found no bruises on the man, no evidence of a struggle. Still, he wasn't drunk, so he didn't just fall into the Tidal Basin. My guess is that two or three men grabbed him, threw him in, then jumped in after him and held him under."

"Oh . . ." gasped Missy. "How horrible!"

"I examined his clothes very closely," said Kennelly. "The evidence is not conclusive, not by any means; but some of the seams in the suit jacket are stretched to the point of separating. That suggests someone grabbed Wolfe and—And did like I said."

"You're talking about thugs," said Szczygiel. "You're talking about professional killers."

"Well . . . Maybe. They wanted it to look like suicide. They wanted it to look like Wolfe killed himself the first chance he got—"

"Because he was guilty and knew he faced hanging," interjected Missy.

"—by throwing himself into the Tidal Basin and drowning," Kennelly finished his sentence. "Which was pretty stupid and doesn't suggest the work of professional killers. They drowned a man who had been a national collegiate swimming champion only a few years ago. I'd say a bunch of hooligans made it up on the spot."

"Because . . ." said Mrs. Roosevelt, deeply thoughtful. "Because Mr. Wolfe knew who killed—Or maybe just to make it appear he was the guilty person and—" She sighed. "It is outrageous!"

"The Tanner woman," said Szczygiel. "She's lying."

"She could be a key, too," said Kennelly. "Who sent her to lie? Maybe we ought to find out."

"How do you propose to do that, Lieutenant?" asked Mrs. Roosevelt.

"I'm just a flatfoot cop," said Kennelly. "Some of my

methods don't meet with everybody's approval. But I'm like you say outraged by how they killed Wolfe. I've already put a guard on Sally Partridge. Who knows? Maybe somebody figures *she* ought to be put out of the way. Or who else? In my judgment, you've been treating some of these heavyweights with kid gloves. Well, one of them is killing people. I think the time has come to start sweating some of them.''

"How do you propose to do that, Lieutenant Kennelly?'' asked Mrs. Roosevelt.

"I won't try to move in on what's really White House business," he said. "But I'd start calling them in here, if I were you. They'll come if *you* call.''

" 'Sweating . . .' '' she mused. "You don't mean— Nothing physical, Lieutenant.''

"No rubber hoses, Ma'am," Kennelly laughed. "I'm talking about uncomfortable, not hurting.''

Mrs. Roosevelt glanced at her watch. "It's quite late," she said. "Should we subject people to—''

"Half past nine," said Kennelly. "People sweat better at night. Anyway, some of them are probably off balance, and it's good to keep them that way. By tomorrow they'll have thought up better stories. By tomorrow they'll have a chance to get together and make up lies that agree with each other.''

"Very well. Can we start in half an hour?''

She arranged for a temporary headquarters to be located in the Cabinet Room. A stenographer was called in to take a record of what was said. In the half hour she had suggested, she made some telephone calls. Stan Szczygiel reinforced himself in the bar at the Willard with a couple of generous shots of gin—explaining to Missy who went with him that he wanted to walk the distance from the White House to the Willard Hotel, to see exactly how long Cranshaw might have taken to walk there the night of the Taliafero murder. Lieutenant Kennelly took his place in the

Cabinet Room as soon as it was ready, called in two more D.C. detectives to act as his assistants, and gave some orders by telephone.

"I hadn't thought of this when I suggested the Cabinet Room," said Mrs. Roosevelt when she joined Kennelly, "but it's ironic that we are using the Cabinet Room this evening. Miss Taliafero was murdered just outside that window." She pointed to a window. "Right out there. Ghastly thing, you know. She was lying on the ground, right out there."

"Criminal investigation is a gruesome business," said Kennelly.

"Well . . . You've begun by—"

"I had Sally Partridge brought in. She's waiting."

"Is that poor young woman under arrest again?"

"No. I sent a car for her, but I had the policewoman tell her she didn't really have to come."

"What do we need to ask her?"

"I'm not sure yet," said Kennelly. "Stan says she knows a lot. Let's just keep her handy, okay?"

"All right. Then what?"

"I had someone else picked up. Ruby Tanner. I suggest you step outside while I question her. She'll talk, later. Loud. I mean, to the newspapers."

"I'll go to the President's study by the Oval Office," said Mrs. Roosevelt. "Please call me as soon as you've finished questioning the woman."

She went through the secretaries' room and the Oval Office, not through the hall where she would be seen. As she left, Szczygiel and Missy returned. Kennelly suggested that Missy, too, not see Ruby Tanner, so Missy went to her own desk in the secretaries' room.

"What I want to know is, what the hell is this?" Ruby Tanner shrilled as she was led into the Cabinet Room by a uniformed policewoman. "The *White House,* f' God's sake! What—"

"Sit down and shut up, Ruby," said Kennelly gruffly.

"Who you—" she began but thought better of it and sat down. She was dressed the same as she had been in the afternoon, and her jaw pumped wildly as she chewed gum.

"Who paid you to come to headquarters this afternoon with that cock-and-bull story about how Wolfe was out all evening the night of the Taliafero murder?" Kennelly demanded.

"Wha'? Paid me? You gotta be outta your mind, Mister Kennelly. Why I—"

"*Ruby.*"

"Hey. No. You got it wrong."

"Do I really? Sure. You just wanted to be an honest citizen."

"I *am* an honest citizen!"

" 'Kay. Have it your way," said Kennelly. He glanced at the policewoman. "Get your 'cuffs, Beth? Put 'em on her and take her in. Lock her up. We'll talk about it in a couple days, Ruby—see if you've got any better ideas."

"Hey, wait a minute!" shrieked Ruby Tanner. She put up one hand, as if to signal the policewoman to stand back. "Hey, what am I . . . ? How kin I—" She deflated. "Look . . . Okay, two guys came. They wanted to know— You know. They wanted to know where Wolfe was the night the lady got killed. I said, hell, he was here, far as I know. And they said, do you have trouble with your memory? They said, we know he was out all evening. Then they said, would like a hundred bucks make you remember better? And I . . . Well, I said, now that I think of it—Okay?"

"For a hundred bucks you remembered Wolfe was out all evening," said Kennelly wryly. "How much did it take to remind you of your duty as an honest citizen—I mean to come tell the D.C. police?"

She stared at the table and shook her head. "Another two hundred," she said.

"What would it take to get the truth out of you?"

Ruby Tanner looked up. Tears welled and began to run down her heavily-powdered cheeks. "He was home at first," she said. "Then he got a call on the phone. That's in the downstairs hall, and I called him down to answer it. After that he made a couple more calls and left his two nickels in the dish. After that he went out."

"So when you told us the other story you were lying," said Kennelly grimly.

She nodded.

"Who were the two guys who paid you to lie?"

"As God is my witness, I never saw either of 'em before and ain't never seen neither of 'em since."

"Looked like what?" Kennelly asked coldly.

"Uh . . . Like what? Like what? A couple of *big* guys, what y'd call husky. Well-dressed. Good-talkin'. Came to the house and—Hey . . ."

"I want *their names*, Ruby."

"Names . . . Hey, there's no way I can tell you. They never said nothin' about names. Names? No names, Mister! No names."

"Is that all you have to tell us, Ruby?"

"What else can I say?"

Kennelly nodded. " 'Cuff her, Beth. Lock her up and charge her with interfering in a criminal investigation, obstruction of justice."

Judge Beresford Kincaid, entering the Executive Wing from the colonnade, encountered the policewoman hustling the handcuffed, struggling, cursing woman out the door. Kennelly, standing in the door to the Cabinet Room, saw the judge stop and watch. He could not have been more pleased. He knew of few better ways to sweat a witness than by letting him see another under arrest.

"Sit down, Judge Kincaid," said Mrs. Roosevelt.

The judge nodded and sat down. "Odd procedure, isn't it? Calling a man at this hour."

"We are investigating three murders, Judge Kincaid," she said.

"Three? You mean . . . Wolfe? I supposed he committed suicide."

"Murdered," grunted Kennelly.

"Lieutenant Kennelly, District police," said Mrs. Roosevelt.

"Who was the woman?" Kincaid asked, tossing his head toward the door.

"A witness who lied to us," said Kennelly.

Judge Kincaid could not suppress a cynical smile. He had been a prosecuting attorney for thirty years before he became a judge, and little tricks to intimidate a witness did not intimidate him.

"Judge Kincaid," said Mrs. Roosevelt, "we are all but certain you did not commit any of the murders. You were presiding at a hearing on the morning when Mr. Skaggs was killed, and you were at dinner with Admiral Horan when Miss Taliafero was killed. Unless you were in some way involved in the murder of Mr. Wolfe, you are clear of the serious charge of murder. On the other hand, you have not been entirely candid with us on a number of points."

The judge nodded. "Okay. I guess I haven't."

"I want a direct answer to one question, if you don't mind. How did you learn of the death of Miss Taliafero?"

The judge stared at her for a moment with a thoughtful frown. Then he said, "Steve Valentine told me. He called me at the Army-Navy Club and told me."

"You had a perfect alibi for the hour when Miss Taliafero was killed. You were at dinner with Admiral Horan. But when Mr. Szczygiel asked where you were at that hour, you said you might have finished dinner by then and left the Army-Navy club. Why did you say that, Judge Kincaid? Why didn't you use your perfect alibi?"

The judge leaned back in his chair. He was not uncomfortable. "You've learned how wide the circle is, Mrs. Roosevelt," he said. "At the time when I first talked with Brother Szczygiel, I don't think he guessed how many men, and who, were involved—and I saw no reason to enlighten him. I suspected—I still do suspect—that Skaggs killed Vivian. And I suspect that Sally Partridge killed Skaggs."

"That would be very convenient," said Szczygiel.

The judge shrugged. "Granted. You don't accept the idea."

"I should like to know, as precisely as you can tell us, what time it was when you received the telephone call from Senator Valentine," said Mrs. Roosevelt.

"What did Dick Horan say?"

She shook her head. "I prefer to hear what *you* say."

"Well, I'm not exactly sure. It was of course after nine."

"Why did he call you, Judge Kincaid?"

"To tell me Vivian had been murdered."

"He called you from dinner at the Army-Navy Club simply to give you the news that a woman neither of you could have liked much had been killed? Surely he had more reason than that."

"Well . . . He called to warn me, actually. The investigation into the murder was bound to disclose the illicit sexual relationships between some of us and Vivian Taliafero. The blackmail was likely to be disclosed, too."

"Had he telephoned anyone else?" she asked.

"Yes. He'd called Burt Oleander."

"Before he called you?"

"Yes."

Mrs. Roosevelt nodded grimly. "The pattern is uniform," she said. "There is no doubt."

Stan Szczygiel shook his head. He saw the pattern she was talking about but didn't yet understand how it identified the murderer. He had questions but decided to hold them.

"Unless Mr. Szczygiel or Lieutenant Kennelly has a question for you, Judge Kincaid, I think we can say thank you. I suggest you may wish to stay in the Executive Wing.

We may see some excitement before the night is much older.''

"I can tell you something you should know," said Judge Kincaid. "Frankly, I had half hoped you would not be able to put enough of the pieces together to see the picture. But apparently you have. So let me supply a missing piece.''

"We'll be grateful for that.''

"Skaggs got the photographs Tuesday night. Wednesday he was on the phone, telling all of us to keep up our payments—because nothing had changed. Everybody had a motive for getting rid of him. *Everybody.* It was possible to understand Vivian, maybe even to have a little sympathy. But not Skaggs. He was scum.''

"Then what about Wolfe?" asked Szczygiel. "What was the motive for killing him?"

"I have no idea. None whatever.''

Missy returned just as the judge rose to leave the Cabinet Room, and Mrs. Roosevelt asked her to find him a comfortable place to wait.

Missy nodded. "Secretary Rinehart is waiting," she said.

Mrs. Roosevelt rose to greet the Secretary of Trade as he entered the room. "Our apologies, Mr. Secretary, for calling you at so late an hour," she said. "I know you will realize we wouldn't have done it except that it is important.''

Rinehart, who was dressed in one of the crisply tailored suits—this one gray—that were an element of his reputation in Washington, sat down uneasily and glanced around the room. He took particular note of the stenographer, quietly but busily taking a record of every word spoken.

"I assume you know that Mr. William Wolfe was murdered last night," said Mrs. Roosevelt.

Rinehart shuddered. "Wolfe? Oh, no!"

"Yes. That is why we called you and others so late on a Friday night. It seems a dangerous killer is at large.''

Rinehart exhaled loudly, making his lips flutter, and he shook his head. "I acknowledged to you, Mrs. Roosevelt, that I did have a relationship with Vivian Taliafero. I am shocked by the manner of her death, then that of Skaggs, now—Are you certain Wolfe was murdered? The papers suggest suicide."

"I have a very simple question for you, Secretary Rinehart," said Mrs. Roosevelt. "It is perhaps not altogether fair for me to ask it, since I believe I know the answer. But I must ask it."

"I will answer truthfully," said Rinehart soberly.

"You have told a lie in the course of this investigation," said Mrs. Roosevelt. "Haven't you?"

Rinehart lowered his head, and his body trembled as though he were sobbing. He nodded.

"And the lie was . . . ?"

Rinehart shook his head. He was in fact crying.

Mrs. Roosevelt spoke softly. "It is not the truth, is it, that you met with Senator Cranshaw on Friday morning to discuss the lumber-import bill? That was a lie, wasn't it?"

Rinehart sobbed and nodded.

18

"As we've heard the various suspects and witnesses tell their stories, Senator," said Mrs. Roosevelt to Senator Cranshaw, "I've been writing some notes and putting them in order. I don't wish to be dramatic, but this is what I've come up with, in the form of a sort of diagram. It deals, as you see, with *time*—the times when things happened on the Tuesday evening when Miss Taliafero was strangled."

She handed him a sheet from a yellow legal pad, on which she had sketched out a rough diagram (see page 229).

She waited for a minute, to give the senator time to study the sheet, then asked—"Do you see my problem?"

"I would suggest, Mrs. Roosevelt," said Senator Cranshaw, "that your time chart is wrong in one vital particular. Vital to me, anyway."

"Which particular is that, Senator?"

He stabbed the paper emphatically with his finger. "You

Time	
8:30	Miss T leaves Mr. Hausser's office.
8:30	Senator Cranshaw leaves President.
8:30–8:40	Miss T murdered.
8:40 (?)	Mr. Hausser calls Mr. Wolfe to tell him Miss T is dead.
8:55	Mr. Skaggs arrives Miss Partridge's house, tells her, Sen. Valentine of death of Miss T.
9:00	Mr. Skaggs, Miss P leave for Miss T's house.
9:05	Sen. V calls Mr. Oleander.
9:05 (?)	Mr. Wolfe calls Mr. Rinehart.
9:07 (?)	Mr. Rinehart calls Mr. Oleander.
9:10 (?)	Sen. V calls Judge Kincaid.

show me leaving the President's cocktail hour at eight-thirty. I know I told you that I was with the President for a considerable time after that."

Mrs. Roosevelt shook her head. "I'm afraid not, Senator," she said. "We've been at some trouble to discover when you left the President. It could not have been later than eight-thirty."

"I left the President and Miss LeHand—" He paused and looked at Missy. "As she can confirm. I was with the President until—"

"Until no later than eight-thirty, Senator," said Missy.

"Has the President expressed himself on this subject?" asked Cranshaw.

"He doesn't have to," said Missy. "After you left, he was helped to take his bath and get into bed, after which he ate his dinner and listened to two albums of records—before Stan Szczygiel called to tell him a body had been found in the Rose Garden. And we *know* for sure when Stan called. It was nine-ten."

"If you had left the President at eight-forty-five, Senator," said Mrs. Roosevelt, "he would have had to do all that within twenty-five minutes." She smiled sadly and shook her head. "Getting the President undressed and bathed and into bed is a laborious process. And only after *that* did he eat his dinner and listen to the 'Rhapsody in Blue,' which lasts more than sixteen minutes, then part of the choral movement from Beethoven's Ninth Symphony, which takes—"

"All right!" snapped Cranshaw. "Maybe I misjudged my time. Maybe I wasn't still with the President when Vivian was murdered. That doesn't prove I murdered her."

"That is entirely correct," said Mrs. Roosevelt. "But now we arrive at other discrepancies in your account of that evening. Tell us again where you went when you left the White House."

"I went to the Willard Hotel. I meant to have a cup of coffee, but I found Burt Oleander in the dining room, and I sat down with him and had coffee and a brandy."

"At about what time?"

"Well . . . Whatever time it had to be. I went there from the White House, either at eight-forty-five as I had thought, or maybe it was at eight-thirty. Between those two times."

"Yes. Mr. Oleander confirms that."

"I suppose he would."

"But I am most curious as to why he would," she said. "Look on down my diagram. Secretary Rinehart telephoned Mr. Oleander a few minutes after nine. So did Senator Valentine. They reached him at home, Senator— in Burning Tree, Maryland. He says he was at the Willard Hotel, but he wasn't. He's lying about that. And so are you."

Senator Everett Cranshaw made no effort to conceal his anger. "I do not believe," he said through clenched teeth, "the President would call me a liar."

"If I am wrong, you will have my most abject apology," said Mrs. Roosevelt. "But my response to your observation is that perhaps you've never lied to the President. I assure you he would call you a liar if he caught you in a lie."

"Mrs. Roosevelt, I—"

He was interrupted by the arrival of Burton Oleander, accompanied by his attorney, James Townley. They would not wait outside the Cabinet Room but brushed past the Secret Service man who was guarding the door and burst into the meeting.

"This meeting is unofficial, unauthorized, improper, illegal, and a gross violation of my client's rights," said Townley heavily. "We protest and demand that it be stopped immediately."

Mrs. Roosevelt rarely showed anger. She did not often become angry, and when she did she concealed it. But now her face reddened, and she pushed back her chair and rose. She pointed a finger at the Secret Service man standing in the doorway.

"Remove this gentleman," she said coldly. "Remove both of them."

"Whatever you're doing here, it's illegal," said Townley in shrill indignation.

"Your intrusion into the White House at this hour, and into this room, is illegal," she said.

"I was called," said Oleander. "I was *summoned*. And I came, with my attorney."

"I'm glad to see Mr. Townley," said Lieutenant Kennelly. "I want to talk to the man who insisted on bailing Wolfe out of jail only a few hours before he was murdered."

"What's the implication of that?" Townley demanded.

"What do you mean, murdered?" asked Oleander.

"Mr. Wolfe was a championship swimmer," said Mrs. Roosevelt. "And completely sober. What is more, the autopsy proves he did not fall and strike his head or anything like that. Mr. Wolfe died as the result of being thrown or pulled into the water and held under until he drowned.

The coroner's report lists murder as the cause of death, not suicide."

"Lawyers studying the principles of evidence," said Townley loftily, "are taught not to build inference on inference."

"I don't give a damn about that, Jim," snapped Cranshaw. "Burt, this thing has gotten serious. They've accused me of lying. It amounts to accusing you of lying, too. You'd better sit down and listen."

"My advice to my client is to refuse to participate in any way in—"

"Will you shut up!" Cranshaw snapped. "Burt—"

"You may remain, Mr. Oleander," said Mrs. Roosevelt. "With your attorney. We will not however tolerate constant interruption."

Oleander nodded to the lawyer, and the two of them sat down. The lawyer, a florid, white-haired man of sixty years or so, wearing round, gold-rimmed eyeglasses, pretended to give his attention to the contents of his briefcase. He made no concession.

"The dinner at the Willard Hotel, Mr. Oleander," said Mrs. Roosevelt. "We were talking about the time when—"

"Mrs. Roosevelt," Oleander interrupted firmly. "I'm sorry, but this constant hair-splitting about minutes—"

"Perhaps you should look at this," she said, handing him the sheet bearing the diagram Cranshaw had already examined.

Oleander frowned over the diagram. Townley looked on, too—obviously uncertain as to just what he was seeing.

"Can you really be sure of all of this?" Oleander asked. "For example, you fix the time of Vivian's death within ten minutes. How do you know she died between eight-thirty and eight-forty?"

"It has to do with the time when she left Mr. Hausser's office," said Mrs. Roosevelt. "Also with the hour of sunset and the schedule of police officers patrolling the White

House grounds. It is somewhat complicated, but there is little question.''

"And you say Ev Cranshaw left the President at eight-thirty. How can you be sure it wasn't at a quarter to nine, as he says it was?''

"Some rather careful detective work, Mr. Oleander.''

"It has to do with the President's bath and dinner and with listening to music,'' said Cranshaw, glumly but not without a note of scorn. "They've worked it out to the minute.''

"None of this proves a thing about who murdered the Taliafero woman,'' said Townley, still staring at the diagram. He spoke more quietly now. "It deprives the senator of an alibi, but it does not so much as *suggest* he killed the woman.''

"He had motive,'' said Kennelly.

"So did a great many other people, I'm afraid,'' said Oleander.

"There was motive and opportunity,'' said Mrs. Roosevelt. "I believe those are two essential elements in the proof of a crime. They would not be persuasive, however, except for another point.''

"I bet this one's speculative,'' said Cranshaw.

She ignored him. "The other point is a question,'' she said. "Why did Senator Cranshaw, with Mr. Oleander's assistance, go to such lengths to create an alibi if he didn't need one? The truth is, Mr. Oleander, that you were never at the Willard Hotel that evening. Neither was Senator Cranshaw.''

"I suppose you can prove that?'' said the lawyer.

"I'd like to ask Mr. Oleander a question,'' said Szczygiel. "Do you often eat at the Willard?''

Oleander shrugged, then shook his head. "No.''

"Did you *ever* eat there?''

"Well . . . What's the difference?''

"How about you, Senator?''

"I'm not sure I want to answer.''

"Since neither of you ever ate dinner there," said Szczygiel, "the waiters wouldn't know you and wouldn't remember you. You couldn't make an alibi involving the Caliber Club, for example, because the personnel there *would* remember if you'd been in."

"Inference on inference," said Townley.

"Both Senator Valentine and Secretary Rinehart telephoned Mr. Oleander at home within a few minutes after nine. He could not possibly have been in the Willard Hotel, or anywhere else in downtown Washington, much after eight o'clock."

"I hear an accusation in this," said Oleander.

"Indeed you do," she said with a crisp little smile.

"Weaving your net, are you?" said Cranshaw.

"Not a tangled web such as you have woven, Senator," she said.

"Am I to understand you are accusing me of the murder of Vivian Taliafero?"

"Yes. And of Joe Bob Skaggs as well."

"Skaggs!"

"A pattern," she said. "You somehow procured Mr. Oleander to lie to make an alibi for Tuesday evening; then you procured Secretary Rinehart to make one for Friday morning. You said you were meeting with him to discuss some legislation. You weren't. He confessed a little while ago."

"Next you're going to tell me I killed Wolfe," Cranshaw sneered.

"In fact, I don't think you did," she said. "I suspect, though, you know who did."

Townley was still staring at the diagram. "How do you know Valentine and Rinehart aren't lying?" he asked. "How in fact do you know one of them didn't kill Vivian Taliafero?"

"We know where Senator Valentine was when Miss Taliafero was killed. His witness has no motive to lie, at least not to lie about that. And Mr. Wolfe told us before he was killed that he telephoned Secretary Rinehart at home a little after nine. The secretary lives in Alexandria and could not have killed Miss Taliafero between eight-thirty and eight-forty and reached home before nine-fifteen."

"How do you eliminate Judge Kincaid as a suspect?" Cranshaw asked. "Or Admiral Horan?"

"They were at dinner at the Army-Navy Club, where both are members and are well known. Senator Valentine reached the judge there by telephone, a little past nine."

"Skaggs could have killed her," said Cranshaw.

"Then who killed Skaggs?" asked Mrs. Roosevelt.

"Wolfe could have killed her. Hausser could have killed her."

"Again, if one of them did it, who killed Skaggs?" asked the First Lady. "Mr. Wolfe was appearing in court at the time when Skaggs was killed. Mr. Hausser was in his office upstairs. Also, if Mr. Wolfe killed Miss Taliafero, who then killed him? And why?"

"What points the finger at you," Szczygiel remarked to Senator Cranshaw, "is the lies you procured to make yourself an alibi."

"Rinehart—"

"Secretary Rinehart is waiting in one of the offices," said Mrs. Roosevelt. "Let's have him join us."

Secretary Herschel Rinehart shuffled into the cabinet room, hunched, a frightened and defeated man. He jerked when he saw Cranshaw and Oleander, as if he were shocked to confront them.

"Mr. Secretary," said Mrs. Roosevelt as gently as she could, "you've confessed that you lied when you told us you and Senator Cranshaw met to discuss legislation on the morning of Friday, July seventeenth. Tell us why you lied."

Rinehart stared at Cranshaw, and his abject expression changed, hardened. He was angry, too.

"He called me and . . . demanded I tell that lie. He said he'd drag us all down the drain if we didn't help him establish alibis for Tuesday evening and Friday morning. He threatened to . . . He said he'd make it all look even worse than it was. That is, if he was arrested."

"Did Senator Cranshaw tell you he killed—"

"Wait a minute!"

"Be quiet, Mr. Townley."

"He didn't say so exactly," said Rinehart. "Not in so many words. But it was clear that's what he meant. Why else would he need an alibi?"

Mrs. Roosevelt shook her head sadly. "Why, indeed?"

"Senator Cranshaw," said Kennelly, "I arrest you for the murders of Vivian Taliafero and Joe Bob Skaggs."

Senator Everett Cranshaw imposed a harsh, hostile stare on each other person in the room—Mrs. Roosevelt, Missy, Szczygiel, Kennelly, Oleander, Townley, and Rinehart. That stare reminded Mrs. Roosevelt of what Sally Partridge had said of him: that he was a foul-tempered, hard-drinking man, capable of hatred and violence.

"Do you want to make a statement, Senator?" asked Kennelly.

He shook his head.

The Secret Service man outside the door rapped discreetly, then opened the door. Szczygiel went to him and returned to the table and quietly told Mrs. Roosevelt that Senator Valentine had arrived.

"Bring him in," she said. "And Judge Kincaid and Miss Partridge, too. We may as well have the whole cast assembled."

"How very nice," said Cranshaw sarcastically. "Even the little hooker."

"If you refer to Miss Partridge," said Mrs. Roosevelt, "she contributed significantly to pointing the finger of guilt at you, Senator. She suggested the guilty party might well be one of the men who couldn't afford Miss Taliafero's exactions.''

"Inference on inference," muttered Townley.

When the others were seated, Mrs. Roosevelt spoke—

"Let's see if we can't reconstruct the sequence of events of the Tuesday evening and Friday morning of last week," she said.

"Inference . . . speculation . . ."

"Oh, be quiet, Jim," growled Oleander.

"Miss Taliafero came to the Executive Wing to collect money from Mr. Hausser. That poor innocent gave her a personal check, and she left his office about half past eight. Mr. Skaggs had come with her and was waiting outside. The White House grounds had not been closed for the evening, and maybe he wandered around a little, looking. That, Mr. Townley, *is* speculation.''

"Thank you," said the lawyer.

"Senator Cranshaw had been with the President and Miss LeHand during the President's customary cocktail hour. That evening the cocktail hour lasted longer than usual, and Senator Cranshaw had a bit too much to drink."

"More than a bit too much," grumbled Cranshaw.

"He came down from the second floor. He told us he left by the South Portico, but in fact he wanted to go west and so left the White House through the first-floor corridor, out into the colonnade, intending to walk through the Executive Wing and leave through the west gate. By chance he encountered Miss Taliafero, either in the colonnade or in the Rose Garden—more likely in the colonnade. In any case, they spoke and began a conversation. He led her—or she led him—into the Rose Garden."

"And what did they say?" asked Oleander.

"We can only guess," said Mrs. Roosevelt. "Something angry. Something about Miss Taliafero's hold on the senator. Something about her demands. He was drunk. That's the word—drunk. He has a hot temper. Need I describe the scene further?''

"Heaven forfend," said Cranshaw.

"He had not meant to kill her," Mrs. Roosevelt continued. "The encounter was by chance. And having done it, he realized he had not solved his problem, only created a new and worse one. The photographs that had been the basis for her blackmail still existed, almost certainly hidden somewhere in her house. He determined that he would go there and try to find them."

"Before Skaggs could get to them," said Kennelly. *"He'd* know how to use them."

"Yes. He had, of course, no idea that Skaggs was somewhere about and had seen him kill Miss Taliafero. So, there ensued a race to the house, to get the pictures."

"Skaggs had to have help," said Valentine, "so he came to get Sally."

"Exactly," said Mrs. Roosevelt. "Senator Cranshaw was unaware there was a race. He supposed he had an hour or so—until the body was found and identified and the police went to search. So he took some time to sober up . . . and—" She paused and fixed her eyes on Oleander. "And to telephone one or more of his fellow victims to solicit their assistance."

"You have no evidence that he called my client."

"That is true, sir. I haven't."

"Hausser called Wolfe, it says here," said Cranshaw, tapping the diagram with one finger.

"Confirmed by both of them," said Mrs. Roosevelt. "Mr. Hausser thought he'd be arrested, since his check would be found in Miss Taliafero's purse. He telephoned Mr. Wolfe to warn him about what had happened. Mr. Wolfe determined to go to the house and get the pictures, and he telephoned Secretary Rinehart and demanded he come help him. Secretary Rinehart refused. But Mr. Wolfe, I think, joined the race for the pictures."

"Skaggs won the race," said Judge Kincaid. "He grabbed the pictures and started calling us all, telling us our payments were to come directly to him."

"Senator Cranshaw entered the house while Skaggs and Miss Partridge were in the cellar," said Mrs. Roosevelt. "Skaggs fired a shot at the senator and scared him off. I suspect that Mr. Wolfe entered the house still later, searched, and found nothing. He was too late."

"So everything was in worse condition than it had been before," said Judge Kincaid. "Now Skaggs had the pictures, and—"

"And it became imperative to murder him," said Szczygiel.

"I decided I might as well have my share," said Sally Partridge, "so I broke into Joe Bob's house to get the pictures. But he was already dead, and the cops were watching the house, and I got arrested and locked up."

"Of the several suspects," said Mrs. Roosevelt, "only four do not have ironclad alibis for Friday morning. Admiral Horan does not. Representative Pierce does not. And Secretary Rinehart and Senator Cranshaw do not because they were supposed to be together and weren't."

"Then why does it fall on me?" asked Cranshaw.

"Again, because you demanded that someone lie for you to create an alibi."

Cranshaw sighed loudly. "It's all very circumstantial," he said quietly.

"Yes. And perhaps Mr. Townley or some other good lawyer will defend you and pick holes in the case."

"Yes. In the meantime, my mess with Vivian becomes public, I am forced to resign from the Senate, my wife divorces me—"

"We all face things like that," said Valentine.

Senator Cranshaw's gaze traveled to the faces of every person in the room once again—this time with less hostility, in fact with resignation.

"Careful, Ev," muttered Oleander.

"Careful, my backside!" grunted Cranshaw. "You'd like that, wouldn't you, Burt? 'Careful, Ev. We'll get you a light sentence. We'll take care of your family while you're in the penitentiary.' Sure. You've used that line before, Burt.''

"Do you want to make a statement, Senator?" asked Kennelly again.

Cranshaw glared at him for a moment, then settled a more moderate stare on Mrs. Roosevelt. "Why not?" he said.

Townley shook a hand at him. "Don't be a fool, Ev," he cautioned.

"I've *been* a fool," growled Cranshaw. "And now . . ." He shrugged. "What the hell . . ."

"This man's emotions have been—"

"Shut up, Burt," said Cranshaw. "Don't you have enough sense to know when the game's over?"

"We have judged correctly, haven't we, Senator Cranshaw?" asked Mrs. Roosevelt.

"Mostly . . . It's true that when I left the President I was drunk. She was out there. She was looking around for Skaggs, I suppose. When she saw me, she started hissing. She wanted money! She wanted this, she wanted that! She—I'm not sorry I killed her. I'll be *damned* if I am!"

"You left her body lying in the Rose Garden, and . . . ?"

"Just like you said. I stumbled off, too drunk to think clearly. I got to a phone and called—I called Kincaid first. You weren't home, Judge. I called Steve." He looked at Valentine. "Your wife thought you were working late. I guessed where you were. Then I called Burt."

"He didn't tell me he'd killed Vivian!"

"The hell I didn't. And you told me I'd better get out to the house before anyone else did, and get those photos. I tried. But Skaggs was there, and he fired a shot at me. So I called you again, Burt. You want to tell what our conversation was?"

"You're out of your mind!"

"You might have the decency, Senator, not to try to involve others in your—"

"In *our* crimes, Jim. Yours and mine and Burt's," said

Cranshaw, angry at the lawyer. "You're going down the drain with me, Burt, Jim. I'm not taking the rap alone. I told you I wouldn't."

"Continue your narrative, Senator," said Mrs. Roosevelt.

"We met the next day. Burt and I. Jim came in during the session. I'd already had a call from Skaggs. He had the pictures, and he'd guessed who strangled Vivian. Burt and I talked. There was no alternative to killing Skaggs. Having the pictures in his possession was worse than having them in Vivian's. We had to kill Skaggs—and we had to make it appear that someone else did it."

"You planned it together?"

Cranshaw glared at Oleander. "*Together.* And it was no difficult matter to rid the world of Skaggs. He wanted to see me. He'd called and said he did. I went over to Alexandria, to his house. He received me like an honored guest. As soon as I was certain there was no one else in the house, I killed him."

"How?" asked Kennelly.

"I beat him to death with a length of iron pipe I'd carried along for the purpose. I knew he carried a gun, so I waited for a chance to get behind him, then hit him as hard as I could from behind. He never had a chance to pull that gun."

"He wasn't carrying it at the time," said Mrs. Roosevelt.

"Okay. The idea was to leave behind clues that made it look like somebody else did it. We knew Fritz Hausser was a hypochondriac who used every kind of pill you could think of, so I dropped a Campho-Lax pill. But more important—More important, I went through the photos. I'd have liked to take them all, destroy them all. I—"

"Leaving behind most of them and taking away only those of Mr. Wolfe and Secretary Rinehart . . ."

Cranshaw nodded. "Made pretty powerful evidence that they were the ones who'd killed Vivian and Skaggs."

"Why *two* sets?" asked Szczygiel.

"Two murders," said Cranshaw. "One of them might have had a perfect alibi for one or both. It was unlikely both of them had an alibi for both."

"I am curious about something, then," said Mrs. Roosevelt. "How did you know we would find the fingerprints of Messrs. Rinehart and Wolfe in the private areas of Miss Taliafero's house? What made you suppose we would understand that some of the photographs were missing?"

"We didn't know about any fingerprints," said Cranshaw. "We knew, though, that you'd come up with a list of names. Vivian was dead. Any thorough investigation was going to discover the fact that she was blackmailing some people. And when you talked to one or two of her victims, they would surely name others. The circle would come complete, sooner or later. You'd know who'd been paying her, and you'd see that some men's pictures were missing."

"How did you decide to incriminate *me?*" asked Rinehart plaintively.

"Or for that matter, Wolfe and Hausser?" asked Kennelly. "How'd you make your choices, Senator?"

Cranshaw turned to Judge Beresford Kincaid. "Why don't *you* answer that question, Judge?"

"The President will have my resignation tomorrow," said the judge. "There was more involved in the Taliafero blackmail than just money. Look at the record. Look at the senatorial votes on the Utilities Holding Company Act. Look at my opinion in *Grayson* v. *Central Electric.*"

"Dictated . . . ?"

"Not dictated," said Valentine. *"Influenced."*

"Senator Valentine," said Mrs. Roosevelt regretfully. "Judge . . . And Representative Pierce?"

"No," said Valentine. "Not even influenced."

"Okay," said Kennelly. "Who killed Wolfe?"

Cranshaw turned his head slowly toward Oleander.

"Prove it!" barked Oleander.

"When we didn't know who did it," said Kennelly, "that might have been pretty tough. Now that we know, it won't be so difficult. You got some toughs on your payroll, Oleander? We'll find out. Now that we know where to look, that won't be tough at all. Bully-boys don't sweat very well. They cave in. We'll find out."

"Do I understand you intend to convey me to jail?" asked Cranshaw.

"That's the idea," said Kennelly. "Two counts of murder. I can hardly hand you a ticket, like for overparking."

"I thought so," said Cranshaw. "And I anticipated it. So . . ."

He reached into his jacket and slowly withdrew a small revolver.

"Cranshaw!"

"Quietly, please," he said. "No one gets excited, no one gets hurt. All I want to do is leave."

He swung the muzzle at Oleander, who turned deathly pale, then at Kennelly who smiled at him and shrugged.

"I'm sorry," said Cranshaw. "Deeply sorry. For many elements of it. But—Well . . . Maybe you can understand."

He backed out of the Cabinet Room, threatening the Secret Service man in the hall with the pistol, then disappearing out of the Executive Wing and into the darkness of the Rose Garden.

Epilogue

The following evening, Saturday, July 25, 1936, the President sent a wire from Down East—

ARE YOU AWARE THAT THIS AFTERNOON THE
DODGERS PITCHER VAN LINGLE MUNGO
STRUCK OUT SEVEN SUCCESSIVE CINCINNATI
BATTERS STOP WHILE LISTENING ON RADIO TO
THE ACCOUNT OF THIS FEAT YOURS TRULY
HAULED IN A SEVEN FOOT SHARK STOP YOU
WILL ALLOW FOR EXAGGERATION IN THE LAT-
TER BUT NOT IN THE FORMER WHICH MUNGO
REALLY DID DO STOP WHO KILLED VIVIAN
TALIAFERO STOP THERE BEING NO WORD ON
THAT SUBJECT I ASSUME A MURDER MYSTERY
HAS DEFIED YOUR POWERS AND WILL REMAIN
UNSOLVED STOP CIVILIZATION WILL SURVIVE
STOP LOVE AND KISSES AND MY BEST TO ALL
STOP

When the wire arrived, Mrs. Roosevelt was sitting down to a light evening meal—cold cuts, lettuce, sliced tomatoes, radishes, cucumbers, carrots. Missy was with her, as was Stan Szczygiel. She read the wire to them.

"A Rooseveltian statement, no?" she said.

Missy tipped her head back and grinned broadly. "The Boss . . ."

Szczygiel laughed for a brief moment, then turned solemn and shook his head. They were not in a self-congratulatory mood.

Senator Everett Cranshaw had escaped from the White House only as long as it took him to drive to a dark block on F Street, where he pulled to the curb and used his pistol to kill himself. The word of his death came back to the White House before the meeting in the Cabinet Room finally ended, an hour after midnight.

Mrs. Roosevelt's thoughts then had been of the senator's family, and she had personally telephoned the Cranshaws' pastor, so that he, and not some impersonal police officer, could go to the home and notify the senator's wife and children.

Now her thoughts were how to protect the reputations, even the feelings, of the innocent. She told Missy they must give some thought and time to that.

In some measure, reputations and feelings were spared. In some measure, they were not.

—As Lieutenant Ed Kennelly had promised, the District police found little difficulty in proving that four thugs in the employ of the Mingo Creek Electric Company—union busters—had murdered William Wolfe. All four were electrocuted early in 1937. Burton Oleander fled to Argentina, where he lived until 1939. In that year he was murdered on the street by a *descamisado* mob that mistook him for a prominent Argentine politician.

—Judge Beresford Kincaid resigned from the Second Circuit Court of Appeals. He returned to the private practice of law in Indianapolis and died there in 1953 without ever having explained to anyone's satisfaction why he resigned his enviable position as judge of a federal appeals court.

—Senator Steven Valentine served out his term as United States Senator from Michigan, then announced he preferred to live in Detroit, rather than Washington, and would not run again. He returned to Detroit. Six years later he was a candidate for the Democratic nomination for mayor but was defeated when the Detroit *Free Press* exposed his illicit relationship with a teenage girl he kept in a Dearborn apartment.

—Representative Gordon Pierce served in Congress until 1971.

—Mrs. Richard Horan divorced the admiral in 1938, citing his illicit relationship with Betty Coughlin, whom he then married. The scandal ruined his chances for further promotion in the Navy, and he was sent to the Pacific and given command of an aircraft carrier, not the battleship he had hoped to command. He was killed in January of 1945 when a kamikaze plane hit the bridge of his flagship.

—Secretary Rinehart served in the Cabinet through the election of 1936, then resigned, saying his business interests were suffering terribly from his absence on government service. He was later elected president of the United States Chamber of Commerce.

—Frederick Hausser continued to serve in the Executive Wing, until 1942 when he enlisted in the United States Army. (He was careful to conceal his chronic ill health.) He became an expert on military government, and in 1944 Major Hausser was appointed military governor of an Italian hill district south of Florence, where he was responsible for preserving many important works of Medieval and Renaissance art that might otherwise have been damaged for want of materials to repair churches and palaces.

—Sally Partridge returned to her job as a cocktail waitress. Late in 1937 she married a jockey, accompanied him as he traveled to tracks around the country, especially to California, and left him in 1940 when she was offered a bit part in a Paramount picture. Interviewed by *Look* magazine in 1954, she proudly showed the reporter thirty-four lines she had spoken in six pictures. She was then married for the second time, to a set designer.

—Ruby Tanner was kept in jail for two weeks on the charge of obstructing justice. Lieutenant Kennelly persuaded her that she could earn her release by keeping her mouth shut, absolutely, about what she had seen and heard.

Lieutenant Edward Kennelly remained with the District police force until his retirement. Mrs. Roosevelt would work with him again during the investigation into the Garber murder in 1939. He was then Captain Kennelly.

Stanlislaw Szczygiel retired. He moved to Florida in 1939, invested modestly in Florida real estate, and by the time of his death in 1961 he was a multimillionaire.

Missy served the President for the rest of her life—until she died in August, 1944.

Mrs. Roosevelt and the others succeeded in suppressing the worst of the Taliafero-Skaggs scandal. It had no impact on the election of 1936. Many years later, Mrs. Roosevelt would shake her head and smile reminiscently about it.

"It was a different world," she said, "when we could keep a thing like that quiet. Even when some reporters found out about it, they could be persuaded not to trumpet it. They could have, of course. But they chose not to. I believe firmly in freedom of the press—absolutely, without qualification—but I must say I liked the ethics of some of the old journalists."

ELLIOTT ROOSEVELT'S
DELIGHTFUL MYSTERY SERIES

MURDER IN THE ROSE GARDEN
70529-X/$4.95US/$5.95Can

MURDER IN THE OVAL OFFICE
70528-1/$4.50US/$5.50Can

MURDER AND THE FIRST LADY
69937-0/$4.50US/$5.50Can

THE HYDE PARK MURDER
70058-1/$3.95US/$4.95Can

MURDER AT HOBCAW BARONY
70021-2/$3.95US/$4.95Can

THE WHITE HOUSE PANTRY MURDER
70404-8/$3.95US/$4.95Can

MURDER AT THE PALACE
70405-6/$3.95 US/$4.95Can